A DARK TRAIL WINDING

Pete Peterson

A DARK TRAIL
WINDING

A DARK TRAIL WINDING

WINDING

•

Pete Peterson

AVALON BOOKS
NEW YORK

Published by Thomas Bouregy & Co., Inc.
160 Madison Avenue, New York, NY 10016

Library of Congress Cataloging-in-Publication Data

Peterson, Pete (F. M.)
   A dark trail winding / Pete Peterson.
      p. cm.
   ISBN 0-8034-9810-1 (acid-free paper)
   I. Title

   PS3616.E84D37 2006
   813'.6—dc22

                              2006018076

PRINTED IN THE UNITED STATES OF AMERICA
ON ACID-FREE PAPER
BY HADDON CRAFTSMEN, BLOOMSBURG, PENNSYLVANIA

To the Fellowship

PART ONE

I drink not from mere joy in wine
nor to scoff at faith—
no, only to forget myself for a moment,
that only do I want of intoxication, that alone.
—Omar Khayyam

Foreword

The mists of morning, often present in this gentle, rolling valley of the Willamette, fall from leaden skies above the vast Oregon Territory of 1850. The clouds from the sea pass hesitantly, lightening their burdens before attempting to scale the haughty, snow-capped volcanic peaks of the beautiful, forested Cascade Mountains.

They come to this land of plenty in a never-ending train of humanity, from the crowded cities, the sterile farms, the slums and poorhouses of the East. They come to begin anew lives that have not fulfilled their promises, or that have taken misguided courses. They are pioneers and empire builders, come to build a new land from a rich wilderness—come to dwell in paradise.

For some the dreams come true, for they bring with them the energy and industry and faith required to face life on life's terms. The spoilers come, too—the plunderers and the parasites—come only to take for themselves that which is earned by the sweat of another's brow. And some, unfortunate ones, bring with them the

3

saboteur of hope, the destroyer of dreams, the enemy within—self. Jacob Eriksson is such a man, trudging a dark trail winding ever closer to the abyss, living in a world of his own making: A world of unsummoned tears, brought forth by painful memories of love and laughter somehow lost, and of long ago joys, now dimmed by the misery of soul. He faces another day, spent alone, unmissed, uncounted.

They call him Jackass Jake. This is his story.

Chapter One

Most folks wake up in the morning. I come to.

Emerging from the oblivion that last night's bender had afforded me, I felt smothered in a blanket of undefined fears. Brilliant flashes of light invaded the blackness behind my closed eyelids. Raw nerves jerked at my body and I was racked by tremors. I tried to work up a spit to swallow for the ragged scratching in my throat, but my tongue seemed to have bark on it. My stomach was queasy, rolling, churning and rumbling. I gagged, pressing my lips tight together to stifle an eruption. Lordy. My head. Didn't recall it being so enormous. My hair hurt. My teeth itched. I let escape a long, shuddering sigh at the prospect of facing another day.

I became vaguely conscious of something worrying the side of my face—something foul, rough, and wet. I jerked my head aside as the sticky warm thing crept into my ear. I had not yet opened my puffed and swollen eyes and already I faced a crisis. With an effort that taxed my limits, I forced open one red-veined eye, focusing slowly and deliberately on a glistening black nose set in a dense thicket of tangled, matted fur above a gaping, grinning maw of black gums and yellow fangs. A vile, searing breath watered my eyes and curled the stubble on my slack jaws. I opened the other eye. I was muzzle to muzzle with what has to be the ugliest animal in existence.

I started to get up, but my reactions were off and I was slow to escape the enthusiastic swipe of a limp, disgusting tongue that wet my face from chin to eyebrows. That dog's tongue must be two feet long.

"Dadgum it, Cur. Can't you learn to crow or something? That's a heck of a way for a man to have to wake up."

The dog hovered over me, as big as a small deer, nagging at me with a sorrowful whine to be up and on with whatever it is we are going to do today. Dumb mutt. Reaching to scratch myself, I discovered I had wet my britches again. I struggled to a sitting position, too quickly, and the loose weight inside my skull slid crashing into my forehead. Stabbing lights filled my head as sour, clammy beads of sweat issued from every pore. Two live coals were embedded in the sockets where my eyes should have been.

Ooooooh. Last night must have been a rip-snorter.

Glancing around at the clutter and jumble around me, I reckoned that I had somehow wound up in the alley between the Golden Egg Saloon and McClure's Mercantile. Muffled sounds of morning activity were creeping into the alley through the walls of the general store. It would be a blessed relief, I thought, to wake just once and know where I was without all this intense concentration. Not even on my feet yet and I was already exhausted.

I slapped absently at my vest pocket looking for a

smoke. No tobacco. I looked down. No pocket. Torn away. Couldn't have hit the pipe bowl anyway.

I was vibrating like a maiden at a mule skinner's picnic. With my hands shaking like they were, I'd have folks waving back at me. I needed a drink. Bad. Anxiously I searched my surroundings.

Hah! My spirits lifted considerably as I spotted the neck of a bottle beckoning from behind a broken crate. Crawling tentatively on hands and knees, I reached the crate and clutched at the bottle with both hands so that it would not escape my shaky grip. Brushing a slug from the side, I pulled the cork and held the bottle aloft toward the light at the mouth of the alley, checking the cloudy contents. Glory. Almost half full. It pays a man to pass out early—leaves enough to start the day.

"Cheers, Cur." I nodded to the dog, who was curious, as always, at this morning ritual.

I pulled at the fiery, amber liquid, swallowed, and waited resignedly for the return trip that my first drink of the day most always makes. Turning quickly aside, I sprayed the ground with the transient whiskey, now mixed with the scant contents of my cramping stomach. Hurriedly, I took another jolt of the stuff. It burned all the way down, but this one stayed to spread a familiar glow throughout my grateful body. While that drink was still working, I downed one more, seeking the welcome calm that I knew would follow.

Cur whined again. I was struggling to remember what had gone on the night before. Where had I been? What had I done? Remembering nothing is nothing new to me. I could ask someone, but I try hard not to talk with folks who know more about where I have been than I do. Odds were, though, that I had not spent

the evening helping the good sisters of the church with
their charity fund collection.

Clambering awkwardly to my feet, I leaned against
the clapboard siding of the mercantile building, thoroughly drained of energy and purpose. I carefully corked
the bottle, looking around for a safe spot to cache it until
I had to have it again. Giving the precious container the
tender care a mother gives her only child, I tucked it se-
curely into a sturdy crate, burned the location into my
memory, then turned and shuffled for the street.

Cur sidled back toward me. The monstrous mutt had
taken to following me around a few weeks back, having
discovered that some of the debris the fun-loving
cherubs of the village chunked my way from time to
time was edible. Seems we needed each other, for I'd
run off all human companions. I glanced down at the
disreputable, unkempt mongrel pressing my leg, wondering if there was not a mangy lobo wolf skulking in
the limbs of its family tree.

"You're in good company, dog. Don't have a very
impressive pedigree myself."

You might not believe it to see me now, but as recently as two—no, two and a half years ago, you might
have considered me a handsome, successful man. I
stand five foot ten, when I'm standing, tall for this day
and time. I know I look older, but I am twenty-four
years of age. My blond hair, though tangled and matted
now, once shone almost white when it caught the sun.
My brown eyes, dulled today by drink, were once lively
and alert. I used to weigh about one hundred and eighty,
thirty pounds heavier than I am now, and none of it was
fat. Clothes hung well on my broad shoulders, and it
was not unusual for heads to turn as I strolled the
boardwalks. But that was then. . . .

I'm Jake. Jacob Eriksson. Jackass Jake, they call me. Not supposed to be here in an alley like this. I never planned it; my mother would not have heard of it. I was raised to be a Baptist, a very southern Baptist. I have been prayed for, over, and at. Baptized and chastised and rededicated. Reckon it just did not take.

I leaned to scratch Cur behind the ear.

"We can't go on like this much longer, my hairy friend."

Pa had been a good man, but cursed with a weakness for strong drink. I recalled now, for Cur's edification, what he had told me of his childhood.

Orphaned by a fire while still a baby, my father had been reared by a Nazarene Bible-thumper and his pursy-mouthed sister in a family spilling over with eleven other ragamuffins. Pa developed the habits and preferences of a loner at an early age among that crowd of assorted siblings, becoming an obsessive reader of books. Outwardly a good and righteous man, the minister under whose care my father had fallen was ramrod rigid in his beliefs, holding that any writings other than the Good Book were worldly and therefore evil. One day he happened in on Pa, who was reading from a book of poetry by the Scotsman Robert Burns. In a puritanical frenzy, the minister took a strap to the spindly boy, screaming that Pa should never bring another such book into his home. That wrathful man of the church continued to thrash the boy, all the while pleading to a loving God to cleanse him of his sins. Carried away by his zeal, the minister came near crippling Pa, who was most of a year recovering from the brutal lashing. When at last he was again able to move around, Pa packed his few belongings in a gunny sack, relieved himself on the minister's Bible and set fire to the barn. Then he lit out, forever carrying the scars of his experience, never looking back. Nobody looked for him, and at the age of ten, my father faced the world alone.

Through his compulsion for reading, Pa became a self-taught scholar and he tried to pass his love of learning on to me. He was the finest man I ever knew, when he was sober; unlovable, exasperating, when he was drunk. But I have many treasured memories of the good times we had together. Pa talked to me as an equal, never treating me like a snot-nosed kid. Early on, we fished and hunted together, as often as Pa could get away, and those times were the best, with just him and me. I came to love the outdoors as a result of those outings, always dreading the return home, for there the fun and good times ended. Mother lived there.

In the evenings, Pa would read to me before the fire, hour after hour. We would talk at length about what we had read, and I reckon I learned without really knowing I was being taught.

"Jacob, you must study and learn, then use what you learn. Don't fritter away your youth," he would say. "Don't waste your life as I have done. Make something of yourself, son. Be somebody."
"You're somebody, Pa. You're somebody to me."

When I was a boy, we lived in the little town of Cole Camp, Missouri, in a small house my mother's folks had willed to her.

Pa, as I said, had a drinking problem, which grew progressively worse with time. He could not hold a job. He tried to stop, I know he did. Many times. But it seemed that the worse things got because of his drinking, the more he would drink. It did not make sense to me then, though I am now beginning to understand. Pa drew further and further into himself and into his jug.

"I'm ready, Pa," I said, enthusiastically.

"Ready? Ready for what? I'm busy, son . . . you run along." His speech was slurred and he would not look at me.

"But you promised. Today's the day of the outing . . . all the boys in school . . . and their fathers."

"I said run along, Jacob! I can't go. Next time . . . perhaps."

I missed the good times my pa and I had once shared.

More often than not, Pa squandered what little money he made on booze, which sparked some highly heated discussions between him and my mother—with her doing the bulk of the discussing, generally at the top of her lungs. Looking back on it now, I reckon every fight my folks ever had was over booze, money, or me.

"Frederick, you've disgraced me for the last time. How could you? The entire town must know what happened by now. I'll never be able to show my face in church again . . . ever."

"Don't start with me, woman! Wasn't my fault. To hell with the town . . . and the church. To hell with Schubaugh and his nothing job. And t'hell with you."

She burst into tears and screamed my name.

"Jacob. Come in here. See how a drunken wastrel treats his wife."

The other kids made fun of my rundown clothes and
they called my pa names to my face.

> *"Leave the boy out of this," Pa told her, burying
> his face in his hands.*
> *"How can I, Fred? How am I to do that? He's
> been fighting again. The parson's wife saw it all.
> He is going to grow up to be just like his father. My
> shame will be doubled."*

They had a migration, and we went.

In the early spring of 1843, with the pious hounds of
convention slavering at our door, with barely the
wherewithall to outfit ourselves for the trail, we abandoned our home and went to Independence, where we
hoped to join a wagon train bound for the Oregon country. There was free land there. We could begin again,
the equal of our neighbors. We could be rid of the reputation our family had gained in Cole Camp.

We made Independence by nightfall, and were
dumbstruck by the spectacle that confronted us. The
little village was spread along the south bank of the
Missouri, unimpressive for the reputation it was gaining as the jumping-off spot for western expansion.
"Manifest Destiny," the politicians called it. But the ho-
tels were crowded and the gunsmiths and saddlers were
kept constantly at work in providing arms and equipment for travelers. The surrounding hills on both sides of
the river, as far as the eye could see, were inundated with
the winking campfires of emigrant parties encamped
there, looking like stars come to ground. The night was
alive with the drone of garbled voices and mingling of
noises from pans clattering, dogs barking, trace chains
rattling, anvils clanging, cattle lowing, the whickering of

horses, and the crying of children. An occasional gun-shot could be heard, whether a mover after his supper or the culmination of a dispute, we were never to know. We were awed, all of us, and more than a mite intimidated.

A sternwheeler, its stacks belching white smoke, was docked at the levee, disemboweling itself of its varied human cargo. Santa Fe traders, gamblers, speculators, and adventurers of various descriptions poured from the cabins on the upper decks, while steerage spewed forth Oregon emigrants in homespun, mountain men in hide suits, Negroes in rags and a party of Kansas Indi-ans, who had been on a visit to St. Louis. On the muddy shore stood a large group of dark, slavish-looking Mex-icans, attached to one of the Santa Fe companies, gaz-ing furtively out from beneath their broad hats. A pair of French hunters from the mountains, with long hair and in buckskin dress, leaned on long rifles as they watched the passengers disembark.

Pa had figured it would be a simple matter to join with others of like purpose to form a caravan of wagons and strike off toward the setting sun. It was a disap-pointing beginning to our anticipated adventure to learn that there were long waiting lists for berths on every or-ganized train. Eager travelers trotted behind wagon masters like puppy dogs hoping for scraps. We had been in camp for two weeks and were beginning to de-spair of our chances of departing for the Oregon Coun-try before the exodus was terminated for the year. We had been told that travelers who struck out after the last day of May hadn't a chance of making it across the mountains before the passes clotted and closed of snow, stranding latecomers. What were we to do?

Chapter Two

It was only by chance that we gained a position in one of the last expeditions to leave that spring. The lady in a neighboring camp refused the wagon master's stern directive to abandon her bulky spinet. Peeved at the woman's obstinacy, the crusty pathfinder turned to my pa, who was standing nearby, and said, "Mister, if you want to go West, have your wagon in line an hour before dawn."

Full of soaring hopes of new beginnings, we began the trek in good humor, but our elation crumbled mile after never-ending mile across those vast plains. From the outset, our journey was monotony defined. Pa put me to gathering buffalo chips, the dried ones, to fuel our cookfires, for there was no wood to be had. We sometimes traveled for days without seeing a tree or a patch of green. Our dreams blew away with the topsoil on howling, blistering winds. Pa became even more withdrawn. My mother turned increasingly bitter, ill-humored and resentful. I felt pushed outside of their

14

consideration—unwanted baggage. I learned then and there that *adventure* is what you call something before you are in it.

The wagons of the train were spread out across the prairie, traveling abreast in a fanlike formation to avoid eating one's neighbor's dust. Even so, the air was thick and travelers' complaints were many. A council was called one evening at which it was decided to split the column into two factions. Those families with only their ox teams and no more than three additional head of stock would comprise one group, which included our family. The other, the "cow column," would travel separately to spare the first group the dust, noise, and insect population attendant with larger numbers of live-stock. It was understood that, once the caravan had entered territory known to be hostile we would again band together for our mutual protection.

I had made friends with a boy named Jesse Apple-gate, whose party was relegated to the cow column. When Pa could spare me from my trail chores, I spent the bulk of my time with that more interesting collection of voyagers. There were three families of Apple-gates with the train. The elder Jesse Applegate, an uncle for whom my friend was named, captained the cow column. He was a powerful presence, and would later become an influential force among the settlers of the Willamette Valley. Charles, little Jesse's pa, and Lind-say, were his brothers. All were driving small herds of cattle and horses to the promised land.

The most fascinating character to my mind, though, was the guide, a real mountain man, a free trapper named Sam Irons. He had taken on the chore as hunter and guide only to earn the money for a new outfit for trapping, as he had lost his gear, his furs, his horses, and darn near his life to a band of Gros Ventres Indians the previous season. He had signed on to guide the train as far as Fort Hall in Oregon Country, where he would depart again for the high lonesome to trap the icy streams for beaver and other pelts. Around the cook-fires, Sam regaled me and Jesse and the other Applegate youngsters with exciting tales of his exploits in the wilderness, of hand-to-hand battles with savages and grizzly bears. As he spun his yarns of derring-do, I pictured myself in buckskins, a Green River blade at my belt, a Hawken rifle in hand. I knew then what I wanted to become.

Each evening, Sam Irons stood ready to conduct the train into the circle he had previously measured and marked out to form the invariable fortification for the night. As each wagon was brought into position, it dropped its team inside the circle, the team was un-yoked and the yokes and chains were used to connect a wagon with the one in front of it.

Night watches were set up with all male members of the train who were able to bear arms participating in turn, starting at eight o'clock at night and ending at four o'clock in the morning. Some nights we had dancing. There were fiddlers and banjo players on the roles, and a few folks with Jew's harps or spoons to supply the music. The womenfolk visited and exchanged complaints. Children romped and frolicked at games. Men gathered to smoke and ponder the future. Then it was to sleep, for the morrow would be a grueling duplicate of the day just ended.

Children and old folks died by the score of the harsh conditions, dysentery, and catarrh during that voyage. There was cholera on the trail, too, though our train was spared that particular terror. Accidents took a heavy toll on man, beast, and equipment—young'uns jounced from wagons and being run over, guns going off in jolting wagons, and such. I heard years later that, all told, some forty-five thousand souls died making the journey. Almost one for every eighty yards of trail. The prairie became littered with household treasures, jettisoned to save weight. Some emigrants lost livestock, oxen, horses or cattle, even dogs, spirited away in darkness by silent, skulking savages.

The Great Plains seemed to go on forever, with nothing to break the boredom but the great herds of shaggy buffalo, in herds so immense that their passing would last for many hours, halting the train and adding to the ever-present stifling dust and the searing, heart-sapping heat. After the first million or more of the smelly critters, the sight of buffalo commences to lose its fascination.

Sam Irons rarely went a day without downing a buffalo, left in the trail for the train's butchers to distribute, but we saw the shaggy beasts only as lumbering black dots in the distance until we neared the Platte. A tremendous herd of thousands upon thousands of the great animals barred our progress as we topped a swell in the prairie. Excitedly, the men of the company snatched up their rifles, sprung to their saddles, and rode toward the massive assemblage of buffalo, starting them in motion with their incautious approach. From the wagons, we could hear the faint pops of the hunters' long guns above the bellowing of the beasts and the roar of stampeding hooves. The ground shook beneath us, frightening the younger children. Sam Irons, returning from a scout, rode after the impetuous riflemen, shouting at them to halt, but his cries were swallowed in

the din. When the dust began to clear, we saw the
abashed hunters returning, heads down, their mounts
spent. Not one shaggy carcass lay upon the prairie
floor. His color high, Irons explained to the impulsive
riders, in a voice that built to a roar, that a shot must be
well placed to down one of the huge brutes, striking it
behind the forequarters, in the lungs. The inexperi-
enced men had shot into the poor beasts as they might a
deer, inflicting painful wounds, but failing to deliver a
single killing shot. Irons angrily informed them that
their actions had not only endangered the caravan and
run the herd out of range of his own guns, but that the
wounds they had inflicted upon the animals would fes-
ter, poisoning the beasts and resulting in a slow and ag-
onizing death from which no man would reap a benefit.
For the remainder of the march, the hunting of buffalo
was left in the capable hands of the scout, whose intimidating, berating outburst had impressed even the most
formidable of the would-be hunters.

At the end of one ten-hour day spent plodding
through the hollows and gorges of a range of gloomy
little hills, we gained the summit and the long-expected
valley of the Platte lay before us. It was a welcome
sight, being a mark of measuring our progress, but one
devoid of any picturesque feature. No grandeur, other
than its vast extent, its solitude, and its wildness. For
mile after mile, a level plain was spread out beneath us.
Here and there the Platte River, divided into a dozen
threadlike sluices, traversed the wasteland, its monotony relieved only occasionally by a clump of scraggly
growth rising like a shadowy island in the plain. No living creature, of fin, fur, or feather, moved throughout
the vast, naked landscape, except the swift little lizards

that darted over the sand and through the rank grass and prickly pear at our feet.

A man named Biddle, leading a group of four wagons, left the train at the river, turning south toward Taos.

We were told by the wagon master that we had passed the most tedious part of the journey, but the next three weeks travel made me consider him a false prophet, at best. Two lines of sand hills flanked the valley to the right and left, broken often into wild, bizarrely sculpted forms, reminding me of the ghost stories my pa used to tell me. Before and behind us, the level of the plain lay unbroken as far as the eye could see, sometimes an expanse of hot, bare sand; sometimes a blanket of long, coarse grass. The bleached skulls and whitening bones of buffalo were scattered all about, the ground tracked by their countless hooves in passage and pocked by indentations where the bulls had wallowed. Leading from every gully and ravine, one could see the deeply worn paths made by the buffalo as they streamed forth, twice a day, to drink in the Platte. The river is a thin sheet of rapid, turbid water, half a mile wide and a scant two feet deep, with low, sandy banks. The water is gritty and unpleasant to drink.

Another man that captured my young imagination was a doctor, Marcus Whitman, who joined us on the Platte and was returning to his mission at Waiilatpu, in Oregon Country. The man's indomitable energy and vast experience in frontier travel were of priceless value to our column of migrants. "Move, move and keep moving," he constantly advised, "for nothing else will take you to the end of your journey. No activity is good for you that causes delay." The brave doctor's extensive medical skills saved us many such possible delays as he tended the sick and assisted in birthings, all on the move. The good doctor, like Irons, would depart our company at Fort Hall.

It was there, on the Platte, that I got my first close-up look at a real wild Indian. Early one morning, a long procession of squalid savages approached the circled wagons. Each was on foot, leading his horse by a bull-hide rope.

"Them's Pawnee," Sam Irons informed us out of the corner of his mouth, "come to inventory what they can spirit away after dark."

The Indians were clad only in loincloths with tattered and begrimed buffalo robes draped about their shoulders. Their heads were clean shaven except for a ridge of hair running front to back along the middle, reminding me of the coarse bristles of a razorback hog's ruff. Irons walked out to greet them, making them a gift of a small amount of tobacco in hopes this would satisfy them in the stead of later plunder. It was not to be, however, for they returned that night to make off with an ox and three ponies under the very noses of the night guards.

We lost our first man to Indians the following day, when the owner of the purloined ox rode out alone in a fit of choler to retrieve his beast. A search party found him before dusk of that day, his back bristling with Pawnee arrows. A sudden storm, bringing ice and hail, wiped clean the plain, preventing a proper retribution against the savages. We moved on.

Upon leaving the adobe outpost of Fort John, a supply point they call Fort Laramie nowadays, the wagons again spread out across the prairie to form a fan a mile wide. The formation was a maneuver to escape the vicious alkali dust that rose in a choking, powdery cloud, giving us and our stock the red-eye and drying our skins to cracking.

An occasional band of Indians added the only color to that miserable, monotonous crossing of cinnamon and sepia expanse. Looking back, I would have to say that it was the most ridiculous trip I have ever made in my life.

> *"I simply can't bear this desolation any longer, Fred. Please, let's turn around. I want a bath. I want to sit on my own porch in the shade. Take us back to Cole Camp, where we belong."*
>
> *"Can't turn back now, Sarah. Missouri is past. We've come too far. We are committed."*
>
> *"Lord help us, we* should *be committed."*
>
> *Mother crawled back into the wagon, tying the flap shut behind her.*
>
> *"How much farther, Pa? We about there?"*

We had come most of a thousand miles when the wagon master told us that we had entered the Oregon Country when we crossed through South Pass, (which was not a pass so much as a wide, even saddle). We were all buoyed and encouraged at the news—until we learned that we still had as far yet to travel to the Willamette Valley as we had come, and over more rugged terrain. It was my first realization of the immensity of these Western lands. The caravan took on fresh supplies at Jim Bridger's new fort, then we struck out again, facing the fresh challenges of wild rivers, deep canyons, and towering mountains.

Upon reaching Fort Hall, twelve hundred eighty-eight miles along the way, at the point where emigrants had to decide whether to go on to Oregon or to turn off to California, Sam Irons and Doctor Whitman both departed the caravan. The good doctor left in the company of a group of Cayuse Indians, charges from his mission in the wilderness, who had come to the fort to welcome him. Irons departed in the dead of night, saying no good-byes. I believe it greatly relieved the man to be free of the press of the "greenhorns," as he called us, who had been his traveling companions. We all hated to see these stalwarts leave us, and greeted their departures with trepidation, for both men had been rocks that we leaned upon.

Pa had not touched a drop of liquor since we left Cole Camp to journey west. He had been irritable and gruff much of the time, but I credited his moods to the travails of travel and to my ma's constant complaints. After a time, the thought of his old habits retired to the farthest recesses of my mind. So it came as a total surprise to me that, while at Fort Hall, my Pa got rip-roaring drunk. I was playing a game of mumblety-peg with the son of a fort trader when I heard the commotion. Pa had stumbled headfirst into a well. They fished him out, but he was dead of a broken neck.

"I knew he would come to a bad end," my mother wailed. "Now we're stranded here in the middle of nowhere, in the wilderness. It's all his fault. Oh, how I wish I were back in Cole Camp."

Naturally, I was devastated by my father's death, but oddly enough, I felt angry too. Pa had promised that everything would be wonderful in the great new land at the end of the trail. Now, he had deserted me. I was ashamed of my angry thoughts, but they would not leave me.

I had loved Pa, and I fondly remembered our earlier times together, full of fun and good humor. Blocking the bad times from my mind, forgetting the pitiful shell of a man he had become before his death, I became the defender and protector of his memory. I deeply resented my mother's constant belittling and berating of him, and I hated her whining about what he had done to her. I never once considered the pain, disappointments, and broken dreams that had caused her to become so bitter and unyielding.

Another man died that terrible day at Fort Hall, of a lingering illness. The fort's bourgeois had Pa and Mr. Richardson laid to rest in a thriving little burial ground outside the walls. The ceremony, performed by our wagon master, was perfunctory, at best, for, by now, death and sorrow were no strangers to the voyagers, and all were anxious to continue the journey.

The following morning, a train of thirteen wagons split off from our original caravan, southbound for California on the Raft River cutoff, as the rest of us prepared to trudge onward toward Oregon's fertile valleys. A Major Gilpin, who had accompanied Freemont on his recent surveying expedition and had elected to return to settle in the Oregon Country, agreed to assume the role of guide and scout for our reduced company. We struck out once more, following the Snake River north and west, deeper into the wilderness, to dare its raging waters and forbidding heights.

With help from sympathetic neighbors in the caravan, my mother and I, having no other recourse, kept on toward our original destination, the Willamette Valley—still more than seven hundred miles away

I was so deep into the grief I was feeling at the loss of my father that I cannot recall much of the next, most treacherous, leg of our journey. I rode and walked and swam and climbed as if in a trance, following the directions of others without thinking, as the miles fell away. Our moving community twice forded the wild waters of the Snake River, first at Glenn's Ferry (then called Three Islands), and again at Fort Boise. More graves at these crossings as entire families drowned in the swirling currents. More graves on the long trail, too, from illness and from gruesome accidents. I remember wondering who, possessed of demons, had conceived that evil journey.

At Farewell Bend, where the Snake veered north and east, the wagon train cut cross-country once more, into the Great Basin, heading across that high desert for its appointment with the mighty Columbia River, to brave its perilous falls and rapids in a wild, final ride to the paradise so long ago promised, and for which so dear a price had been extracted. The end of the Oregon Trail suffered no weaklings, for only the strong survived.

Ma and I were forced to halt at a small settlement on the Columbia River, shy of the Dalles, when our trail-weary oxen could go no farther. Fear and uncertainty engulfed us both as we watched the white canvas tops of the wagon train disappear around the bend. Soon the caravan would take to the river, converting wagons into rafts and boats for the last hazardous segment of the six-month trek to Fort Vancouver and the Willamette Valley. More would die on the river, but the majority of those brave and hardy travelers I'd come to know so well would survive to begin fresh and productive lives in a brave new land.

I was a scrawny youngster of fourteen then, all arms and legs, and I felt desperately alone in this strange new country. It was the land itself that proved to be my ally, for I loved the forests and the mountains, the crystal waters, and the mild weather. Rain fell almost constantly, in a silent drizzle that somehow had a soothing effect on me. When worried or frightened or angry, a walk in the forest, in a light mist, soon had me calmed and feeling that everything was going to be all right.

We lived in the old wagon, Ma and me, for we did not have the know-how to build a more suitable shelter, and we had no money to buy a house or to have one built.

My mother and I became estranged. Like many a long-suffering wife of a drinking man, she took to the Book—instructing me, in minute detail and during every waking hour, in the evils of drink and in the torment of eternal damnation and hellfire, for which I was surely destined if I did not toe the mark. That big old Conestoga wagon got smaller and smaller. I came to hate the sound of my own mother's voice.

The fact that Pa had not left us a stake was one of Ma's oft-repeated complaints. We had only a few dollars from selling the sorry brace of gaunt and broken oxen that had pulled our wagon over the Oregon Trail. A dry milk cow and a twelve-year-old gelding named Socrates, plus our meager store of belongings, completed our legacy. The arguments between my mother and I grew in frequency, intensity, and bitterness.

Charitably for us both, Ma soon met a mealy-mouthed deacon at the church—a widowed sawyer with bad feet and a six-year-old daughter with crossed eyes. A match made in heaven. Within a few months they were wed.

The deacon was barely bringing in expenses at his trade, so he and my mother decided to return East to settle on some farmland he held title to, somewhere in Ohio. I pitched a ring-tailed fit, stomping and hollering, demanding that I be allowed to stay behind. You could have knocked me over with a broom straw when no protest was voiced. Not a one.

The day came for them to leave, and I watched them onto the raft that would take them downriver to Fort Vancouver. My mother, teary and smiling, waved goodbye. The deacon stood somberly on the deck, picking his teeth with a splinter. His hand rested on the shoulder of my new cockeyed stepsister as she looked both up- and downriver simultaneously.

There was a moment as the raft poled away from shore and caught the current that I wanted to cry out for them to wait—a moment of fear and a panicky feeling of isolation.

Then they were gone, and I was alone.

Chapter Three

The feeling of abandonment passed.

Somewhat tenuously, but filled with a spirit of adventure, I turned my back to the river and made my way to the wagon to set up bachelor's quarters and take inventory of my assets.

There was the wagon, of course, the only home I had known the long months on the trail from Independence. A .44 Adams five-shot percussion revolver, an excellent handgun that had been my father's prized possession. An old Springfield rifle, .54 caliber, with a broken mechanism. Two bullet molds and a tin of black powder. A double-blade ax. A crosscut saw. Assorted hand tools. Saddle, bridle, and assorted tack. The bay gelding, Socrates. A change of clothes, long outgrown. Some of Pa's old things, still too large. Basic cook gear we had used on the trail. Bedding. Lanterns and fuel. A shovel. Coffee, tea, salt, and other staples. A bait of food that would last awhile—and the books!

Pa once had a thirst for learning that, until recent years, had surpassed the obsessive thirst that killed him.

He had been a teacher for a while in Cole Camp, and he had loved reading. During the long, cherished sessions before the fire, I had learned to love it too. He had taught me to read early and well. I often became lost in some treasured volume, always dreading the coming of the final page. Here, I had inherited a library to fill my leisure hours for years to come. Most likely, through some clever trading, I could even improve my collection. Space and weight had been critical considerations when packing a wagon for the long trip west, so folks were mighty careful in choosing what they brought along. As a result, books selected for the trip were generally fine ones, and were highly prized. The books Pa had chosen were no exception: Burns, Bacon, Scott, Cervantes, Defoe, Plato, Socrates, Keats, Shakespeare, Petronius. Books on philosophy, military tactics, mathematics, law, theology, astronomy, mythology. Texts on Rome, Marco Polo, Ghenghis Khan, Hannibal, Greek philosophy, literature, history.

Some of the writings were beyond my comprehension at the time, but I enjoyed reading them nonetheless, losing myself in the meter of the phrasing and the beauty of how the words were strung together.

When my mother and the deacon floated away into the sunset, I was two months shy of fifteen and ready to meet the world on my terms, or so I thought. A naive mind paints rosy pictures of the independent life, but I soon found that being on my own was a harsher reality than I had imagined. The deacon had left me with a small purse of gold coins, a gesture for my mother's benefit, I am sure. Or perhaps he reasoned that it was a small price to pay for one less mouth to feed and one less passage back to the farm in Ohio. At any rate, my grubstake was soon dissipated, though I had hardly been living high on the hog. In that small settlement there was no work for a boy alone with few skills to offer. However, I often gained meals for doing small chores for motherly types with soft hearts. I developed a sorrowful look that could bring tears to the eye of a river pirate. But the pickings got meaner, I got leaner, and I made plans to leave the little town at Starvation Creek.

I sold the cow to a logger's wife for two dollars and a bag of dried beans and I traded the family bible to the parson at the church for a jenny mule. I soaked the wheels to tighten the spokes, greased up the hubs and the axles, hitched the mule and the gelding to the wagon and I moved out. Striking south along the eastern slope of the Cascades, I crossed west at an unnamed pass, headed for the green and fertile valley of the Willamette, our original destination—my father's original dream.

I set up camp at the edge of a fetching little meadow with a grove of stately fir trees at my back. The site was within a half-hour's ride of the village of Tuality Crossing, downstream from camp on the banks of the clear and sparkling, turbulent Clackamas River.

My money and stores were about gone, my belt tightened to the last notch, and I was living mostly on fish caught from the river's rocky banks.

I was no great shakes at shooting the handgun. I spent hours practicing with it, tucking it in my waistband and drawing quickly, pretending to be an Indian fighter, but I could not have hit an old muley cow if I was to tie it to a tree. The rifle was still busted. Anyhow, both guns were of too large a caliber for small game, and would leave nothing but hair around the hole the bullet made. I would not have known how to properly dress or care for the meat of a deer, elk, or other large animal, even if I could have killed one. I had been brought up in towns, and was no hand at surviving on the abundant bounties of the forests. I did know how to set a snare for rabbits, and would happen across a nest of pheasant eggs in the meadow occasionally, so I made do.

I agonized at it until I put together a passable shelter. Using deadfall timber and utilizing a natural rock out-cropping that formed a sizable indentation under an overhang on the mountainside, I erected a lean-to of sorts. I had watched others build these make-do shelters, so I knew more or less how to go about it. A meandering shaft formed by a crack in the rock of the overhang served as a natural chimney. With the placing of a few stones, I had a serviceable fireplace, though it leaked a bit during heavier rains. Doubling the canvas canopy of the wagon, I made a door. Trenching around the perimeter of the shelter kept it dry inside, even in a frog-strangling rain. The lean-to was situated low on the mountain, so snow was not a great worry. Besides, the weather here was surprisingly mild, though wet a good part of the year.

Much of my time was spent in the forest above my camp, reading my books, getting to know the birds, animals, and plants that lived there. Chipmunks, squirrels, and camp robber jays became my friends. When I sat quietly, deer would browse within a few feet of my touch. Black bear and Wapiti elk went about their daily routines, paying me no mind, and though I had never seen it, I knew a large mountain lion lived in the area, for I had seen its sign. Pesky raccoons made it necessary to lock up all my edibles. I had surprised them more than once inside the shelter, playing fast and loose with whatever they could get into with their grubby little paws. The woods were surprisingly free of bothersome insects, though at the river's edge, swarms of what the Indians call "no-see-ums"—mean-minded, flying bloodsuckers so tiny one has to look twice to see them—sometimes sent me hightailing it for cover. Their bites are downright painful.

Thick green moss covered the forest floor of my mountain like rich Aunt Hannah's fancy carpet. It blanketed the rocks, the trunks of trees, and fallen logs. The underbrush was sparse, so moving about in the forest was a leisurely activity. Delicate ferns of several varieties grew all about in unbridled abundance and lacy lushness. I came to believe that if there really had been such a place as the Garden of Eden, it must have been located right near that mountain.

To that point in time, I had been thinking and acting like a boy, but my situation forced me to realize I had best grow up almighty fast. I would not starve, surrounded by edible plants and berries, fish, and small game, but I would have sold my sister, if I'd had one handy, for a platter of ham, eggs, biscuits and gravy, or for a thick slab of any kind of red meat. So, catching and mounting the mule, I nosed it down the mountain toward the village to find work. It was not far, so I rode bareback. Both the mule and horse had gotten on well on the lush grasses of the meadow, and both were fat, their coats sleek and shiny.

The town of Tuality Crossing was small. All the businesses were situated along one unpaved street not more than four hundred yards in length, except for a sawmill and the livery, which sat back on either side of the main cluster of buildings. It looked to be a pleasant place, clean, the stores and shops painted and cared for. There was a general merchandise store that also supplied the community with feed and grain. A combination dining hall and six-room boardinghouse. The town barber, who served as dentist, veterinarian, and undertaker as well, had a chair in the rear of the town's only saloon. There was a small café with a bakery, and a smokehouse. One empty building had been a freight office. The faithful held Sunday services in the deserted freight office, sitting and singing praises on split logs hauled in for the purpose. There was no preacher. The holding of services was passed among the members of the small congregation. The town had no schoolhouse, and I reckon the youngsters got what education was available to them in their own homes. Within hollerin' distance of the last building sat a blacksmith shop and a boot and harness maker in one large barnlike structure. A good-sized corral, now empty, adjoined the back of the barn. A covered bridge of new lumber spanned the river in the background, glistening in the sun like fresh-panned gold.

Quickly canvassing the length of the street, I landed a job in Mr. Sweeney's saloon as a swamper, sweeping up and emptying spittoons, rolling empty kegs to the shed out back and mopping the wood plank floors. Ma would have thrown a conniption fit, me working in such an establishment, and I suppose I got a perverse satisfaction from that knowledge.

I did not mind the work and I enjoyed being around the people, all whoopin', hollerin', and having fun. As I wiped tables, I would occasionally drink the beer left in the mugs and buckets. I developed a strong liking for the feeling it gave me, though a taste for the foul brew was a long time coming.

When not working or scavenging, I could most usually be found sitting on the porch in front of Sweeney's, a mug of beer in hand, reading one of my books. Mr. Sweeney took to calling me "Scholar," I read so much. On the day of my sixteenth birthday, I was engrossed in a pulp magazine I had acquired from a passing drummer. The book was a blood-and-thunder tale about a daring road agent who robbed rich tyrants and cruel landowners preying upon folks less fortunate than themselves. The author, Edward Judson, had been a passing acquaintance of Pa's. He wrote under the pseudonym of Ned Buntline.

The evening sun cast a brilliant crimson glow along the undulate outline of the distant coastal mountains, and I was straining my eyes in the failing light to see the printed words. A dark shadow crept across the pages of my book. Startled, I looked up. And up—and up—and up.

There was a big man standing before me. Tall and lanky, with a scraggly beard that reminded me of a hedgehog's backside. His slouch hat looked older than me by years. He was decked out head to foot in buckskins, soiled by seasons of sweat and miles of rugged trails. A large knife, a Green River blade, hung in a beaded scabbard at his waist. He leaned slightly on the longest rifle I have ever seen, the scarred and weathered butt resting on the boards of the porch. The large bore barrel of the gun extended well past his towering shoulder. A powder horn on a tooled shoulder strap hung loosely at his side. The moccasins on his feet had been thoughtfully fashioned by skillful hands and beaded in a simple but striking Indian design. He smelled strongly of the forest.

Light gray penetrating eyes, displaying a zest for life

and a youthful curiosity that made a liar of his stern countenance peered out from deep beneath shaggy brows. Lines of trial and hardship were deeply etched in the tanned leather of his face, but there were also telltale tracks of triumph, humor, and benevolence.

Taken aback by his powerful presence, I sat dumb, waiting for him to speak. When he did, I was sorely disappointed. I had expected the roar of a prairie stampede, the crash of thunder, the booming resonance of a vengeful god demanding homage. Instead, his voice was soft, almost meek.

"I'm Cawkins," he said humbly, "Lafe Cawkins, late of Montgomery County, Arkansas. I been watchin' you, boy."

My first impulse was to run. Watching me? Why? What was I to this long drink of water? I had not stepped on any toes I knew of. Hadn't hurt a soul. Reacting defensively, I blurted out, "Don't take much to amuse some folks, I suppose."

Wrong. The outsized stranger's face reddened under the weathered tan and his long body tensed beneath its buckskin trappings. Me and my smart-alecky mouth. That kind of wit can get a body killed in some circles. Hastily, I put on my most fetching grin. Closing my book on the index finger of my left hand to mark my place, I bounced awkwardly to my feet to thrust my open hand in his direction.

"Happy to make your acquaintance, Mr. Cawkins." Heavy on the *mister*. "I am Jacob Eriksson, sir." Heavy on the *sir*.

The tension broken, Cawkins' face brightened in a wide smile. One tooth was absent from its place among the white, gleaming ranks of its companions.

"I'd admire to learn to read," he said, blushing slightly.

Lafe Cawkins and I struck a bargain. I would teach him to read and to cipher, he would teach me to shoot and to hunt, necessary and vital skills for any man choosing to live the frontier life.

Lafe was a man of the mountains, friend to the likes of Jim Bridger, Vasquez, and Joe Meek. He had ridden with Jedediah Smith, Stalkin' Sam Irons, Broken Hand Fitzpatrick, and Kit Carson. He was as out of place in a town as I would be at tea with the ladies of the church. A fall had left Cawkins with a badly broken leg, caused when a cougar had spooked his horse, tossing him over a bluff into deadfall. The leg had not healed sufficiently as yet to stand the rigors of the rugged life of a trapper, so Lafe was passing the time serving the village as part-time gunsmith and part-time hunter, supplying meat for the tables of the dining hall and for Mrs. Thackery's smokehouse.

Our reading lessons began that first night after I had finished swamping out the saloon. We went up the hill to my shelter, Lafe Cawkins' home being where he laid his bedroll, and by lantern light, began an experience in which I would gain as much as I would give.

I relished the prospect of passing along the ability to enjoy the magic held captive on the printed pages of my treasured books. Pa used to tell me that a joy shared is a joy multiplied, and I believe that to be so. How many times have you been thrilled by the brilliant colors of a sunset, calmed by the gentle babble of a brook, warmed by a baby's touch, entranced by the song of a lark—and wished that you had someone with which to share those special moments? I looked forward to the companion-ship and the conversation, as well, for I was much alone.

Lafe had no formal education, had never learned to read or write more than his own name, but his was an agile and eager mind. He took quickly to the lessons. After learning his letters and how to sound out the com-binations and the words, I had him read aloud, then would aid and correct him as we worked. We pro-gressed rapidly through a primer I had borrowed from the smithy's wife and, before we knew it, were into my own books. We would read aloud, in turn, then share what we had learned in lively discussion. Lafe and I learned much of one another in the process.

Lafe Cawkins was born the third son of poor home-steaders in a family of ten children, back when Arkansas was a frontier territory. By necessity, he learned to pull his own weight by the age of seven or eight, helping to clear the timbered land for planting, clawing, prying, and hauling countless rocks and stones from poor soil to plant crops that, more often than not, met with disaster. Hunting game for the family larder, he developed an unerring shooting eye at a tender age, for it was vital to simple survival that each shot fired count for meat on the table. Lafe took off on his own at age twelve, working when he could find employment, living off the land when he could not. It was a mean, poor way to live, but it raised no weaklings.

At age fifteen, hardened by the rigorous existence he'd been forced to, Lafe was working the riverfront with the likes of Mike Fink. When Fink joined Ashley's party on a fur trading expedition up the Missouri, Lafe was part of his crew. In a boat-to-shore battle with a warring band of Delaware Indians, Lafe so impressed the expedition's leaders with his accurate marksmanship they plucked him from the boat crew and made him a hunter. He hooked up then with the famous mountain man, Jedediah Smith, and, when they reached the American Fur Company outpost, he stayed on, becoming a trapper. Lafe had been in the mountains since, traversing and trapping the myriad streams of the Rockies, the Bitterroots, the Sierras, and the Cascades from the Platte to the Pacific, from the Tetons to Taos. He knew the Indian tribes of the frontier as few men knew them. He had fought them and lived with them. The wilderness was Lafe Cawkins' home, and he wanted no other.

At night, we studied the books in pursuit of Lafe's education. Each morning, we took to the woods to work on mine. I proved to be an apt pupil myself. I already possessed a deep love of nature and the out-of-doors and I was eager to learn how to live in harmony with my surroundings

Lafe fixed my broken rifle and converted it to percussion fire, which was easier to handle than flint, less prone to damage or misfire, and had fewer external parts to snare on foliage. I already owned a fine handgun in the English-made Adams revolver. I was blessed with a good eye and quicker hands than most men, so with minimal instruction from Lafe, I was soon a dead shot with rifle and pistol—and I had the ability to get into action fast. Visibly impressed with the speed and accuracy of my shooting, the mountain man felt dutybound to set me straight on the responsibility a man assumes when he takes up a gun.

"Man totin' a gun is announcing that, if need be, he's ready and able to use it, and here in this country, most carry guns because they are needed. Needed, not only for putting meat in the pot, but to protect them and theirs against varmints on the trail, against hostile Indians, and against any man who don't respect the rights and lives and property of others. And Jake, this is a country's got aplenty of them kind.

"It's easy to think of yourself as good with a gun, and almighty fast. But many's the man that's greased lightnin' when shooting at broken branches and bottles, that'll freeze dead in his tracks when there's a body shootin' back. It's more needful, by far, to put your first shot where you want it than to be the first to put lead in the air. I've seen gents shot to doll rags and still get the best of a firefight. So make every shot a tellin' one.

"Never call a man unless you aim to kill him . . . and never kill a man, red or white, unless there's no way around it. 'Cause, son, that's a load you carry with you wherever you go."

The following months were filled with forays into the forest to hunt and to learn the ways of the land. Experience soon taught me that the killing of game was the easiest part of living off the country in this land of plenty. There was much, much more to learn. With the patience of a saint, Lafe Cawkins taught me the habits and behavior patterns of the creatures of the wilds—finned, furred, and feathered. He taught me how to read sign and to follow a game trail. I learned to skin and butcher elk and deer, and to take only the choice cuts.

"Isn't it a terrible waste to leave so much meat?"

Lafe looked up from skinning a fresh-killed doe. "There's times you'll have to pack your kill a lot of miles up and down over mighty rough country. If you're forced to range wide to find game—and that happens more often than not in winter—you may be days on the trail." He wiped his blade clean on the moss covering a fallen tree. "If you take it all, from toenails to eye-brows, you'll wear down your pack animal and have no room for more choice meat should you run across it."

Lafe went on to assure me that nothing is wasted in the mountains, and, as he spoke, a shadow drifted across the carcass of the downed deer. Looking up, I saw a vulture circling far above. Deep in the forest, a crow screamed its invitation to dinner.

I learned from the trailwise mountain man to move lightly and silently through the trees, stepping first on the balls of my feet to *feel* the forest floor as I moved. I learned to catch the slightest motion from the corner of my eye, and to distinguish natural sounds and move-ments from those out of concert with my surroundings. Lafe showed me how to find wood and tinder for a fire, even when the forest was drenched with rain, and taught me that I should always carry a dry fire starter in my pockets. I learned ways to spot quick shelter from a storm. He pointed out how to go about choosing the most likely spots for making campsites that offered shelter from the elements, but that were defensible as well in case of attack.

I loved it all. This was how I wanted to spend my days. All my days. I was as contented as a tick on a fat hound.

Lafe could read now, better than most, and could write passably. These were skills not many men of his ilk had mastered, and he was justifiably proud. The mountain man had developed a deep appreciation of books, and was grateful to me for having taught him.

"It'll make life on the mountain a damn sight less lonely," he said.

The time was long past when Lafe was fit to return to his trap lines and I knew he had stayed overlong on my account to complete my schooling in the ways of the wilderness. I could make out on my own now—live off the land if need be, though I would never be as skilled and practiced as the mountain man. I watched with sinking heart as Lafe made ready to return to the high country.

Lafe Cawkins and I rode down the hill to the village in silence, both having a head full of words to say and no easy way of saying them. We tied our mounts at the smooth and polished hitchrail in front of the Golden Egg and I followed Lafe through the batwing doors. We crossed the saloon to an empty table near the west wall at the rear. Mrs. Thackery's six-year-old, her youngest son, was squirming and fussing in the barber's chair as he got his first store-bought haircut. Skaggs, the barber, was voicing a frustrated complaint.

"Miz Thackery, can't you calm this young'un? He's tougher to trim than grandpa's toenails."

Sweeney placed a bucket of beer on the bare wood table between us, left two mugs, then hurried back to the bar to greet two loggers as they burst laughing and shouting through the door. Lafe reached the bucket and carefully filled my mug, pouring the golden liquid down the side of the glass, so as not to form a head. Sliding his empty mug aside, he turned toward me, the first to speak.

"I got no kin remaining who I'd know by sight, or care to see . . . and living the way I do, there's few men I can call friend. I'd be proud to have you as my partner, if you'd care to come along." He shifted uneasily in his chair. "I got to go down to Oregon City to replace the horse and pack mules I sold when I come down off the mountain. While I'm gone, give it some thought."

My face lit up like sun off a high mountain lake, and I blurted out my reply.

"I don't need to think on it. If you hadn't invited me, I'd have tracked you down. I was taught to read a trail by the best, you know."

Outside again, Lafe mounted his horse. We shook hands and he turned the big buckskin to leave. Turning in the saddle and looking back over his shoulder, he said, "Sell your horse and ride the mule. She's a better animal."

"Aw, Lafe, dadgum it. What'll folks think, me riding a lop-eared mule?"

"A body wouldn't fret so much on what folks think of him, if only he knew how seldom they do."

Smiling, he rode away.

I watched him down the street and into the shadows of the covered bridge over the cresting river. Me, Jacob Eriksson, a trapper and a mountain man. I could hardly believe my good fortune. I jumped into the saddle and raced up the hill to my shelter, yelling at the top of my lungs like some fool kid.

Chapter Four

I woke to the sound of melting snow trickling off the eaves of the cabin. The nutty aroma of fresh coffee served to coax me from my blankets. Tugging on my boots, I shuffled to the stone shelf above the fireplace and took down a tin cup, wiping it clean of dust with my shirttail. Pouring the cup full of simmering coffee, I took a healthy pull, burning my lips on the rim. The heat felt good on the way down. Lafe liked his coffee strong enough to float a beaver trap, and this brew would suit him just fine. It was thick enough and tasted rank enough to cure catarrh and angry the blood.

Opening the door, cup in hand, I was greeted by a glorious morning, with an infant sun lighting the eastern sky like cream fresh from the pail. A warm Chinook wind teased and caressed my face, carrying its false promise of an early spring. These sudden thaws are usually followed shortly by the last hard storms of winter.

Stepping away from the cabin, I looked back over my right shoulder at Mount Jefferson raising its hoary head over the firs on the rim at the back of the canyon, like a bald man peeking over a picket fence. Songbirds, absent during the heavy snows, appeared as if summoned and frolicked giddily in the trees. The magnificent evergreens, now called "Douglas fir," were named for a young botanist, David Douglas, who came to the Oregon Country with other scientists a few years back to study the flora and fauna of the Great Northwest.

Lafe had chosen a site for the cabin tucked against the north wall of a shallow box canyon high on the shoulders of the Cascades, on the eastern slope. An outcropping in the rock wall above us overhung the roof, reaching halfway to the opposite face of the canyon. The log structure was partially protected by rock on three sides, from the elements, and from possible attack. Passersby could not spot our location unless they happened within a hundred yards of the canyon mouth, except from high above on the south rim.

Lafe had walked into the forest alone, as he had done every morning since I had known him. I had no notion what this daily ritual meant, and I did not ask, figuring each man's thoughts are his own.

Lafe Cawkins was the most remarkable man I had ever known, seeming to possess some inner strength, some power he could call upon as needed. I had never seen the mountain man really angry, seldom even flustered, though he often had good cause. Lafe seemed to take everything that happened in stride, accepting all that went on as part of his day, completely at peace, with himself and with the world around him.

There was a time, on one of our hunts, that I had carelessly mis-tied a pack load of choice elk meat on the mule. The ropes gave way, dumping the whole shebang into a deep ravine. I exploded in a fury, throwing rocks and sticks, and hurling invectives at the innocent mule. I expected Lafe to land right in the big middle of me for my stupidity. Instead, he packed the bowl of his pipe, lit it, and sat in his saddle watching my tantrum, smoking peacefully.

Finally, matter-of-factly, Lafe told me, "When you're done with whatever it is you're busy doing there, we got huntin' to do."

He grabbed the mule's lead and started away, me following behind, hanging my head in embarrassment. Lafe turned, looked down into the ravine and observed with an ornery grin, "There'll be some mighty happy critters down there today gettin' served up breakfast in bed."

It was near the end of my second winter in the wilderness and I had never felt more content, more whole. There was a new look about me, as I was not all cowlick and Adam's apple now, but had fleshed out, hardened by the rigors of my environment. At five-ten, I stood a bit taller than most men in these parts, yet still fell a good four or five inches short of my long-limbed companion. I weighed in close to a hundred and seventy pounds, I reckon, and not an ounce of it fat.

We were to hunt that day, far afield and lower down. Our store of meat was uncomfortably low, and what game might be left at this altitude would be skittish because of the close-in winter hunting we had been forced to. With luck, we just might bag a fat bear, lured from its warm winter bed by the thawing breeze of the Chinook. Fat is the hardest of commodities to come by in the wilds, for most wild game is mighty lean.

I trudged knee-deep in snow to the corral, which was set at the rear of the canyon, sheltered by a thick stand of timber. Shivering in the shade of the trees, I readied our horses and a pack mule. I now rode a rangy little mustang, mouse-colored with a spotted rump, which I had picked up in trade from a band of friendly Wishrum Indians. Tough, wiry and mountain-born, the horse had proved himself a sentinel worth any ten men. The previous fall, it had alerted me to three Umatilla braves creeping into camp where I lay rolled in my blankets. The scar on my cheek, where an arrow had burned me, still itched on occasion, keeping my memory fresh. The Indians turned tail after I winged one.

As I led the horses and mule to the cabin, I smelled the last of our bacon frying in the pan. Lafe had our packs ready.

We'd had a good hunt. On the second day out, Lafe bagged our bear, a three-year-old. It was a mite gaunt, having burned its store of fat during its winter sleep, but we had the hide and would have tallow to last until spring. I downed an elk calf. Lafe got a big buck and a doe. With the mule loaded, we headed back toward our canyon.

A party of six Rogue Indians passed us on their way south from a hunt. They looked to have been successful, too, for their pack horses were heavily loaded with fresh meat. We gave each other wide berth, neither side wanting trouble with plenty of meat for the cookfires.

With horses acquired since the coming of the white man, the tribes of the Plateau and Great Basin—Yakima, Nez Percé, Umatilla, Cayuse, Flathead, and all the others, including the feared Modocs—could range further for game, bringing home more meat for their villages. As a result, the local Indian societies changed, becoming more like those of their mobile cousins of the Great Plains to the east—the Sioux, Cheyenne,

Shoshone, Comanche, Blackfoot. Many western Oregon tribes still did not use or need horses, and some were only now acquiring them, but in that neck of the woods, the transition was complete.

That night we camped low on the mountain in a grove of alders, a nearby brook flowing full with snowmelt. A clearing, where the sun had fashioned dark patches in the white blanket of winter, yielded a feast of tender grass shoots for the stock. Over a slow fire I broiled a pair of thick steaks cut from the haunch of the calf I had bagged, and Lafe surprised me with a pan of biscuits he whipped up from makin's he had brought along. There was not a diner in any city restaurant better fed on that warm starlit night. With full bellies and warm feelings, we smoked before the small fire.

Turning in, I laid awake in my blankets, hands clasped behind my head, gazing up through the tangled black maze of bare branches at a bright quarter moon bullying its way across the star-encrusted sky. I fell asleep with a smile on my face.

We awoke suddenly at dawn to the muffled, echoing sound of gunfire from far down the slope. Hastily breaking camp, we packed up and moved out. The shots had not been rifle fire, but pistols, so it was not likely the ruckus had been any Indian hunting party. Knowing that someone might be in dire need of help, Lafe and I took off in the direction of the commotion, keeping well up the mountain under cover of the trees. After the better part of an hour, the report of one lone shot bounced off the trees in the forest around us.

Almost there, we tied the horses and mule well back in the brush, then, creeping to the edge of the trees, looked down at the source of the trouble. A lone wagon stood belly deep in drifted snow, most likely settlers that had been trapped in winter's grasp. Six horses stood tethered in hasty fashion in a semicircle surrounding the scene. Their riders, those we could make out, were in the process of looting the wagon, throwing and scattering clothing, hurling pots and pans in random arcs, laughing and hollering.

Renegades! One of the bands of lawless and ruthless men roaming the country, preying on innocent and isolated settlers, trappers, and travelers. One of them, jug in hand, stood on the side of the wagon, relieving himself and patterning a cussword in the snow. Lafe, unwinding his long rifle, a Kentucky .64 caliber, took a quick bead and let go a shot. A hole the size of a water bucket blossomed where the man's gut had been a moment before. Firing right behind Lafe, I knocked one winding from where he stood on the wagon seat. The renegade spun back, landed in the snow and, stumbling and grasping his shoulder, ran caterwauling for cover in the trees behind the wagon, to where the rest of his bunch were already retreating.

Lafe and I then moved swiftly, humping it back into the forest, as shots rattled the trees behind us. Moving higher and away, we found a vantage point where we were well hidden and we stopped to survey the situation. The owlhoot that Lafe had blasted lay crumpled across the collapsed canopy of the wagon, his blood forming great splotched patterns of crimson on the dirty buff canvas. Four of the half-dozen horses had bolted at the firing. One was now grazing forty yards off. Two were still ground-tied. The others would likely wander back if the silence lasted. Two bodies, only partially visible from our previous position, lay sprawled in the snow behind and to the left of the floundered wagon. A man and a woman. The settlers.

The woman was stripped of her clothes and lay naked, a hole in her forehead. The blood from the wound formed a halo of pink in the snow around her head. No doubt the renegades had each taken their turn with her, then killed her and the man to avoid being found out.

"Keep close watch."

Lafe moved off on silent feet, back toward where we had picketed our animals.

I sat there, sick to my stomach and somehow ashamed, looking down on the scene of violence and carnage that had disrupted the quiet and marred the beauty of the pristine wilderness. What sort of lowly scum would so brutally violate their fellow human beings; snuff out the precious lives of others just to obtain what they had not earned? They deserved no mercy. Indians may kill those who invade their homes and trespass uncaringly upon their hunting grounds, or to prove their worth as warriors. That is how they live and have lived for century upon century, and it is not my place to fault them. But we, white men, are of a different culture and different teachings. Nowhere that good men gather are such actions as these sanctioned or tolerated.

Lafe came scrambling back with a welcome pot of coffee, a bait of jerked venison and a few hard, stale biscuits.

The horses spooked by gunfire had wandered back to the scene of the massacre, and now the saddled animals pawed at the thinning snow for graze. We noticed, for the first time, the deteriorating carcasses of two mules, long dead. By the looks of it, the desperate settlers had been forced to eat the team to keep from starving. For those poor souls to have endured that misery, gone to those lengths to ensure their survival, only to be set upon and murdered, set my pot boiling and I let it be known in a long, loud tirade.

"It's a hard country," Lafe said grimly.

We did not talk as we sat and watched, and nobody was moving around down below. The sun climbed high overhead. We peeled off our coats. The forest had come to life again, its creatures intent on the daily tasks of survival. We watched as a hawk swooped from the heavens to collect a ground squirrel in its talons, then disappear over the treetops, announcing its success in a screech of triumph.

"Now that sure as shootin' beats saddle sores," said Lafe, a hint of a smile playing at the corners of his mouth.

We had seen five men at the wagon. Six horses wore saddles. Where was the other man? Had he been off in the woods on some evil errand of his own? Or was he watching us even now? Lafe thought not, for we were well hidden and enjoyed a good field of vision, but what he was about and where he was worried us throughout the day. With the coming of night we moved away, back to the horses, and made a cold camp.

"They'll be gone come mornin'," Lafe predicted, "and we'll move down and have us a look-see. I'll keep first watch. You'd best get some sleep. I'll wake you midway through the night."

The morning dawned gray and overcast, a light mist falling, mixed occasionally with snow. I shook Lafe from his blankets and we made a small fire, the rising smoke dissipating in the boughs of the fir above the flames. We ate cold jerky, washed down with a pot of coffee, then put out the fire. After rubbing down the stock and securing camp, we crept back to the edge of the forest to study the scene below. The raiders' horses were gone. Nothing stirred. We waited, listening for sounds not of the wilds.

The bodies of the man and woman were lying in the snow as before. The flesh of the woman's stark corpse had assumed a gray-green hue. Some scavenger, probably a coyote, had gnawed at her vitals during the night. My gut churned as I willed my breakfast to stay put.

The thieving killers had not bothered to carry off or bury the body of their dead henchman. They had dumped him onto the ground, finished ransacking the wagon, then covered him with a red and white checkered oil cloth from the settler's rifled stores. I felt the hackles rise on the back of my neck, becoming angry all over again. I glanced over at Lafe Cawkins, crouched a few yards to my left. I could read no feeling in his pacific expression. To a stranger, he might have seemed cold and callous, unaffected by the plight of the innocent folks below, but I knew that just wasn't so. Lafe was a caring man—patient, gentle, and unassuming, with an almost reverent respect for the rights and freedoms of others. He especially valued and respected womenfolk, as did most men in the West, and he always treated them with courtesy and deference. I knew that the grotesque sight of the ravaged remains of this poor soul must be wrenching his innards.

Though I had never seen Lafe Cawkins truly angry, I knew the abilities and total toughness of the big woodsman. I could well imagine what he must be like when he got killing mad. I surely would not want to be the fool to buck him, once his blood was up.

"We got buryin' to do."

Lafe spoke through gritted teeth as he started forward. We approached with stealth, but the area was deserted. Finding a shovel in the wagon, I started in to dig three graves, mindful to separate the hole for the renegade from the others.

Lafe rummaged through the strewn clothing and rubble and came up with a dress. He gently and reverently clothed the outraged corpse of the woman, now charitably past shame and embarrassment. Then he wrapped her in a colorful counterpane, an intricately embroidered quilt that would be her shroud.

Crossing to the man's body, Lafe shouted out in surprise.

"Jake! Come a'running. This one's still alive."

The man was breathing, but the spark of life was dim. He had been shot twice in the chest, one bullet piercing a lung, and he had lost a sight of blood. Both ears had been notched by bullets in some sadistic display of marksmanship. Tracks in the snow where he lay showed that a coyote had come to investigate and, sensing life, had loped quickly away.

As gently as possible, we carried the gravely injured settler to a sheltered spot in the woods. Covering a bed of fir boughs with a blanket, we laid him down to have a look at his wounds. The poor man's body was frightfully gaunt, showing the ravages of near starvation. Building a fire, I heated water in a pan from the wagon and began to bathe the clotted blood from the ugly holes in his chest. Very little new blood flowed from the wounds, and I reckoned that he was about bled out. The man's breathing was faint and erratic, his pulse alarmingly weak. I wiped blood, bubbled with air from the pierced lung, from his lips. The poor fellow did not have a chance in a hundred of living through the night, but I would let no man die alone.

Lafe had buried the other bodies, then gone back up the mountain after our gear and mounts. I readied the grave dug for my patient, so slight were his chances, and was building up the fire when Lafe returned with

our mule and horses in tow. While he staked the animals on the snow-patched grass of the clearing, I
started coffee and put a couple of elk steaks to broil.
Then I walked over to check again on the dying settler.
There was no change in his condition. I put a venison
stew to simmer on the off chance he might regain consciousness and be able to take some nourishment. I
spooned a bit of water between his slack lips, but he
coughed and it ran down his chin to the blanket.

Having eaten, and after checking the patient, Lafe
and I turned to our beds, trusting to the horses to warn
us of any intrusion into camp. We were both exhausted,
more from the ordeal than from any physical exertion.
It started to rain, so I rolled from my blankets to fashion a tent over the unconscious settler with my slicker.
Crawling back into bed, I fell immediately to sleep.

Toward dawn, I dreamed.

*The wounded man was calling to me. Calling for
help, from deep in a dark pit. Two of the renegades
held my arms, preventing me from responding to
the agonized cries for mercy from the tortured
creature in the pit. The other raiders danced
around the edge of the yawning hole, laughing
wickedly and hurling rocks at the helpless wretch
deep within the bowels of the black crater. One
man stood deep in the shadows, watching. I could
see nothing but his eyes, burning through the darkness like the evil, glowing eyes of a cat.*

I sat bolt upright, my forehead covered with sweat.
Lafe woke up too, and we heard a moan coming from
the makeshift tent. Lafe stoked the fire and added fuel
from the stockpile we had gathered and covered with a

groundcloth. I bent over the man and looked into eyes wide with fright.

"They . . . they c-come s-sm . . . smilin'. Smilin'! Passing the time . . . of day." He spoke haltingly, straining to get the words out. "Never . . . had no chance. They grabbed me . . . helt me. Stripped the clothes from my woman. Made me watch. Watch, while they . . . took her. Had their way, each in turn. All except the big one. Mean eyes, he had. He grabbed Ellie . . . dragged her back . . . into the brush."

"Ellie? Who's Ellie? Your wife?"

"No . . . no. My daughter. Little Ellie. Twelve years old . . . he dragged her away . . . screamin'. Was nothing I could do. Nothing . . ."

"Shhh. Rest now," I said.

He shook his head. "No, no time. Find Ellie, find her." He coughed. A terrible, racking cough that brought a trickle of blood to the corner of his mouth.

"Find my girl . . . Ellie. Sister. Get Ellie . . . to my . . . sister, in Salem."

His head fell back and he closed his eyes.

Chapter Five

We buried the murdered man in a shallow trench next to that of his wife, marking each grave with a simple cross of fir branches secured with rawhide. With heads bared, we stood in silence, each with his own thoughts, each sending them on their dark journey in his own way.

The sky darkened suddenly as we turned from the fresh mounds of black earth that marred the white shroud of snow surrounding them, and a lament of the wind wailed through the trees above us. An eerie hush had crept into the surrounding wood, as if the creatures of the wild had joined in mourning the tragedy that had invaded their realm.

There had been a girl with the wagon. Going over the ground, we found where she had bolted toward a nearby wood, pursued by a large man, who caught her in a few giant strides and dragged her, struggling, into the timber. Further searching revealed no body, no grave—so, hopefully, the young victim was still alive.

We sifted through the rifled remains of the settler's

belongings, searching for something that could tell us about them—where they were headed, next of kin, anything that might be helpful. Lafe and I agreed that we had to try to find that little girl. Lafe found a strongbox with the hasp broken. Any valuables, of course, were gone, stolen.

"There's a few papers here. Bill of sale for the mules, and one for the wagon. Looks like a letter from a banker in Northfield, Illinois . . . the terms of purchase of a dry goods store owned by our Mr. Warren. First name was Marcus, accordin' to this. Here's an envelope addressed to Marc Warren in Northfield, from a Lavinia Pettigrew in Salem Township, Oregon Country. That must be the sister he spoke of. No letter in the envelope."

The rest was a hodgepodge of items, the stuff of hopes and dreams now dashed and broken.

I turned up a box of clothing that had evidently belonged to the girl. Ellie, the man had called her. On impulse, I took a print dress, folded it and slipped it inside my shirt. We took an ax, a few dried apples, a fry pan and a bolt of calico cloth, and tied them in a canvas on the pack mule. Lafe and I figured we had as much use for those things as wandering Indians.

We struck out to find little Ellie Warren. Every hour that passed diminished our chances of finding her alive and in one piece—if we were not already too late.

"Sooner or later they have to kill that little girl," Lafe said. "It's the noose for 'em if they're found out."

"Yeah. I know."

As we rode away, I glanced back over my shoulder, surveying the scene with sadness. I had read somewhere that man's greatest gift is decency of mind. Some men do not even come close.

The trail of the outlaw band was easy to follow in the

slush and mud of the melting snow. It had not rained hard enough to erase their tracks, so we followed at an easy pace, Lafe leading the way.

That night we camped higher on the mountain, within four hours travel of our cabin in the canyon.

I woke at first light, shivering in my blankets. It had turned cold during the night, the winds of winter chasing the warm Chinook breezes back to April where they belonged. Peeking out from under my hat, I saw a dreary landscape blanketed with six inches of new snow.

"Dadburn it!" I jumped up, pulling at my boots. "Snow." I slapped my hat angrily against my leg.

Lafe was sitting on a log, smoking his clay pipe. He looked at me like my brain was frostbitten. He smiled.

"Seems so. Not real unusual for February in these parts.

"No need frettin' over what we got no control of, and not much chance of staying on them killers' trail in this. We got no choice but to go home. We'll put away our stores, leave the mule, then start out again in the morning, sweeping the country. It'll take a passel of luck to cut their tracks again, but if we search toward the settlements, there might be a chance."

He knocked the dottle from the bowl of his pipe into his palm, holding it out of habit until the ashes were cold, then dumped it into the snow.

"Put on a pot of coffee. We'll eat at the cabin."

We topped the rise in front of the canyon before midday, the sun a faint glow in the leaden sky. Lafe threw out a long arm, stopping me in my tracks. A faint wisp of smoke was rising from the cabin's stone chimney.

We backed quickly out of sight and, dismounting as one, rifles in hand, we crept back to the crest of the hill and peered over.

"Lafe . . . those are our two mules they've got tethered at the side of the cabin. And they have our winter's catch of furs loaded up on them."

Six horses stood blowing and stamping in front of the door, saddled and ready to ride. A man stepped from the brush, buttoning his pants, and moved toward the door. The same marauders that had massacred the Warren family!

Easing back down the hill, we rechecked our weapons while we put together a plan of attack.

"I done for one of them renegades at the wagon," Lafe recalled. "That leaves five, counting the man you winged. There's six horses saddled up, so it figures that the girl is still alive and able to ride.

"Looks as if these here are some ol' boys need hard and straight convincin', Jake."

Lafe's hackles were up and there was fire in his eyes. His lean body tensed, long legs bunched beneath him like a coiled spring.

"It ain't pilgrims and little girls this time. Let's us just go down and see can they run the gauntlet."

We moved out swiftly, me following Lafe's pointed finger directing me to the right along the rockface on the north, where the cabin stood. Lafe went left along the opposite wall. There was good brush cover on both sides.

Stealing quietly and carefully to within fifty feet of the horses, I peeked around the base of a large, lichen-covered boulder. I was rising to move when the click of a gun's hammer behind my left ear stopped me flat-

footed. Caught like a greenhorn picking daisies. I had
been so intent on watching the cabin that I was careless
in checking the cover around it—a violation of one of
the primary rules of survival that Lafe had tried to
pound into my head.

"Never lose your patience . . . never shortcut your
precautions," Lafe had preached, "for a shortcut is
sometimes the quickest way to somewhere you wasn't
headed."

A voice behind the gun said, "You arrived just in
time. We had about given you up for lost."

I turned slowly and looked up at a bear of a man. Not
as tall as Lafe, but well set. He stood a good two inches
taller than me, massive through the chest and shoulders. I had seen buildings that looked less solid. He
wore a tan, wide-brimmed hat with a flat crown, of the
type worn by gamblers on the riverboats back in Missouri. A black mustache curled upward at the ends of
his mouth and his cheeks were clean shaven. He had on
a heavy wool coat, red and black plaid, with a fur collar. Under other circumstances I might have recognized
that he was a fine-looking gentleman, but in this situation I was not all that interested in how the man was
turned out. Without a doubt, this was the renegade that
Warren had described on his deathbed. The man with
the mean eyes. The one who had carried the girl away.

"Who do you think you are, Mister," I asked, for lack
of anything to say, "stealing a man's stock and goods?"

"I know who I am, my clumsy young friend. I am
Malachai Winter . . . not that you will have any use for
that information after today. And I know you. You are
one of the heroes that shot up my men back there. I'll
kill you for that . . . and your partner."

For him to introduce himself by name did not help my peace of mind, for he must have been confident I would not live to tell it.

Winter motioned me toward the cabin with the barrel of his pistol. Now that we were in the open, I could see the tracks he had made when he sneaked into the brush. *Keen observation, Jake, if a trifle too late.* I walked through the door with his gun prodding at the base of my skull.

A drawn and frightened young girl sat huddled on the dirt floor near the fire with a blanket around her shoulders: Ellie Warren. The dirt on her cheeks was streaked with dried tears. She did not look up as we came in.

The air in our neat little cabin now stank of cheap liquor, old leather, and the sour proximity of unwashed bodies. Two of the bandits were sprawled on my bunk, playing with a dog-eared deck of cards for pulls on the jug that sat between them. One, no older than me, wore a sling and a fresh bandage on his right shoulder. He looked to be a dim-witted sort. He sported a blank look on his slack face and had small, close-set eyes. Long hair fell in grimy, tangled ropes to his shoulders, and he had a sparse and scraggly growth of whiskers on his upper lip and chin. He hummed continuously, low and off-key. The other, a Mexican, won a hand of cards and reached for the jug. He smiled to expose a mouth full of long, tobacco-stained teeth. He was older than his partner, short and slender, with a whip-quick look about him. The liquid from the jug leaked from the corners of his mouth as he drank, running down his neck onto his dirty shirt front. His mama would be proud.

Two men? Where were the other two? Outside afoot, surely. All of the renegades' horses still stood at the door. I prayed that Lafe was on his toes, and a sight more alert than I had been.

The tall jasper holding me captive, who I figured to be the leader of this sleazy crew, spoke with surly amusement.

"You arrived not a moment too soon, my young friend. We had been about to leave, given up on you. I should have hated to miss your demise. What name would you like carved on the marker?"

"You're as arrogant as you are worthless, Mister. Jake Eriksson is the name . . . but I figure when I finally go down, they'll just carve, 'Here lies the man who killed a smug and sorry scavenger named Winter.' "

An evil, humorless chuckle escaped Winter's lips.

"You speak distinctly for one whose teeth have been pulled, pup. Where is your companion?"

"Rode down to the settlements for help. Last night. He'll be back soon with a posse of friends. If you're half as smart as you seem to think you are, you'll get your mangy crew away from here while you can . . . leaving the girl with me."

Shots rang out from up the canyon. Four reports, one more resonant than the rest. Lafe's Kentucky long rifle.

"Seems my associates have met your friend, Mr. Eriksson. Do make yourself comfortable."

Malachai Winter holstered his pistol. He was that confident, that smug.

I listened hopefully for more reports from Lafe's big gun. The throbbing silence grew heavier as the knot of fear in my gut swelled to painful proportions. After what seemed an eternity, the door swung open and the two remaining members of the gang came stomping in, heading straight for the fire.

"What did you do with him?" Winter asked. "Where's the body?"

"We couldn't get to him. He crawled off into a blackberry thicket. But don't worry, he's hit hard. Bleedin' like a stuck boar. We got two, maybe three shots in him. If he ain't already dead, he will be by nightfall."

My heart sank. Was it true? Was my partner out there dead, or dying? I had figured Lafe Cawkins too tough to go down. I dared not believe it.

"Mount up." Winter was irritated, not liking loose ends.

"We'll find their horses and take them along, and we'll burn the cabin. If he is still alive, he'll die soon enough, with no horse and no shelter. One-Eye, get the girl. The rest of you, move."

The oldest of the group, a small, grizzled man in dirty buckskins and a fur cap, moved to do as he was bid. A ragged scar started at the man's scalp line, continued across his right eye and down to his chin. His blank eye loomed stark and white in the wizened, rugged planes of his face.

"What you dragging her scrawny butt along for?" one of the others asked. "She'll just slow us down. Kill her."

With sudden, savage fury, Winter backhanded the outspoken bandit with all the force in his massive frame, sending him scooting across the earthen floor and careening into the opposite wall. The chastened outlaw made a reflexive move toward his gun, then, seeing the rage in the leader's face, thought better of it. He stayed where he had fallen, gingerly massaging the reddening welt on his cheek.

"My decision . . ." Winter roared. "Mine! I'll decide when and where it is time for her to die."

Then, as quickly as he had exploded in fury, a studied calm overtook him. He looked sternly at each man in turn and said through clenched teeth, "Let us not lose sight of who is in charge here, shall we not, gentlemen?"

They herded us out into the snow, the girl and I. The fellow who had spoken out of turn, a trickle of blood leaking from one side of his nose, mounted one of the saddled horses and disappeared around the corner of the cabin. He returned with the fur-laden mules.

If we were to stand any chance at all, now was the time I must make my move. They had not bothered to tie me, either through lack of concern or as a way of toying with me before putting a bullet in my head. Well, I might wind up dead, but I'd damn sure go down fighting.

As I tensed, ready to spring, the renegade tending the mules flew from his horse in a spray of blood, half his head missing. As his body hit the ground, the report of the Kentucky long rifle was heard echoing through the canyon.

While the bandits stood motionless in momentary shock, I grabbed the girl by her spindly arm and, dragging her with me, rushed in the direction of the big boulder, where my rifle still lay in the snow. I plunged for the safety of the rock, rudely pushing the girl ahead of me. Winter got off a snapshot that hit the heel of my boot. A numbing shock traveled up my leg. At that same instant, another of the outlaws, the dim-witted hummer, left his feet as a charge from Lafe's big gun hit him full in the chest—dead before he hit the snow.

I turned swiftly and sighted on the Mexican. He was fighting his mount, spooked by the firing and the smell of blood. I squeezed off a shot as he was slipping the toe of his boot into the stirrup. The charge caught him in the small of the back. The horse bolted, dragging the body, hanging by the foot and bouncing crazily through the snow.

The one they called One-Eye had gone back to grab the lead rope on the pack mules when the big .64 caliber Kentucky roared again, dropping the lead mule in its tracks.

"Leave it," Winter shouted from the rise at the mouth of the canyon. One-Eye held his rifle in one hand like a pistol. He fired in my general direction, then hightailed it after his disappearing leader. I let them go without an answering shot.

Silence descended into our canyon once more. I sat in the snow shivering, not from the cold, but from the near-escape. The ugly specter of sudden and violent death hovered like an evil fog over the blood-splattered, snow-crusted landscape. Too ever lovin' close for comfort.

I pulled myself up straight and turned, walking slowly to the bushes where I had left Ellie Warren. She was crouched there in the snow, cringing, in a fetal position. No expression whatsoever showed on her face. I led her to the cabin, took the shoes off her feet and the wet blanket from her shoulders. Then I lifted her gently onto my bunk. Covering her with a fine bearskin, I turned to build up the fire. When I looked again, Ellie was hard asleep.

I turned my thoughts to Lafe. If he was wounded, as those two bandits had said, he would likely need help getting back. I chuckled. Wounded maybe, but Lafe was a far cry from dead. The rugged man of the mountains had played all kinds of hob with those killers. His shots had come from the lip of the canyon, high on the south rim. Mighty fancy shooting. Firing downward is

ticklish at best. Yes sir, Lafe Cawkins was a man with
the bark on.

It looked as if our young houseguest was tuckered,
and would sleep until I got back. She would be all right.
I went over the rise at the canyon entrance to where we
had tied our stock. I headed the mule, still loaded with
meat from the hunt, toward the cabin, knowing it would
head for the lean-to. Then, leading Lafe's big buckskin,
I pointed my mustang's nose straight up the mountain. I
knew the exact location from which the shots had
come. The only spot on the whole rim with a good field
of fire into the canyon. I rode as close as I could and
tied the horses, then climbed a jumble of rocks to the
ledge where Lafe should be.

There he was, lying facedown in firing position. Lafe
was unconscious, but his breathing and pulse were
strong. Checking him over, I saw that he had been hit
twice. Once in the shoulder, once in the fleshy part of
the leg, the same leg he had broken before. He would,
no doubt, have a few prime words to say about that.
Lafe had lost a considerable amount of blood, and it
could be that the cold was all that prevented his bleeding to death. As gently as possible, I struggled with his
dead weight across my shoulders down the face of the
rockfall. It's a pure wonder how he got up there with the
shape he was in. I was hard-pressed hauling him down.

Hoisting Lafe to lay face down across the saddle, I
tied his feet and arms together under the horse with a
string of rawhide and we went home.

Wrestling with Lafe's big, limp frame, I got him into
his bunk and stripped him down to his skivvies so that I
could tend his wounds. Both shots had missed bones
and vital organs. The shot to the shoulder had passed

right through, and I had to dig lead out of his leg. I was mighty thankful that Lafe was out cold and couldn't holler. He was shot up, true, and would need considerable rest, but he was a sight better off than those misguided, recently departed gunmen who had sought to take him on.

Going back outside, I tended our stock and hung the meat from the hunt. The dead mule and the dead outlaws weren't apt to stray, so the burying could wait until morning. It had been a hellishly long day. After lugging our pelts back to the cache, I went to the cabin.

I checked the sleeping figures on the two bunks, the contrast in their sizes striking. I put a pot of coffee on the fire. Spreading a blanket on the earthen floor, I waited for it to brew. I never heard the pot pop as the last of the coffee boiled away.

Chapter Six

A month passed.

Lafe's wounds were healing well in the clean mountain air. I knew he must be feeling better, for he had gotten as cantankerous as an old sow with a new litter. He took to calling me "nurse," and his "little angel of mercy." I offered to put a bullet in his other leg.

Lafe Cawkins had spent his life outdoors, an active man and a man of action. He did not take to lazing abed, and I came near having to hog-tie and sit on him to keep him from moving around and reopening his wounds. He had done so several times, despite my playing mother hen.

"This here lying flat of my back is like making love to a skunk," Lafe complained. "I maybe ain't had all I need, but I've had just about all I can stand."

Ellie Warren had fleshed out some on a steady diet, though she still weighed less than a full bucket of water. A healthy color was coming back into her cheeks and she seemed to have more energy and vitality. It was hard to measure her physical progress for she was a solemn child not given to play and frolic. Ellie had a pretty little face, but there was no life in her eyes, no spark. I could detect no smile upon her lips or in her heart.

When Ellie came to us, she was wearing only her bloodied underthings and the blanket that was wrapped around her. I was grateful I had stuck that little dress inside my shirt that day at the wagon, the day we buried her parents, for it was all she had for clothing until we could improvise a wardrobe. I had dug into my possibles and come out with a couple of old shirts and a pair of pants I had long outgrown. Still, they were too large by a mile for her tiny frame. Lafe almost opened his wounds laughing when I tried them on her for size, and, I must admit, it was a comical sight. But together, for it turned out that she was a fair hand with a needle and thread, Ellie and I cut them up and altered them to a passable fit.

While lying abed, Lafe put together a coat for Ellie from some skins from our cache. Though he had to stop every so often to rest, he insisted on doing it for her himself. His skill at tailoring put me to shame, for he had fashioned many a suit of buckskin in his years as a man of the mountains. Ellie came as close to showing pleasure as she had been able to do when Lafe slipped that coat on her. She would not let it out of her sight, she was that taken by it. I finally convinced her not to wear it inside the cabin. Lafe had made the coat of prime fox and marten pelts, alternated in a patchwork pattern, and I thought it was as fine a wrap as I had seen on ladies of fashion in the cities of the East.

Ellie still had not uttered a word.

I spent much of the time while Lafe was laid up reading aloud from our store of books. His favorites were the epic poems and adventure tales of Sir Walter Scott, though I secretly felt that none of the heroes of those mythical flights of fancy could stand up to his own exploits. Several times I noticed Ellie listening intently as I read.

When at last Lafe began to hobble around the cabin, I started going out to hunt for fresh meat or to fish in a pool at the base of some small falls, just around the hill. The pretty little speckled trout made fine eating, and it was a welcome change from our usual diet of red meat. I was never gone more than half a day. Each time I rode out, Ellie would sit on a firelog outside by the front door and watch me ride from sight. And each time I returned, she would be sitting in the same spot, watching for me.

Nearing the end of the second month after the shootout, the snow had gone from our little box canyon, except for patches under the trees where the sun could not reach. There was still deep snow on the lofty peaks, but days in the canyon were filled with sunshine and songbirds and fresh-blooming flowers of a hundred kinds and colors. Hoping to spark some interest in the girl, I spent an hour or so each day acquainting her with the names and calls of the wide variety of birds that filled the mountains with music. She paid close heed to my efforts, but showed no real pleasure in it.

I decided to take Ellie on a hunt, thinking she might enjoy the outing. As I sat her on the saddle in front of me, I thought I saw her smile, though it might have been wishful thinking on my part. We rode off into a grand and sunny day.

Riding in the hushed forest, it was hard to imagine this the scene of the violence that had turned all our lives inside out just a few weeks ago. It had been an obscene insult to nature to have invaded her peaceful province with angry combat. It was my own feeling that murder and gunsmoke were as out of place here as those things would be in a church.

Stopping at the edge of a meadow, I spotted a sleek doe, browsing peacefully, her long, graceful back dappled by the sun filtering through the branches above her. Dismounting, I wrapped the horse's reins around a convenient branch, leaving Ellie in the saddle. Dropping to one knee, I took my shot. The doe took two leaps and fell.

I turned to smile at Ellie. She was gone. Vanished.

I looked anxiously in all directions and spotted the print of her dress disappearing into the forest. Rushing recklessly through the trees, I raced to catch her, branches slapping at my face and snatching at my clothes. I swept her up in my arms. She was trembling in fear, her wide eyes filled with tears of panic.

How could I have been such a blasted idiot? The child had been living in constant dread of gunfire and violence, blood and slaughter. Without thinking, I had reawakened her sleeping horrors, doubtless undoing whatever progress she may have made toward recovery. If I had been physically capable of doing it, I would have kicked my own rear end.

I walked with her back to the patiently waiting mustang, talking softly, cooing, trying to calm her. Mounting my horse, holding Ellie in my arms, I rode slowly back to the cabin with guilt riding heavy on my shoulders, leaving the carcass of the doe to the scavengers of the forest.

Lafe was hobbling about on a stout oak staff in front of the cabin the day the Indian came.

The red man sat his pony at the crest of the rise that

slopes into the canyon, looking proud and straight and tall.

Lafe shaded his eyes against the morning sun, then let out a whoop that brought me scrambling out the door of the cabin, my rifle in my hand. Lafe was three-legging it up the hill as fast as he could go, showing a grin that could have stretched from the Columbia to the Klamath.

Three Bears was of the Cayuse nation, and was far south and west of his people's lands. He had come to find Lafe Cawkins. Lafe had lived among the Cayuse for several years, and Three Bears was an old friend. Both had lived in the lodge of Wolf Robe, a widely respected leader in his society, the man who sent Three Bears to fetch my big friend. Old Wolf Robe had not given a reason; Lafe Cawkins asked none. It was enough that Wolf Robe wanted him to come—that he was needed. He would go.

Lafe explained to Ellie and me that his own Indian name was Bear-Upon-the-Mountain. I thought it suited him well.

The Cayuse brave knew enough English to carry on a halting conversation, but Lafe was fluent in the Indian's tongue, so they spoke mostly in his language. The two friends talked and laughed at length, and I found myself caught up in the mood of the visit, leaning forward and grinning as if I knew what they were saying.

He was an impressive-looking man, this Cayuse warrior. Tall and slender, with a sinewy power that rippled his bronze skin whenever he moved. He wore an open vest of wolf fur over his bare torso. A long, decorated breechcloth hung almost to his knees over leggings of russet elkhide. Soft leather moccasins on his feet, decorated with the simple and elegant beading of his tribe, and a necklace of the long claws of a grizzly, completed Three Bears' costume.

Lafe told Three Bears of how Ellie had come to be with us . . . of the massacre at the wagon. He told how she was carried off by the renegades, and described the shootout in the canyon. He explained that Ellie could not speak—or would not—and he spoke of her rekindled fears that day of the hunt.

Three Bears said that he understood Ellie's silence, insisting that it was a shield the Great Spirit had given her to protect her from evil spirits that wanted to live in her memory. And that when the evil spirits were driven away, she would speak again. I hadn't any way of knowing if he knew what he was talking about, but it made a kind of sense to me.

Then they talked of the renegades. Both men knew about One-Eye. One-Eye Charlie Riddle. Lafe had told me previously that he had known him at Rendezvous, a gathering in the mountains of trappers and traders at the end of the fur season.

Mountain men, as they were commonly called, was a simple term for a very special and adventurous breed of men, perhaps unique in history. They came to these meetings from all over—from every lonely mountain range where beaver dam the streams. They came to sell furs, drink and get drunk, fight till outfought, shoot till outshot and generally have a hell-raising good time after a long and lonesome winter. These hard-bitten individualists faced all manner of hardships, deprivation, and unforeseeable dangers on a daily basis in their cruel existence in the mountains and along the streams. They trapped the beaver, whose pelts satisfied the dictates of fashion in the cities of the East and in Europe. They dared to put their lives on the line against the un-

forgiving elements of bitter cold, vicious winds and
sudden storms; against avalanches and accidents, hostile Indians and voracious animals. They faced loneliness and boredom too. One can easily understand why
these staunch and rugged men, the free trappers, ea-
gerly anticipated this annual event.

Indians came to Rendezvous, too, by the hundreds.
The trappers, traders, and Indian warriors faced off
against one another and among themselves in hair-
raising contests of skill, marksmanship, and bravery.
The mountain men traded and got drunk with the Indian
braves and trysted with the Indian women. The way
Lafe told the last warmed my blood and quickened my
pulse, though I hadn't any such experience first hand.

Anyway, Lafe explained that Charlie Riddle had gotten that scar and lost his eye in hand-to-hand combat
with a Mandan brave in the Bitterroots, the brave scalp-
ing him and leaving him for dead. Full of holes from
the Indian's blade, old Charlie had crawled and stumbled almost thirty miles to a trapper's cabin, living off
roots, grubs, and berries along the way. The ordeal had
taken better than two weeks, but Charlie lived to become One-Eye.

"Charlie never was a likable sort," Lafe explained,
"but he turned poison mean after that. Took to killing
Indins. Any tribe, didn't matter. Squaws, papooses,
warriors, old folks. If he could kill a Indin and get away
with it, he done it."

All the tribes knew One-Eye and considered him
bad medicine. The people of every Indian nation would
hail the brave that brought in Riddle's head as a great
warrior.

Neither Lafe nor Three Bears had ever heard tell of
the man who called himself Malachai Winter.

"Seems a man to stay shy of," Lafe said. "He's low-down mean, no disputing that. Uncommonly canny too. You notice, Jake, that we never seen him till he was downright sure he had the upper hand and figgered there'd be no man alive could point an accusing finger his way. Might be that he is a known man somewhere. He'll use others to do his killing if he can. If he can't, he'll do it hisself . . . any way he can.

"Might be, too, you're the only man can name him for what he is. He won't like it a bit knowing you're walking around. You'd be well advised to sleep light, walk wary, and watch your backtrail."

Lafe stopped to light his pipe with a brand from the fire.

"And don't be forgettin', the girl has seen him. He won't know she can't speak up to point him out. This whole country would be up in arms to know what he's done, and he seems a man who'll want to be sure of his own safety . . . by whatever means.

"Me and Three Bears will be leaving in three days. I want you and Ellie out of here, too, before Winter—if that's his actual name—comes back in force to tie up his loose ends. Take her down to Salem to Mr. Warren's sister, that Lavinia lady. She'll be safe among all them folks. And they're kin. They'll be able and willing to do for her.

"Take our cache of pelts and sell 'em for the best price you can get. It won't be much, for the glory days are past for our kind, and our whole catch won't bring what five prime pelts would've been worth five, six years ago. But it'll be enough for a stake for you. You're a likely young feller, Jake, and can make of yourself what you will.

"I'll do whatever it is Wolf Robe needs done, and

then I'll come back and find you. I can't say when, but that's my word and you can put it in the bank."

The days passed all too swiftly and it was time to go.

At the first gray hint of dawn, we made preparations to leave the canyon that had been our home. My heart was heavy at the thought of our taking separate trails. Lafe Cawkins was my partner and my good friend— my only friend. His leaving would be like losing a piece of myself. I was worried that his wounds were not healed as they ought to be for such a long trip. But I respected his need to go, so I said nothing.

"Take care of Ellie."

I nodded. "I'll be watching for you."

I had slipped my volume of Walter Scott into his packs. They turned and trotted to the top of the rise. Lafe stood in his stirrups silhouetted against the rising sun, and raised his arm in a farewell salute.

An important chapter of my life ended with that final salute.

It was late in the spring of 1846 when, the next day, we rode out of the morning fog on Coffin Mountain following the course of the Santiam River into the wide valley, heading for the bustling settlement of Salem on the banks of the lazy Willamette. Brilliant rhododendron brightened our path as we crossed the gently rolling, lush valley, the air warm and moist and sweet.

The Oregon Country had undergone sweeping changes since I had arrived with the first great emigrant train of '43. The Reverend Dr. Marcus Whitman and his lovely wife who were on that train, were firmly ensconsed in the mission they had established at Waiilatpu, east of Fort Walla Walla. It was said they were converting heathen savages hand over fist to their "saving grace of Christianity." I was not at all sure that the heathens really needed all that converting. From what I had seen of Three Bears and heard of Wolf Robe, most Indians seemed to be far more spiritual than a lot of the white folks I knew, left to their own beliefs. But Dr. Whitman was a sincere and dedicated man, devoted to his calling and strong in his faith, inflexible as that belief might be.

A man named Samuel K. Barlow had just opened a toll road around the southern slope of Mount Hood, easing and shortening the route from the Columbia River to Oregon City in the valley. A mighty impressive achievement, powered by the sweat of one man's brow and the strength of his purpose.

The country's first newspaper, *The Oregon Spectator,* had started publishing in the capitol, Oregon City, a thriving town on three levels, overlooking the thunderous falls of the Willamette. George Abernathy was governor of the provisional government. And Jason Lee, who came here as a missionary, but had been bitten by the political bug, was petitioning the Congress back in the States to have the Oregon Country declared a Territory of the United States.

The empire builders had come.

Chapter Seven

The sun was low in the western sky when Ellie and I arrived in Salem. As we walked our mounts down the main street, I saw a sign on a storefront proclaiming, *Pettigrew Freight and Cartage Co., Caleb Pettigrew, Prop.* The name of the sender on the envelope found among the Warren's belongings had been Lavinia Pettigrew. With luck, this could be the same family. If not, they would surely know of any others in the community with the same name.

Leaving Ellie on the mule, I went inside the office, an eight-by-ten room with a plank floor and bare walls. A small counter holding a wire basket filled with papers and bills of lading divided the room. A square wooden table and a ladderback chair were the only furnishings. Mr. Pettigrew had gone for the day, but the clerk on duty, a wrinkled gnome of a man a scant five feet tall and wearing spectacles as thick as my thumb, directed me to the Pettigrew house. He was cute as a speckled pup. I had an urge to pat him on his little head, but I thanked him instead and walked back outside.

Crossing the plank walk, I remounted the mustang, took Ellie in tow, and in a matter of minutes we found ourselves in front of an imposing two-story home set inside a white picket fence. The lawn was green and well groomed. The entire yard was skirted with well-worked beds abloom with a kaleidoscope of flowers— zinnias, marigolds, petunias, moss rose, hollyhocks, geraniums and snap-dragons. A most unusual thorny tree, a monkey puzzle I discovered later, stood sentinel on the grass. A man and a woman, who I guessed to be in their late thirties or early forties, were sitting in wicker chairs on a wide covered porch, talking and watching the sun sink behind the coastal mountains.

"Mr. Pettigrew," I called out. "Jacob Eriksson. May I come up and have a word with you, sir?"

He looked at us, trailworn and haggard, smiled broadly and motioned us through the gate.

With Ellie standing slightly behind me, I stood at the base of the steps. I hesitated, swallowed hard, then started to explain my sad mission.

"Pardon me. Ma'am, are you the Lavinia Pettigrew had a brother named Marcus Warren?"

The lady jumped from her chair, the color drained from her face.

"Had? Has something happened to Marcus?"

I slapped at my forehead with the heel of my hand. *Handled that real smooth, Jake.*

"Sorry, that was stupid of me. Yes, ma'am, I have some tragic news for you folks."

I briefly recounted the story, leaving out for the moment the most shocking and grisly details. With tears welling in her eyes, Lavinia Pettigrew invited us inside. She descended the porch steps and bent to put her arm around her niece's shoulder to lead her into the house.

Ellie balked and looked up at me. I nodded my assur-
ance and they went in through the screen door. I
stopped Mr. Pettigrew at the door.

"Sir, I need to make arrangements for my stock and
find safe storage for my goods, then I'll come back and
tell you what happened up there . . . at least as far as we
were able to figure out."

His voice breaking slightly, Mr. Pettigrew said, "We
have a large stable in the back. There is plenty of room
and feed. Your goods will be quite safe in one of the
empty stalls." Mr. Pettigrew put his hand to the nape of
my neck. "You look tired, son. You go in and have some
supper. Be my pleasure to do this. We are greatly in
your debt."

Now I am not generally one to let another man take
care of what is mine to do, but to tell the truth, I was bone
tired, and so hungry that the lives of my mules were in
real jeopardy. I thanked him and went into the house.

Ellie was already seated at the kitchen table. She had
a steaming bowl of stew in front of her and a thick slab
of fresh-baked bread, spread heavy with fresh-churned
butter, in her hand. I knew she must be as hungry as I,
but her eyes kept falling shut so, finally, after setting
my supper in front of me, Mrs. Pettigrew took her hand
and led her away for a bath then to bed.

It had been a long time since I had eaten a meal not
thrown together by me or Lafe, and neither one of us
were any great shakes in a kitchen. I fairly demolished
that pot of stew and the better part of a loaf of bread,
heaped thick with strawberry preserves. I was a mite
embarrassed, and said so. Mrs. Pettigrew passed it off
with a smile.

Mr. Pettigrew came in from tending my stock and securing the furs. He sat down next to me at the table. His

wife came with a cup of coffee for him, refilled mine, then excused herself to go upstairs and make up a bed for me. I objected, not wanting to put them out, but they would hear nothing of it. It had been almost four years since I had slept in a real bed between real sheets, the last time being in our home back in Cole Camp. It sure enough sounded good.

While his wife was gone, I confided to Mr. Pettigrew that there were parts of the account of the tragedy in the mountains that he might not like for his wife to hear. I told him how Malachai Winter had dragged Ellie into the woods alone, and how much time had elapsed before she came under our care.

"Of course I can't be certain what, if anything, was done to the girl during that period, but taking into account the nature of the situation and Ellie's half-dressed and soiled condition when we got her away from the outlaws . . ."

I doubted seriously that they had taken her along because they loved kids, but he nodded his understanding, sparing me the pain of voicing my fears. I touched on the carnage she had seen, and on her unreasonable fright that day of the hunt.

"She has not uttered a word since the shootout on the mountain," I told him.

"Mr. Eriksson, Lovie will want to hear everything you have to tell us regarding what happened out there . . . every detail, no matter how ugly.

"She's a strong woman, my wife. We were among the first to settle in this valley. We came to this country following a pathfinder, not a guide, and there was trouble and hardship on the way. We had our share of confrontations with Indians, and Lovie fought by me shoulder-to-shoulder. Truth is, the first set-to we had with savages, she buried more of them than I did. I watched her dump all the possessions she held dear into the dust of the Great Basin, to lighten the load in the wagons, and I've seen her go three days without more than a sip of water. She never complained or had a regret she gave voice to, and even when the going was roughest, there was never a morning or a night that she didn't have a smile for me. That's the kind of woman you'll find here in the West, for the most part, and Lovie's the cream right off the top.

"After we had conquered the trail and it looked as if our tribulations were behind us, we lost our baby daughter, Charity, to pneumonia. She had come late to us, and we both cherished her greatly."

He drank the last of his coffee.

"So you see, Mr. Eriksson . . . I think perhaps my wife's a better trooper than I am. You tell her. You tell it all."

Lavinia Pettigrew reentered the kitchen.

"I've heated water for your bath, Mr. Eriksson, and laid out some clean clothes of Caleb's. When you've finished, do come back in and let us talk."

"You bathe in the house, ma'am?"

She smiled broadly at the surprise on my face. "Out on the sleeping porch . . . in a big tub, all the way from the East."

I soaked for the biggest part of an hour in the big galvanized tub, up to my nose in warm, sudsy water, coming near to drowning once when I dozed off. Hating to leave the bath, but knowing the Pettigrews waited in the kitchen, needing to know how their loved ones had come to disaster, I toweled off and dressed in the too-snug shirt and trousers laid out for me, then went back in to join our hosts.

We talked through the night, and with a rooster crowing in the morning mists, I went to my bed.

I stood in the carpeted waiting room with the Pettigrews as the doctor entered from the narrow hall.

"She is in good health . . . still a bit thin." He paused, searching to soften the words, but finding no way around the hard truth. "The girl has been brutally violated, physically. Repeatedly. I cannot possibly imagine the kind of fiend who would assault a young and innocent child in this manner. I should be the loudest spectator at the hanging of such a man."

Mr. Pettigrew pressed his wife's hand in his as Dr. Fox continued.

"But this other thing, her inability to speak . . . I just don't know. I can find no physical disability. There have been similar occurrences reported in battle, and the outcomes varied. They are just beginning to study matters of this kind in Europe, and little is known as yet. I am sorry. I just don't know."

I thought of what Three Bears had said.

"Ellie will be all right . . . in time," I told them.

They looked at me oddly.

Caleb—we had agreed to use given names—directed me to a dealer who bought our furs for four hundred dollars and change. I kept my mouse-gray mustang and one pack mule, selling the other mules for sixty dollars apiece. I had never seen so much money in one man's pocket in all my life. Not in mine, for sure.

At the general store, I bought a suit of clothes off the rack. Black coat, gray striped trousers, gray shirt, and black string tie. I chose a fine pair of black cowhide boots with a walking heel, and a gray hat with a high crown and a wide brim. Getting a store-bought shave and haircut, and smelling of bay rum, I strutted onto the plank walks of Salem feeling like a Ned Buntline hero. Leaving my buckskins and the other gear with the animals in the stable at the rear of the Pettigrew place, I set out to "see the elephant."

Leaning my elbows on the bar of the Three Sisters Saloon and Dance Hall, I watched a card game while I drank a rye whiskey and beer, then another, and decided to take a hand. Having a tolerable head for poker, I won a few modest pots to start. After six hours, I left the game eighty dollars richer. What was happening here? Life just cannot be this easy.

Heady with success, I crossed the muddy street to a restaurant recommended by the bartender. I ate a fine steak, blood rare, fried potatoes, hot biscuits with fresh butter and apple blossom honey, cream gravy, and mustard greens. Topped that off with half a hot apple pie with cheddar cheese, and a pot of coffee. Finishing with a snifter of fine peach brandy, I paid my bill, walked into a quiet, cool, starlit night and inhaled deeply.

"Jake, my man . . . this town life might be just your ticket for a spell."

Not wanting to put Caleb and Lavinia to task, I had taken a room at Ma Cutler's boardinghouse for the night. "Ma" Cutler was a big, fat man with a long red beard, named Geoffrey Cutler. He had been a camp cook for Fremont and Kit Carson on their Oregon Trail survey expedition in '42. We hit it right off, Cutler and I, and talked for an hour before I went up to my room— him doing the biggest part of the talking, having more to tell.

I crawled between clean cotton sheets on a feather mattress a yard deep and, by lamp light, read from odes by Keats.

My eyes grew tired, so I closed my book and turned down the wick on the lamp, but sleep would not come. Reflecting in the darkness, arms crossed on the pillows behind my head, my mind drifted back to the tragedy that had robbed Ellie Warren of her parents and her speech. It had been a brutal and senseless act. Two lives had been callously snuffed out, and a young girl's life had been so shattered and scarred she might never recover, though I hoped that one day her right to live a normal life might be restored. Only time would reveal the answers.

The events in the mountains had left their mark on me too. I had faced death and danger, as we all had, and I had been forced to take a good hard look at what I was made of. I stood up well enough under fire, and knowing that was a comfort. I suppose no man really knows how he will react to adversity until he is tested. But I had been mighty scared, too, and had been shamed by it, until I confessed my fear and my shame to Lafe Cawkins.

"Fear is a downright necessity to a man," Lafe had assured me. "It's the very key to surviving out here. Lord knows, I got it in ample supply, as does any man who loves and respects life and its rewards. It don't reflect on a man's worth or mettle to be afraid . . . it's how he toes up to the line in spite of fear that takes his measure. And Jake, you stack up fine."

The firefight with the renegades also left me with a sense of my own mortality. A bullet plays no favorites. A man can never be certain when his number might come up, so it is vital for each of us to do what he can with today. It could well be the only chance he gets.

I was a grown man now. It was high time I figured out just who and what I was, what I intended to do with my life. Lafe once warned me that, "The hound that runs with his nose in another dog's backside, he don't get the coon." I resolved that from here on out I would chart my own course. With that resolution in my mind, I drifted off to sleep.

With little Ellie delivered to the safe bosom of loving relatives, my job was done. I was on my own again for the first time since meeting Lafe Cawkins.

At liberty as I was, I decided to take a ride over to the coast. I had never seen the Pacific, or any other sea. I had heard that the coastline of the Oregon Country is one of the most scenic in the world. As I left the boardinghouse that morning I stopped to talk with Geoffrey Cutler about my intentions.

"Thought I would ride over to the seacoast for a few days and have a look-see. I'm sure you will be wanting to let the room, but I wondered, would you be willing to keep my possibles in safekeeping while I'm away?"

"Sure enough, I will. You will love that country over there, son. It's a land that sticks in a man's mind for all his days. I'll fix you up with new quarters when you get back. Enjoy the trip."

I dropped in at the freight office to tell Caleb of my plans. He was kind enough to offer me the use of a big, black mare for the trip and said he would gladly board my mustang while I was gone. The little gray had been ridden hard of late, and could use the rest.

Then I sauntered over to the Pettigrew house to have breakfast with Lavinia and Ellie. Keeping fifty dollars for my needs on the trip, I left the rest of my poke with Lavinia for safekeeping. I went out back to the stable for Caleb's mare and the pack mule, waved good-bye to Ellie, then headed for the general store in town. After filling my order for supplies, I packed the mule, mounted the black, and headed west out of town, full of a spirit of adventure.

Clearing the town limits, I followed the lazy Willamette south a few miles to a ferry crossing and, for ten cents, rode the ferry to the west bank. Then I cut southwest, cross-country. I rode at an easy pace through the gentle valley, enjoying the sunshine and solitude, away from town and folks. I took a notion to stop before sundown to make camp on the banks of the Siletz, and to fish for my supper. A half hour of angling netted me a fine panful of sunfish, which I rolled in yellow corn meal and fried in hot bacon grease. Served up with a potato roasted in the coals and bacon-flavored dandelion greens, I was eating high off the country.

After cleaning the dishes, I took an easy stroll along the river, watching a brilliant red-orange sun making silhouetted scallops of the rounded tops of the Coast Range mountains, gentler and friendlier than their sometimes forbidding inland cousins, the Cascades.

I fell asleep that night to the river's song and awoke to the smile of the sun to continue my journey of pleasure and discovery. I had read much about the tropical rain forests and South Sea paradises of romantic legend, and knew that this lush, green world through which I was riding must rival any other spot in the world for sheer beauty. Even the creatures seemed more leisured, not having to wander far afield for food, as it was all around. The moisture in the air was a tangible thing, carrying the gift of abundant life as it crept inland toward the valleys.

I happened across a short, heavy-set Indian walking

on the trail. One of the coastal tribes, Clatsop, most likely. His manner was friendly and relaxed. Apparently out on a lark, he traveled unarmed. We swapped smiles as we passed.

The breeze picked up farther along, the smell of salt air quickening my pace. The trees thinned slowly. I could hear the muted roar of the surf on the wind. Topping a small rise, I was greeted by a blue ocean stretching forever in all directions. Crashing, pounding waves broke brilliantly white upon the shore, leaping and beckoning for my attention. Inviting white beaches extended from horizon to horizon, punctuated with random artistry by black upthrusts of rock. Proud, rugged monoliths reached from the sea to scrape the sky. The whole vast expanse roared its welcome.

Overwhelming! I would have swapped my horse and saddle for someone special with which to share that moment—Lafe, Ellie, Pa.

Anxious to get closer, to touch it, I picked my way down the cliffs to the beach. Picketing the animals and relieving them of their loads, I pulled off my boots and began to walk the sparkling sands in my bare feet. It was a glistening new world, filled with sights and wonders to last a lifetime. I played in tidal pools that teemed with life forms I had never seen, nor even read about. Giant strands of seaweed had been washed ashore, as long as trees are tall. Beautiful gemlike agates lay by the thousands upon the sands. It was more than a backwoods boy from Missouri could savor in one fell swoop. I stripped off my clothes, rushed yelling into the surf and swam in the sparkling waters, frolicking like an otter in a pond.

Cutler had told me how to dig clams from the wet

sands, and I captured Dungeness crabs from a pool where they had been trapped at high tide. Building a fire of driftwood, I cooked my meal on the sands, as men have done from the dawn of time, a guest of the bountiful sea.

I laughed at the antics of sea otters as they splashed and played beyond the breakers. I marveled at the grace of the large white gulls rising swiftly and effortlessly into the sky on powerful updrafts of wind, gliding on silent wings, hanging motionless in midair, swooping low to catch another lift and beginning the process once again. I was a wide-eyed kid again, thrilled and taken with a newfound toy.

I watched the sun set flame to the waters. Then the sea swallowed the sun and cooled the heavens to allow the moon to play, and the sea was rewarded with a silver crown.

I stayed six days, roaming up and down the coast, walking the beaches for miles, collecting agates and sand dollars and shells, sleeping on the sand, romping in the surf.

On the seventh day, a storm swept in off the sea, so, reluctantly, I headed inland again toward the peaceful valley. Having wandered south twenty miles or so from where I had come to the coast, I chose to take a different route back, across Alsea Summit and circling Mary's Peak.

I camped twelve miles inland in a cozy cave under a dry waterfall, its stream having changed course long ago. The wind howled fiercely, driving a hard rain before it. The stock and I remained dry and unaffected by the storm's fury throughout the day.

Travelers had often used the cave. Indians mostly, I

figured. There were signs of old fires and a supply of dry wood, thoughtfully left for the next passerby. I made a mental note to replenish the store of fuel.

With the coming of morning the storm had passed, leaving a steady drizzle trailing after as a reminder of its might. I staked the horse and mule to graze alongside a meandering, spring-fed stream and returned to the cave to put a pot of coffee on to boil. Relaxing with a smoke at the mouth of the cave, lulled by the peaceful silence of the forest in the mist, I almost missed the warning as the ears of both horse and mule shot up in alarm.

Chapter Eight

Snatching my rifle from atop my blankets, I crept near the animals so that I could quiet them if need be, then searched the trees for whatever had spooked them.

I heard them before I saw them—a line of riders on the trail, not twenty yards from where I crouched unseen. The horsemen seemed to be grumbling about something. I caught, "powerful poor pickin's" and "rotten . . . ," but could not grasp the gist of it.

Then I froze. Trailing the main group of riders were two that I knew—One-Eye Charlie Riddle and Malachai Winter! A chill of fear sent a shiver through me, as my memory once more felt the barrel of a pistol at the base of my skull. I watched them, out of sight. Thank heavens they had not seen me.

After I pulled my stomach out of my throat, I settled down to consider my options. There were too many hardcases in that bunch for me to tackle alone, no question.

Should I follow them now, and risk being seen or heard? Or should I wait, then track them to their hideout, a safer action? I admit it crossed my mind, too, just to hightail it out of there. But no, those hoodlum predators had to be made to face up to what they had done to Ellie Warren and her folks. They must not go unpunished. I elected to wait until they were safely away, follow their trail, locate their base of operations, then ride for help.

I drank my pot of coffee, paced nervously, checked and rechecked my weapons. Then, after cleaning up the camp and restoring the woodpile, I started on the trail of the renegades. I had counted seven men. There were probably more in camp. I would need plenty of help, for this crew was bear-dog mean. The beauties and wonders around me were forgotten as I followed after the group of desperadoes, now an hour and a half ahead of me. Would they post sentries as they neared their home stomping grounds? It was likely. Winter had proved to be a cautious man.

Intent on their tracks, I rounded a narrow and curving section of trail. A sharp drop of forty-five or fifty feet to a deep river in a rocky gorge on my right led me to crowd against the steep bluff on the other side.

Suddenly my horse reared in fright as a slide of soil and rocks came rumbling toward us from above. A hurtling rock struck my head, knocking me from the saddle, just as the full force and weight of the slide reached me, carrying me over the side, followed by the screaming, flailing pack mule. In the racing confusion, I thought I heard a piercing and evil laugh above the deafening roar as the deluge of rock and earth enveloped me. I was unconscious before I stopped falling.

Malachai Winter leaned back in his chair, a broad smile on his face. He was talking with One-Eye Charlie

Riddle, mountain-man-turned-killer. Winter filled his lungs with smoke from a long, black cigar, exhaling slowly.

"It is most fortunate that you spied our young friend lurking off the trail, One-Eye. Are you positive he died in the slide?"

"Got to of. If the fall didn't do him, he was kilt when that pack beast landed on him. I can go down there and put a ball in his skull, though, if you want."

"No, no . . . it's much better this way. A tragic accident. No questions, no speculations, no problems. Stay away from there. Someone will find him . . . eventually."

My first awareness was of total blackness, and of a numbing cold gripping my left arm. Slowly returning to my senses, I realized that it was the middle of the night, and that my arm lay in running water. I lay very still, afraid to move, trying to locate myself. It took several minutes to remember what had happened. My thoughts were murky. I fought to bring them into focus. Then the pain made itself known, from the marrow in my bones outward. I was stretched out on jagged rocks that stabbed into my back, and it felt like every blasted rib I owned was busted.

There was no feeling in my lower body. Alarmed, I reached quickly toward my legs, stopping my move as a slashing, immobilizing pain brought me up short. I lay back, panting heavily, my head humming. More gingerly then, I slid a hand down, discovering that the body of either the horse or the mule—I could not see which in the dark—was across my legs, pinning me down. Groping blindly, my hand hit the oilskin cover of the pack. It was the mule.

My mouth was so dry my tongue felt like a piece of

rope. Careful not to jerk around, I reached to the water, cupped my palm and painfully brought my hand to my lips. I did it again. And again. I still wanted more, but it was mighty hurtful going, so I stopped for the time being. I could hear the lonely sounds of the night over the rush of the river's flow at my back.

Gritting my teeth against the throbbing pain, I started pulling the largest and sharpest rocks from under my back. There was a passel of them. Getting that done, I kind of melted, exhausted. I lost consciousness, whether in sleep or weakness, I don't know.

The sun's impudent glare on my closed eyelids woke me. I lay there a minute with eyes closed, not really wanting to see how much of a fix I was in. I tensed and tested each muscle from my scalp on down. God Almighty, I was sore. Everywhere. Badly bruised in the fall; not fatal, but often more vexsome than broken bones. I could not move my legs at all. Opening my eyes, I saw the dead pack mule lying across them. The fall had broken the poor beast's neck.

Looking around, I saw no sign of the mare I had been riding. It figured that after I was knocked out of the saddle, the panicked horse had escaped in front of the slide. Probably still running.

Blast it. My rifle. It was still in the saddle boot on the mare. Slapping my hip, I found my handgun still in its holster, the flap fastened over the grip. Drawing the gun up in front of my face, I checked the load and the action. No damage that I could see. Fully loaded.

I could use the gun to signal for help, but who would hear me? That outlaw bunch I'd been following, most likely. Eliminate that for now. Looking again at the mule, I saw that the pack was within my reach. There was a bait of food and some ammunition in the pack.

Struggling to rest on my elbows, every move a torment, I strained to pull my legs from under the carcass of the mule. No chance.

Squinting skyward, I saw vultures circling, patiently biding their time, secure in the knowledge that all living creatures eventually come to their supper tables. I considered the fix I was in. I would not starve for a while yet, anyway. Nor die of thirst. I had the Adams .44 to defend against marauding predators and scavengers. But I could not see how, by my own efforts, I was going to escape the dead weight of the mule's carcass. I was trapped and without help.

Would that gang of toughs discover me here? If they did, I was a goner. Winter would not play with me this time. He would make sure that I was dead meat. I vaguely remembered hearing laughter as I dropped over the lip of the trail. Had the outlaws caused the landslide? I looked up to the ledge from which I'd been swept. No movement. No sign of help, but no sign of enemies. Lying flat again to ease my discomfort, I slept once more.

Judging by the sun, it was mid-afternoon when I woke, my head throbbing like a Modoc war drum. Two vultures, more daring than the rest, had descended and were perched on the carcass of the dead mule, tearing at the flesh with vicious beaks. I screamed at the ghoulish scavengers and they departed in a rush of flapping wings that stirred the air around me. A man forgets what large birds the ghoulish things are when he is watching them circle high above.

My heart was racing. I felt feverish. Thirsty again, I fumbled with the pack on the mule's stiffening form until I found a tin cup. I twisted around to fill it from the river and drank deeply. Mmmm, better.

Inspecting the carcass that held me captive, I could see that the major part of its weight was resting on top of the larger rocks. Maybe, just maybe, I could dig under my legs, removing enough sand and rock to allow me to pull them free. Well, I had nothing else to do. Nothing at all.

I chewed on some jerked venison from the pack, drank more water, then using the cup as a scoop, began to dig. I worked in short intervals until dark, pausing often to ease the pain. In exhausted slumber I forgot my bumps, breaks, and bruises.

When dawn crept into the gorge, my head and shoulders were lying in shallow water. I sat up with a start, wincing at the sudden movement. The river was rising! In panicked frenzy I took cup in hand and began to dig furiously.

After half an hour of steady digging I stopped to rest and to eat a bit of jerky. I would have killed for a cup of Lafe's strong, black coffee. There seemed now to be some feeling in my legs. The pressure had been relieved somewhat by the frustratingly slow excavation process. Steeling myself against the pain to come, I pulled with all the strength I could muster.

Nothing.

I started to dig again.

The mule's body was now stiff and swarming with gnats and flies. Good. It would not sag back down on my legs.

I worked another hour. The river was still rising, but slowly, and I kept on with my methodical chore.

I tried again to pull my legs free. They moved! About six inches. I dug some more.

I rested and drank, then braced myself to try again.

This had better do it. I did not think I had the strength for another try.

Slowly—slowly—moving an inch at a time.

Then I was free!

Puffing and wheezing, I briskly rubbed my numbed legs to get feeling back in them. I loaded up what I could carry in my pockets out of the pack, then sat on the dead mule and smoked, trying to figure how best to tackle the long trip back home. I would stay to the river bank. There was not a chance in hell I could climb that bluff to the trail with my ribs all stove in. The bank would be no picnic either. It was a mass of jumbled boulders, brush, drop-offs and fallen timber. But I would have water, and places to hide if the need arose.

"I'm not getting any closer, sitting here on my dead mule."

I started. It was slow going, crippling along like some old fossil with lumbago. By nightfall, I could still see the body of the pack mule in the distance behind me. Three days later, I stumbled onto the floor of the valley.

For six weeks I lay in an upstairs bedroom of the Pettigrew home, recuperating from the fall.

A passing settler had brought me in his wagon from where I limped from the mountains to the doctor in Salem. I had five broken ribs and a broken bone in my left foot, severe bruises and cuts, and a pulled muscle in my back. Painful injuries, but nothing that time would not heal. The doctor notified Caleb, who insisted I spend my convalescence with him and his family. Grateful, I thanked him and apologized for losing his mare, offering to make good the loss. He dismissed the apology with a wave of his hand.

"Don't give it a thought, Jake. That mare is known all over the valley. Someone will find her and bring her home."

And someone did.

The local law came to see me, got my description of the band of raiders I had seen, but nothing ever came of it. We came to believe they had passed on out of that part of the country.

Ellie assumed the responsibilities of tending to my needs, and was constantly at my side. I was not totally bedfast, so we spent a part of each day reading, weather permitting, on an upstairs porch. She still did not speak, but she seemed to be more animate and interested in what was happening around her.

Eventually, I was mobile and feeling better, about to go berserk with cabin fever. Expressing my gratitude to the Pettigrews and to Ellie, I moved back to Ma Cutler's. I picked up where I had left off the night before leaving for the coast. Getting decked out in my struttin' outfit, I went to meet my destiny in the saloons and at the gambling tables of the Oregon Country.

Where did I go wrong? What misguided decision did I make that led me to this?

The changes that took place over the next few years were practically imperceptible on a daily basis. But, in retrospect, I see that they were both rapid and profound. My perceptions and my priorities changed, my values deteriorated. Mostly, my actions and attitudes became centered upon my own gratifications and desires. I did not see it coming, so I could not get out of the way. I can't explain it, this transformation of mind and of soul, for I do not understand it myself. When did the end begin?

It started, I guess, that first night on the streets of Salem. Plucked from an environment of clean, free, and simple living in my mountain canyon home, removed from the strong and steady influence of my friend, Lafe Cawkins, I had been whisked into the heady atmosphere of unearned freedoms and instant pleasures. Plenty of money, fine liquor, good food. I had a wildcat by the short hairs and no way to let go.

My early luck at cards had me convinced that easy riches were mine for the taking. Why should a man spend his life up to his backside in freezing water in a remote mountain stream trapping smelly little animals for the fur on their backs to make a few dollars to buy what he would need only to go right back and do the same dadgum thing, year after miserable year? It made no sense.

The fine new clothes, the heavy wallet in the pocket of my coat, the comfort and pleasure of a soft bed and a warm room—all these things played a part in the seduction of my purpose and principles.

Strange, new, and seemingly wonderful things were happening to me. I was discovering pleasures that had never been a part of my life experience, that I had never dreamed possible. A carefree lifestyle—no hardship, no danger, no hard work. It seemed I was living the romantic life of a character from one of my beloved adventure stories.

It had been preached to me as far back as I can remember that honest toil and selflessness are the basis of a content and satisfying life. I was raised on *don'ts*. Don't drink whiskey, don't smoke, don't run with women, and don't play cards. I rejected such restrictions and set about proving the pious, prudish purists wrong. Hide and watch, brothers and sisters, for Jake has found an easier, softer way.

The evening following my move back to the boardinghouse I had promised to have supper with the Pettigrews. As I headed through the gate to the house, Ellie came prancing proudly out the door, sporting a brand new outfit. She stood on the porch, smiling shyly, awaiting my reaction. I made a big fuss over her and we went in to supper. It was good food and good company, but I was nervous and uneasy, wanting to get to the poker tables for an early start. After dessert, I made my apologies and headed for the Three Sisters.

The gaming tables were full when I reached the saloon, so I stepped to the bar to pass the time while I waited. I was watching a game at a nearby table, both elbows on the polished counter with my back against the bar, when a young woman sidled up to me. She moved next to me and rubbed against my arm, smiling as if she had known me all my life. Startled, I looked down into the face of what I knew right off to be what my mother called a "painted woman." I blushed at the girl's brazen familiarity and, taken aback as I was, could not think of a thing to say. No problem. That little gal knew all the words. I bought a bottle of champagne, (it was the only thing she ever drank, she said), and we went to a table. She was not what one would call a pretty girl, but what we called "plain" back home. But she knew how to put that paint to good purpose and she smelled mighty pretty. Then she commenced to explain what she would like to do for me, and to me, and I felt myself growing excited. She lived just upstairs, and invited me to her suite to finish our champagne— and I'll guarantee, there was nothing plain about that little filly at all. Later that evening, when I came back down the stairs, I was a lot calmer, a little wiser, and two dollars lighter. Finding a poker seat open, I played cards until dawn.

I stayed a month more in Salem. My days and nights were spent at the gaming tables, my evenings in the suites above the saloon in the company of one of the several young women who worked out of the dance hall. Fine whiskey flowed like water, and my luck at cards held steady.

Tiring of the same faces and small stakes, I made plans to head north—to Oregon City, Champoeg, and the Hudson's Bay Company—hoping to hurry along my rise to the ranks of the wealthy. I fully intended to stop and tell Ellie and the Pettigrews good-bye before I left, but I got into a game and pulled out of town late. I promised myself to get back this way soon.

I spent the next two years and six months in the saloons and gambling houses of the Oregon Country. My luck ran hot, then cold, then hot again. The longer I would sit at the tables, and I could be found there at most any hour of any day, the more I drank. And the more I drank, the worse the fickle cards fell. My fat bankroll began to look a trifle gaunt.

I killed a man in Vancouver, exposing him for the cheat he was. Word soon spread throughout the country that Jacob Eriksson was a man to be reckoned with, quick and accurate with a gun. Figuring to live up to folks' image of me, I became cocksure and belligerent. Moody and irritable, filled at times with a sense of impending doom, I did not know what was going on with me, or why. I seemed helpless to change my direction. I drank more and more to still the building discontent I felt. Visions of Pa nagged at me, for no reason I could put a name to, and I dreamed of my mother reading to me from the Book—the story of the Prodigal Son. My know-nothing friends, meaning well, hinted that I might be drinking a bit too heavily, but they could not possibly understand the pressures that plagued me. Besides, no one was going to convince me that I could not drink like a man.

My luck at cards finally left me, and I found myself without a copper to my name. Trading on my modest reputation as a man good with a gun, I landed a job as a shotgun guard on a freight line, hauling goods and supplies from Oregon City to settlements along the Columbia and in the Willamette Valley. Between runs, hoping to change the bad fortune that dogged me, I spent my idle hours in card games wherever I found them, playing hard and drinking harder.

One rainy night at the Dalles, on the Columbia, my luck came back to me. In a lively game played in a logger's shack, I cleaned the table, winning over two hundred sixty dollars. It was late fall. The gale-force winds rushing down the Columbia River Gorge were cold and penetrating, pushing a stinging rain horizontally before them. To celebrate my good fortune, I stopped at a tent saloon to buy a bottle, then started through the storm to my bunk in the storeroom of the freight office. I never heard the shot that struck me down.

Next morning, the driver of a freight wagon found me lying in the blood-stained mud and rain. My guess was that a disgruntled player from the game the night before, having been cleaned out, decided to recoup his losses with interest, for I had been robbed of all my winnings. Shot in the back and unable to work, I lost my job as shotgun guard. Seemed everything I had touched of late had turned sour. Rotten luck. For the life of me, I did not understand.

After a period of recuperation in the home of a fine, church-going family who took me in, I worked odd jobs, anything I could find. Naturally, I drank every chance I got to kill the pain, of my wound and of my situation.

I am hazy on most everything that happened from that time to this, having been stricken with frequent lapses of memory, but I eventually wound up here, where I started years ago, a swamper in Sweeney's Golden Egg Saloon.

Jackass Jake, the pitiful town drunk. The sum of my assets a column of wasted years.

PART TWO

What lies behind us and
what lies before us are
tiny matters compared to
what lies within us.
—Ralph Waldo Emerson

Chapter Nine

Jackass Jake paused where the alley opened into the street. Glancing in both directions, he turned suddenly, having decided in answer to some inner call to return to the crate where he had hidden the bottle.

"May as well finish it off now and get on with my day."

Cur, the rangy dog that had become his only companion, followed resignedly at his heels.

Jake retrieved the bottle, viewing with dismay the piddling amount of cloudy liquid remaining. He threw the cork over his shoulder and shakily raised the bottle toward expectant lips to drain it. Suddenly the bottle burst in a thunderous explosion of glass and spray!

What the . . . ?

In total fright, Jake stared at the shattered neck of the bottle in his still-raised hand. Jerking his head around, he tried to focus on the mountainous, shadowy form filling the mouth of the alley. The fuzzy specter advanced toward him, smoke curling from the long barrel of the rifle hanging casually at the end of a long right arm. An astonished expression of sudden recognition crept over Jackass Jake's slack features.

Lafe Cawkins!

Looming over the trembling derelict, Lafe drew back a mighty arm and swept it forward with awesome force, knocking Jake flying across the alley. Cur scurried to avoid being flattened by Jake's limp body as he skidded to a halt against the side wall of the saloon. He lay there shaking his pounding head to clear it. Slowly, Jackass Jake raised his rheumy eyes to focus of the massive figure towering above him.

"What in blazes did you do that for?" Jake whined.

Lafe Cawkins looked down at the pitiful shell of the young man who'd been his closest friend. With slow, studied deliberation, he took aim and spat contemptuously onto the rubble under Jake's head. Lafe began to speak in a low rumble that built to a thunderous, angry roar.

"Look at you! You're a mighty poor excuse for a man.

"You look terrible and you smell worse. When was the last time you washed up, Jake? When was the last time you ate a decent meal?"

Bile rose in Jake's throat at the mere mention of food. He needed a stiff drink.

"I've had some bad luck, Lafe," Jake said, averting his eyes from the mountain man's intense and scathing gaze.

"Bollocks! You put yourself in situations where bad things were bound to happen to you. Luck had nothin' to do with it. A man don't waltz in a pig pen if he don't want a mess on his boots."

Jake climbed shakily to his feet.

"You don't understand . . ."

"Oh, I understand, boy. I reckon I understand better'n you're ever apt to.

"You're killin' yourself by degrees, Jake. I'll fancy you don't recollect half of what you do one day to the next. Right?"

"Yeah, maybe, but . . ."

"No 'but' to it. You're destroyin' your fine mind with that poison. A mind that loved books and beauty, that loved the land as I love it. Loved to learn, just for the learning. I should've put that bullet right between your red and yellow eyeballs. You're better off dead than the way you are now.

"You stolen from me, Jake. I ain't talkin' about the furs. That don't matter. But you've robbed me of your friendship and understanding. You've taken from me a man I been able to share my thoughts and dreams and fears with, without so much as a 'by your leave.' That makes you a low-down thief of the cruelest sort."

Having heard the shot, Dutch Cabiness, the deputy marshal of Tuality Crossing, rounded the corner of the saloon, sidearm in hand. A handful of curious towns-folk followed close behind. Seeing the size and fury of the mountain man, they all stopped short and backed up a step. Then, seeing it was only Jackass Jake getting his comeuppance, Dutch slid his pistol into the holster on his hip and hustled the onlookers out of the mouth of the alley, as Lafe roared on.

"You've turned your life and your soul over to that damned jug, leaving nothin' of what you used to be but a shamed and frightened shadow.

"A beggar and a parasite is what you are, Jake . . . and a cringing coward, afraid to look yourself in the eye. And when you do, afraid to climb off your belly and change what you see there. Called on to face up to what you been doing, you fold like a bad poker hand.

"You're a worse drunk than your daddy ever was."

Those last words hit Jackass Jake like a cold bucket of water. The ultimate insult. He clambered to his feet, filled with a fury like none he had ever known. Jake swung with all the might he could muster at the source of his outrage. The puny blow fell impotently on Lafe's buckskin-coated chest, and Jake fell against him, defeated, sobbing beyond his control.

Lafe wrapped both big arms around the racking frame, holding his friend, unashamed and unmindful of what the small, reconvened group of onlookers might be thinking. He held him that way until the sobbing slowed, then stopped, cooing to Jake as one might to a child with a skinned knee. His right arm tight around Jake's shoulders, Lafe turned and led him from the alley, past the curious cluster of people and down the street.

Lifting Jake's slumping body as he might a sack of salt, Lafe sat him on the saddle of his big buckskin. Swinging up behind, he turned the horse toward the mountains that loomed dark and somber in the morning haze.

Cur fell in behind and trailed along, cowed as if the big stranger's fury had been directed at him.

Morning dawned in the forest. The hesitant sun, strained by towering firs, dappled the sleeping camp like the back of a frisking fawn. A camp robber jay hopped restlessly from limb to limb, impatient for the kitchen to open. Returning from the night's scavenging, a raccoon paused in passing to peer curiously from behind its mask at the sleeping interlopers, then shuffled on.

Jake jerked and tossed fitfully in his blankets. Lafe sat up, scratching his beard, and arched his back to work out the cricks. Gently shoving Cur's massive head off his leg where it had rested through the night, Lafe pulled on his moccasins. Unwinding his big frame, he crossed to a ring of stones to lay the morning fire.

Lafe noted Jake twitching and flailing about. Shaking his head, he returned to his tasks.

"You got a long road ahead, ol' son."

Jake woke in sudden fright and lurched upright, not knowing where he was. Waiting for awareness to overtake him, he sat with his chin on his chest and slowly cast a wondering eye over his surroundings. His body launched into a racking coughing spasm, then stilled again. With watery eyes, Jake saw Lafe's long arm extend a cup of coffee in his direction.

"Mornin'," Lafe said.

Shaking his head in refusal of the proffered cup, Jake rose tentatively and, with no small difficulty, made his way to the brush at the edge of camp. Having relieved himself, he fumbled at his belt with unwilling fingers, then headed back to the fire. Cur met him halfway and turned to escort him, big tail waving like a parade banner.

Sinking wearily before the fire, Jake sat cross-legged.

"What now?" he asked.

"That's up to you."

"I've got to get to work. I'll lose my job."

"Nobody's holding you, but it's a far piece back to town, and you ain't got no horse."

"I can't do this, Lafe."

"Probably not. Depends on how bad you want to. That's up to you too."

Jake reached for the cup of coffee, spilling most of it onto the ground as he drew it along the long route to his mouth. Using both shaking hands, he captured a mouthful. It felt good on the way down. It did not feel as good on the way back up.

"Lafe, blast you, I *got* to have a drink."

"None around here, ol' son. Like I said, town is thataway."

"You are a hard man."

"These is hard times. And it's a hard country."

They stayed at the camp five long days. It was a living nightmare for Jackass Jake.

When the alcohol he demanded was withheld, Jake's body rebelled with a fury, wreaking merciless revenge on its disobedient occupant. He shook uncontrollably. Cold, toxic sweat poured forth from every pore, soaking his clothing head to foot. His vision blurred and his eyes watered continuously. His legs refused to support his weight. He crawled on hands and knees to the latrine at the edge of camp to answer his body's frequent demands, then crept back again in humiliation. Jake's teeth chattered. His voice became weak and broken. In full revolt, his stomach hurled back each unsolicited offering. His muscles cramped in painful spasms. Each time a twig of the fire blazing in the clearing popped, Jake would jump as if a howitzer had been fired next to his ear.

"God," Jake cried to himself, "just let me die!"

It was the first prayer that Jacob Eriksson had uttered since he was a child. The first one he had ever fully meant.

Each time that Jake closed his eyes, bursting lights streaked through the blackness. He heard sounds that

were not there. His brief periods of sleep were invaded
by bizarre and frightening dreams.

*Jake watched in horror as his father walked in
slowed motion to a deep well to plunge headfirst
into a bottomless blackness. When Jake lunged to
help him, he could not move his legs. Looking at
his feet, Jake saw his mother clutching his ankles
with both arms, grinning wickedly.*

*Malachai Winter stood with hobnail boots on
the naked corpse of a woman, pointing a huge pistol, the opening of the gun barrel as large as a tin
plate. With his other arm, Winter held little Ellie
Warren by the neck. As Jake rushed toward them,
the gun exploded time and again, blowing huge,
bloody holes in his chest as he ran. When Jake
reached to grab him, the grinning outlaw floated
swiftly away over the mountain, above the trees,
still clutching Ellie, her eyes wide with fright. She
was screaming, but there was no sound.*

*Indians with the heads of wild animals ad-
vanced in a picket line through the walls of his
hotel room as Jake sat screaming in a big four-
poster featherbed. The Indians lifted a huge vat
filled with whiskey, pouring it over Jake's head
and the covers of the bed. Jake reached fran-
tically for a cup. He held it under the flowing
liquid. When he looked into the cup, it had no
bottom.*

Lafe observed all this turmoil and anguish matter-
of-factly, going about his camp duties and ministering

to his friend in his misery. When Jake threw off his blankets, thrashing about in delirium, Lafe covered him again and blotted the cold sweat from his brow with a damp cloth. When Jake retched, the big man cleaned away the foul mess and spread dust and fir needles over the stain on the forest floor. Lafe spooned water into Jake's mouth. He wiped his chin of drool and spittle. He talked constantly in a low tone—rambling talk—though he knew Jake was not listening. Lafe talked only so his young friend would know that he was there for him.

After three days, though weak as a day-old kitten and sore from muscle spasms, Jake's torture eased, and he felt as if he might not die after all. He ate a bowl of broth that Lafe had put together from venison and grain. It tasted good to him and, for the first time, he was able to keep something down. Lafe dug into his supplies and began mixing a concoction in a cup, stirring vigorously, as Jake sat shaking, and watching.

Lafe handed the cup to Jake.

"Drink."

It looked thick and terrible. Warily, Jake lifted the cup to his lips. He took a tenuous sip.

"Yecch." Jake spit. It was a sweet, sweet mixture of honey, raw egg, some kind of bran, and water.

"I can't drink this slop, Lafe, it's too blasted sweet. I'll lose it."

"That's all right," Lafe assured him, a slight smile playing on his lips, "we got plenty."

Jake gagged some, but he got it down and it stayed. He glared at the mountain man.

"Next thing you'll have me doing is kissing a horse's rump."

Lafe chuckled. "If you figger that'll help you stay

sober, by all means, have at her." He broke into a full laugh.

Jake could not see the humor of the situation.

That night, for the first time in recent memory, Jake slept the night through.

On the fourth day, Jake woke feeling reasonably well. At Lafe's none-too-subtle hint that he had become a bit fragrant, he walked a hundred yards to a small, cascading stream to bathe himself. Jake looked around and noticed the beauty of the forest. He gargled with the fresh, cold water from the spring and spat it out. Using his finger and a pinch of soda from Lafe's pack, Jake brushed the film from his teeth. He plucked a nearby sprig of mint and chewed it. Dipping his head in the stream, he rose and shook the water from his hair like a wet coyote.

Jake started back up the path, flushing a variety of birds into the trees. Cur met him partway, his tail busy, and walked with him back to camp.

Jake walked and fidgeted around the clearing all that day, trying to help with the camp chores, nervous and jumpy as a stud horse in a gelding chute. He ate two full meals—solid food—with no ill effects. Sitting that night watching the fire dance, his thoughts jumping around, Jackass Jake smoked a pipe, feeling somewhat at ease.

The morning of the fifth day, leaving Jake sitting on his bedroll, Lafe rode from camp, saying only that he would be back before long.

While Lafe was away, Jake wandered around the small camp, discontent to sit in one spot for too long at a time. The thought entered his mind to go through Lafe's belongings on the off chance he might find a bottle. He dropped that notion when his stomach spasmed just thinking about it. He recalled then, too, that Lafe never drank spirits of any kind. Jake figured that was why the sanctimonious sonofagun did not understand.

Lafe was back within the hour, leading a saddled horse. He'd had it staked out in a grassy meadow not three miles from where they now were. Jake stared in astonishment at the mouse-gray mustang with the spotted rump. His own horse. His father's Adams .44 revolver hung in its belt from the pommel of the saddle.

"How? How'd you get my horse?"

"I backtracked you before I fetched you up here. I got the horse and saddle from the hostler you sold them to for drinking money. He let them go cheap because there ain't nobody been able to fork that ornery mustang. The gun, you left as collateral with the barkeep at the saloon in Vancouver, where you killed that poor feller.

"Your buckskins is in the pack on your horse. Your rifle's in the boot. Ammunition in the saddlebags, along with a bait of grub.

"I left your books and other possibles with Cutler in Salem. Anything else you might of had is lost, I reckon."

Jake choked back the tears.

"Lafe, I . . . I don't know what to say."

" 'Thank you' might be nice."

They broke camp and mounted up.

"I'm headin' back to our cabin in the box canyon," Lafe said. "That's good country, and there's still a market for beaver, marten, fox and such. You're welcome to come with me, or you know the way back to town." Lafe turned and started down the trail.

Cur sat looking back and forth between the two men, then got up and trotted after Lafe's disappearing horse.

Jackass Jake hesitated, then, muttering under his breath, started following after. He broke into a trot.

Chapter Ten

They topped the rise, and after looking the situation over carefully, Lafe Cawkins and Jake Eriksson started down the canyon to the cabin. Cur took the lead. A string of four horses, picked up on the way, trailed behind.

There was no sign of human intrusion into the canyon, at least not of late. The lean-to for the stock had fallen in on one side. It was still solid. They could fix it easy enough. The corral fence was busted in two places, no big thing.

A couple of raccoons had to be run out of the cabin. They had gotten in through the chimney, or perhaps through a tear in the oiled cloth that served as a window pane. A skunk had dropped by, too, not many days ago, and pack rat nests were all around. The leather hinges on the door were in sad condition; new ones would have to be made.

Everything else was in tolerable shape, considering. They were partners again, and they were home.

The year was 1850. Much had happened in Oregon since the two friends had left the canyon on separate trails—events of which Jake had taken little notice, or had missed entirely.

1846 had seen the northernmost boundary of the Oregon Country set at the forty-ninth parallel in a treaty with Great Britain. That was the year that Lafe had gone north in response to his friend Wolf Robe's summons, to help the old subchief in disputes between his people, the Cayuse Indians, and officials of the Hudson's Bay Company. He would also help try and calm a growing discontent among the more traditional members of the tribe with the teachings, edicts, and proclamations of the Reverend Dr. Marcus Whitman, who ran a mission there for all the tribes of the Great Plateau. (Jake had known Whitman, and knew that the man allowed the Indians no margin of tolerance when it came to conforming to his religious teachings.)

All hell broke loose in 1847. The Cayuse attacked the mission, killing Whitman, his wife, and twelve others. The whites called it a massacre. The Indians felt they had cause. Measles had swept through the Cayuse, killing dozens of tribal members. Dr. Whitman had done what he could, but had not been able to stay the wave of death. Tribal tradition held that members of a dead man's family had the right to kill the medicine man. And to the Cayuse, Whitman was just a "medicine man" who had been unsuccessful.

President Polk had declared Oregon a territory of the United States back in '48, probably to get old Jason Lee, the political-minded missionary, off his back. Also in 1848, the Umatilla Indians fought a battle with federal troops. Unrest was growing among the tribes. Even those Indian societies that had always shown peaceful tolerance for white intruders were beginning to offer resistance when the push of white men began to crowd them off their lands.

Lafe's friend, Joe Meek, the mountain man, was now a United States marshal of the Oregon Territory. This tickled Lafe mightily, for he knew Meek for a yarn-spinning rascal who had tiptoed the line between the law and the situation at hand a time or two himself. That Meek was a shirt-tail relative of the president's wife could have been a factor in his appointment.

A new law, the Donation Land Act, had been passed by Congress just that year, 1850, granting free land to settlers. The immense territory covered the area between the forty-second and forty-ninth parallels, and from the Rocky Mountains to the Pacific Ocean, so there was plenty of land available for the taking. A new influx of emigrants were even now headed this way. Many of the early settlers had abandoned their lands in '49, heading south for the new gold finds in California, and the territory's population had dwindled. This latest wave of newcomers would more than compensate for the loss of the fortune seekers.

Yet, all these things had left the peaceful mountain canyon unchanged, and the healing magic of the wilderness was beginning to work its wonders on Jackass Jake.

The partners were nooning one day in early summer by a lovely little falls that cascaded over a rocky bank covered with a lush, green growth of ferns. Lafe pulled out his pipe and filled it from a doeskin pouch. He gazed at Jake, leaned back against the moss-covered trunk of a big fir tree six feet across at the base. Cur was content, lying his big head in Jake's lap.

"I know what you've been goin' through, Jake. Know just how you been feeling. Been there myself."

Jake looked at Lafe curiously, not knowing what he meant, waiting for him to continue.

"Never told you why I felt duty-bound to go traipsin' off when old Wolf Robe hollered." Lafe lit his pipe, savoring the inhaled smoke as it caught in his lungs. "I told you my Indin name is Bear-Upon-the-Mountain, and that's a fact, but that wasn't the first name they give me.

"Some years ago, I was called, Coyote-Who-Falls-and-Cannot-Walk." He smiled faintly, remembering. "Some Indins don't have much respect for a coyote. They figure he's cowardly, feedin' off another animal's courage and effort."

Lafe grabbed a handful of berries off a salal bush. He dropped half into Jake's open palm and popped the rest into his mouth.

"Don't go figgerin' you're the only child ever had a liking for the jug. I drank enough whiskey in my day to float a war canoe. Started suckin' on a jug when I let loose my mammy's teat. I never drank every day like you done, because, living the life I do, it wasn't always to hand. But I always put in a goodly supply, and anytime I got hold of a bottle or a jug, I done 'er up proper . . . throw away the cork and loose the tiger."

Jake squirmed where he sat, not sure he wanted to hear this.

"Well, after a spell . . . after a lot of years, in fact . . . that ol' jug commenced to handling me, instead of me handling it. Seems as if I could never get enough to drink, but I always drank too much. Got to where I couldn't handle nothin' . . . didn't want to and didn't care. All I wanted was the good feeling I got out of that jug. Then, after a time, even that wasn't working for me, and I drank just to feel normal. I was between a rock and a hard place. I couldn't live with liquor, and I surely couldn't live without it."

Jake nodded his understanding without realizing he had done so.

"I had stampeded off all my friends," Lafe said. "They'd taken all they could stomach. Now I've come to understand the fearful way I'd been treating folks . . . but then I figgered the whole world was out of step except me, and that nobody understood. My whole life was caving in on top of me, but I kept doing what I was doing . . . and I kept getting what I was getting."

"Why didn't you say something about this when you pulled me out of that alley?" Jake asked.

"You was in no shape to listen," Lafe reminded him, "let alone understand."

Jake shrugged as the mountain man continued to share his troubled past.

"I was wandering around the Clearwater Range near Hell's Canyon, doing a little trapping and a lot of drinking. And Jake, I was a mighty lonely man. I became wishful of cashing in my chips, but I didn't have the heart for it. Not to do it myself, anyhow. I had no will to live . . . just an instinct to survive.

"That's where Wolf Robe come in. He was leading a hunting party after bear. Him, Three Bears, who was just a sprout then, and two others, Red Elk and Sees-Far. They come upon me, laying out cold on the trail, a sorry sack of skin and bones, as I hadn't been eating. They slung me on a pack pony, one of the few horses the tribe had in them days, and finished their hunt with me bouncing on my belly on that pony. I figgered both me and that bear was dead meat.

"They hauled me back to their village, and Wolf Robe stuck me in a 'sweat hut.' That's a little bitty house where they pour water over hot stones, making steam, and it's supposed to purify the outer body. The Cayuse use it to drive away bad spirits when they're took sick. And the young men go there when they're fixing to become braves, to have visions, and to offer themselves to the Great Spirit. Ofttimes, they'll cut off a finger or a toe, or slash their arms, to prove to the gods they're serious. Then they go out in the wilds for a week to ten days. They stay out there, not eating, until they've had their vision and made contact with the Great Spirit. That purifies the inner body. When they come back they are braves.

"Most white folks think Indins are savages and heathens. I haven't found that to be so. All Indins are spiritual, to the extreme. Some, like your Dr. Whitman, are forever trying to save them from themselves."

The big dog, Cur, yawned and stretched, arching its back, then trotted off into the woods to run down a fat rabbit for its supper. Lafe knocked the ashes from his pipe and suggested that Jake put on a pot of coffee.

"White folks figure God lives in church," Lafe continued. "But not the Indin. He don't put his gods in a box. His gods live all around him, in the mountains, in the skies, on the plateaus, and on the prairies. He finds them in the rivers and the streams. His gods are everywhere and he treats the land with respect and reverence, so's not to offend the gods.

"Anyways, old Wolf Robe stuck me in this sweat hut and left me there . . . and Jake, I'm here to tell you, I was mighty sick and sorry. I shook and I sweated and I hurt and I cussed. Most miserable I ever been, before or since. Like you must have felt those first few days, remember?"

Jake nodded emphatically that he did. He would never forget.

"Well, I was in just such a shape. I was hurtin'. Some squaw would come in, time to time, to give me water, or clean me up, then pour more water on the stones . . . and I'd cuss her and Wolf Robe and everybody I ever knew that I figured got me into that fix.

"I seen things while I was in that hut. Seen 'em in my mind's eye—Horrid, frightening, terrible things I find it hard to think on to this day.

"After a few days of sweating in that hellhole, I calmed a mite. Least enough I wasn't afraid to pick my nose for fear of putting an eye out. They started trying to get some food down me then, and at first I'd give it right back to them, just like you done. But after a try or two, I could keep 'er down and felt better for it. And they made me drink that honey and bran stuff I made up for you. That's where I got the recipe."

Lafe reached to take the cup of coffee Jake held out. He sat silent as he sipped it down. Then crossing to the pot in the edge of the fire, he refilled his cup and continued to share his story.

"After six or seven days, Wolf Robe pulled the flap of that sweat hut and peered in at me. 'It is time,' he said, and he walked away. After a couple of false starts, I got to my feet and follered after him, weak as a bobcat kitten.

"Never have figured why Wolf Robe bothered with me. A pitiful specimen, and a white man to boot. He could just as easily have killed me, or left me lying out there in my own vomit on the trail. Instead, he done what he could to straighten me out, and he taken me into his lodge. The old red rascal has a second name, sort of a title, among his people, The Care-Giver . . . and I reckon that explains the why of it.

"I could speak a sight of Cayuse, having spent years in that neck of the woods, and Wolf Robe, he had a smattering of English from trading with the Hudson's Bay folks, so talking back and forth was no big shakes. He did remind me, time to time, that I'd ought to do the listening, and mostly that's what I done."

Lafe glanced up through the trees at the position of the sun, now halfway to the horizon, and said, "I been palaverin' and worrying your ears quite a spell. You ready to head back to the cabin and see to the stock?"

"Don't stop now," Jake protested, a note of panic in his voice. "Finish your story. Please."

"All right, then. I had told Wolf Robe all about my woes . . . my hard luck, nobody understandin' me, being so lonely and trying so hard. I pointed a finger of blame in every direction but my own. Well, he let me do my whining, then he started talking, and he made it mighty plain I was just to listen.

"There was an evil spirit in the jug, he said, that'd captured my mind and had made a slave of my soul. It was an almighty powerful spirit, who bound even the strongest warrior in ropes of rawhide, tying him with knots no human man could untie. He said that every time a man would drink of the jug, it would wet them rawhide ropes, which would dry in the sun and tighten up until a man lost his senses, started thinking crazy. And if that man kept on drinking from the jug, them ropes would get tighter and tighter until he couldn't breathe, and then he would die. Now I didn't want to hear none of that. I didn't want no evil spirit inside me,

tying my young self up. So I asked him how could I run
off this spirit, and he says, 'You cannot.'

"He seen my lower lip hit the ground and the hope go
out of my eyes. I was in deep despair, knowing I was
doomed to live the rest of my days tied to that jug, with
that old evil spirit running loose inside me, tightening
them bloomin' knots."

Lafe paused to fill another pipe. Jake leaned forward
from the fallen log he was sitting on, hearing his own
feelings in what the big mountaineer was saying, hearing a smattering of hope, and wanting him to get on
with it.

"Then Wolf Robe says, 'There *is* One who can rid you
of the evil force. The Great Spirit alone has the power.
But He will not come to you. You must seek Him.'

I asked him who this Great Spirit was, and how did I
go about gettin' hold of Him?

" 'Each man sees the Great Spirit with his own eyes,'
he told me, meaning, I reckon, that every man must picture his own god . . . have his own understanding. 'You
will find Him all around you, in the trees and in the forest. When you are alone, He will hear you call Him.
Man's voice is small, but the Great Spirit will hear you
in the silence of the forest.'

" 'The Great Spirit will untie the knots and loosen
the bonds, but you must ask. You must ask as the sun
rises, for Him to place your feet safely upon the path
that is each day, for the evil spirit of the jug places
many snares and traps along the way. The Great Spirit
is good, but He will let you be bad. It is your choice.'

"You've likely wondered why I walk out alone of a
morning?"

Jake nodded that he had.

"I go out and I talk to that Great Spirit, and I ask Him

to direct me. And then, Jake, I listen. Sometimes it's harder for me to hear Him than others. But it's always there, my direction for the day. A feeling that comes. If it don't feel right, I figure I got it wrong, that I'm not hearing what He is saying, and I listen again.

" 'You will never be safe from the evil spirit, for he follows you always,' Wolf Robe says. 'If you stray from the path of the Great Spirit, you will be lost, and the evil one will have you. You will be a slave again.

" 'The evil spirit will place many rocks upon the path, blocking your way. You must not turn back. You must not leave the path to go around the rock. The evil spirit waits to trap you. You must move the rock and go on the way you have been shown.

" 'Sometimes the rocks are too heavy, and you cannot move them. Then you must ask the Great Spirit to help you move the heavy rock, and He will help you. If you do not ask, He will not help. He will let you be trapped. Do not ask Him to move the rocks alone. He will not. Do not ask Him to move the rocks you can lift by yourself.'

"Ol' Wolf Robe must have seen I wasn't buying his whole packet, because he smiled and said, 'You do not believe. You do not have to. Believe that *I* believe. All you must do is do it. If you do it, someday you will believe.'

"Then he told me, 'If you will not do it, go now into the mountains and become lost, for I will not watch you die.'

Now I wasn't too all-fired anxious to be off on my own just yet, so I done like he told me. It was a simple thing, but not an easy thing for me to do, asking some big spirit for help when I didn't even know if He was around, and if He was, was He paying me any mind. I kept getting in my own way, always trying to figger reasons why it wouldn't work.

"But, in spite of me, not because of me, things began to change. I can't tell you when it happened, but one day it come to me that it'd been a long spell since I'd even thought of taking a pull off that jug . . . and for me, partner, that was one hellacious jump ahead.

"I was strong again and feeling good. I'd commenced to go on hunts with Three Bears and some of the other braves, and pull my weight. I was feeling pretty smug about the way things was going until one day Wolf Robe summoned me and set me down. 'Now we must begin,' he told me. I didn't know what in blazes he was talking about. Begin? I figgered I was through it. I'd done everything he'd told me to do, and now he was fixin' to start me over from scratch.

"He explained that I'd harmed folks, doing what I oughtn't do, or not doing what I'd ought've, and that until I had set things right, I'd never be free from the evil spirit . . . that them slights and wrongs would gnaw at me and I'd fret on it, so I'd be forced to pull the cork and let the evil spirit out of the jug. For by long habit, I'd drunk whiskey to ease my hurting and in avoidance of facing up to whatever was unpleasant to do.

" 'If you have stolen another man's robe, you must replace it with a finer robe. If you have slept with another man's wife, repay him by leaving his wife alone. If you have killed a brother in anger, or because you wanted what he had, change your ways and kill no more for wrong reasons.'

"He told me to go alone into the sweat hut and to think on it until I knew all my wrongs. If they were buried in my head, I was to root 'em out, or the rot would spread. I had to get square with myself before I could start getting right with others. Then I was to go back and tell him what I'd found out.

"When I had done that, Jake, it was like a whole new world opened up for me. I knew what had to be done, and I wasn't afraid of doing it. Wolf Robe sent me off to start righting those wrongs, telling me that if a particular thing couldn't be done or undone, not to fret on it, but just don't do it no more.

"He taught me that if ever I see a man in need of help that I'm able to give, that it is my bound duty to offer that help.

"I lived in the lodge of Wolf Robe for better than four years. I learned a lot from that ol' Indin. Most important, I reckon, I learned to know myself.

"If I find somethin' ugly about *me* that I want shed of, the Great Spirit will help me move that rock.

"I do the best I can every day . . . and some days I just don't measure up. But I can start again with a new dawn, doing what I can do, being what I can be.

"I don't never want to forget those dark days before Wolf Robe picked me up. Nor do I want to forget the pain and the misery of those first days in that sweat hut, for I don't ever want to run that gauntlet again. By asking that Great Spirit for help, I'm not helpless, but a bigger man for it.

"The purpose of a man's life is not happiness, but worthiness . . . and by becoming worthy, he becomes happy."

The sun was sinking behind the mountains. The dell where they sat lay in dark shadows.

"It ain't so much what a man does that's so all-fired wrong, but what he becomes as a result of it. I'm a free man, Jake. Free to choose my own burdens. Free not to pick up the jug."

Lafe stood and brushed the fir needles from his buckskins.

"You might or might not understand what I been try-ing to tell you today. You might or might not cotton to it. That is your choice, and you're free to make it. If my way appeals to you, I'll help you all I can . . . but it's you will have to do it. It don't come to you free of ef-fort, but to me it has been worth the price."

They mounted and rode toward the cabin in the mountain dusk.

"And Jake . . . if you try it, and it don't work for you," Lafe said, grinning, "you can always get your misery back."

Jake lay awake a long time that night, staring with open eyes into the black interior of the cabin.

First light, and Lafe slipped out of the cabin and headed into the forest.

The things Jake had heard the day before were prey-ing on his mind. He watched from the cabin door as Lafe disappeared into the trees, followed by the dog. Jake stood a moment, watching the first silver rays of the morning sun illuminate the high ridges to the east. Setting his hat on his head, Jackass Jake walked toward the light.

Chapter Eleven

A year had passed since Jackass Jake and Lafe Cawkins had returned to their canyon in the Cascades.

Lafe made several trips to the settlements to pick up supplies during that period, but each time Jake elected not to ride along, claiming he would rather stick close to protect the horses or to run the trap lines. The bare-bones truth of the matter was that Jake was afraid to venture out, to be again where there were saloons and gambling houses and temptations of every description. Like a kid learning to ride, Jake was unsure of himself, and of his seat in the saddle of right living.

Lafe was again getting ready for a trip. Cur watched closely, whipping his tail to and fro in expectation of new adventure.

"Get your gear together, Jake. You'll be coming along this trip. We're going into Salem."

The name of the town hit him like a rock in the pit of the stomach: Salem! That was where Jake had gone crossways to begin with. Thrown off the straight and narrow track into a dark whirlpool of whiskey, gambling, harlots, and high living that had sucked him in an ever-downward spiral to an existence of degrading pain, loneliness, and self-loathing. Jake did not dare chance it. He remembered vividly what it had been like for him only one year ago, and he never wanted to revert to that miserable existence. He had not gotten into that fix on purpose then, so what was different now? He was getting on fine right here, right now. Why chance slipping back into the same stinking sewer? He felt strong physically again. The rugged life he led in these mountains might not be conducive to comfort, but it did build strength. And Jake felt at peace with himself at last. No, sir. He would hole up here.

"I'd best stay right here, Lafe. There's things I ought to be doing. I'll just stick close and keep watch . . ."

Lafe interrupted him with a big hand on his shoulder. "It's time, Jake."

Jake stared intently into Lafe's firm, reassuring gaze and knew he was right. Yes, it was time.

They rode to Salem by the same route that Jake and Ellie Warren had taken years before and a lifetime ago.

As the day wore on, Jake started feeling better about having come along. In fact, he was starting to look forward to the experience. He wanted first to make a stop at Ma Cutler's to be sure that his books were still in safekeeping. He would pack them back to the canyon on the return trip. He and Lafe had about worn the covers off the two volumes that were at the cabin now.

Jake was curious, too, to see how little Ellie Warren was faring. Could she speak now? Or was she still mute as a result of her terrifying ordeal in the mountains? He felt a strange stirring inside when he pictured the sad little girl in his mind. An evasive, uneasy feeling he could not quite put a finger on.

It would be pleasurable to visit with Caleb and Lavinia Pettigrew again, though Jake felt sheepish at the prospect of facing them. It embarrassed him to realize that they must be aware of his boozing, gambling, womanizing, and other misadventures. This was a big country, but there were few secrets here.

Cur raced back and forth between the legs of the two packhorses that were loaded down with pelts. The dog especially delighted in teasing the little roan, which would snap at it testily as it darted in and out. Jake called the dog to task for its pestering performance and Cur fell in alongside the gray, looking disgruntled. Jake looked down at the dog with wonder. Cur had fleshed out and his coat was sleek and shiny. An abundance of strenuous exercise had transformed him into a fine, strong beast. Still the ugliest mongrel in creation, Jake thought to himself, but certainly a different animal. *Far as that goes*, Jake chuckled silently, *I'm a different animal myself*.

When they got to within sight of town, Jake's jaw dropped open with surprise. The place seemed to have doubled in size since he had last been here. The offer of free land in the Oregon Territory had brought a horde of new settlers streaming across the Oregon Trail, each seeking his own brand of happiness. New settlers needed supplies: tools, stock, furniture, lumber, seed— all manner of goods. Those who had rushed off to the gold fields of California had needed outfitting, too, for the trail and for the task of extracting their fortunes from the streams and hillsides of their El Dorados. Thus, the old merchants prospered, new businesses sprang up like toadstools after a rain, and the townships and settlements of the valley grew and thrived as commerce flourished. As Jake and Lafe rode closer, they could see stately new homes raising their proud gables two, even three stories into the air. New businesses crowded the streets, and pedestrians scurried along the boardwalks, one occasionally darting across in front of a loaded freight wagon or a fancy carriage. The spectacle was a mite intimidating to men whose notion of heavy traffic was a brood of quail crossing the trail.

They pulled up at the edge of town.

"I'll take the furs and sell them," Lafe said. "You stop off and see to your books, look around if you like, then I'll meet you . . ." he pointed, "at that barber shop catty-corner across the street yonder. We'll get ourselves cleaned up and then have us a store-bought meal. I hear they got beef on the bill of fare at some of these places, and I aim to try it. I've never eaten any."

They went their separate ways, Cur following Lafe and the packhorses. Jake went along to the livery to leave his mustang to be cared for, then on to Ma Cutler's. He asked for Geoffrey Cutler at the desk in the plush new lobby. The building had been enlarged and was now a full-fledged hotel, renamed Government House when the territorial capitol was moved from Oregon City to Salem.

The portly, red-bearded proprietor came in through a door behind the registration desk wearing a chef's hat on his head. Recognizing Jake, he broke into a broad smile. Cutler pumped Jake's arm and invited him into the dining room for a cup of coffee, removing his hat and apron as he walked. Yes, he had Jake's books. They were still safely locked away in his office. The two men were enjoying a long and pleasant conversation until

Jake, suddenly mindful of the time and of his appointment with Lafe, made his apologies and rushed toward the front door.

A light drizzle had begun to fall. The boardwalks glistened silver in the muted afternoon sun. A cluster of men stood on the walk in front of the hotel, talking in concerned voices of a general Indian uprising to the south involving a coalition of five tribes—the Rogue, Klamath, Modoc, Shasta, and Umpqua. Jake overheard of a pitched battle on the Rogue River in which a number of settlers and miners had been killed.

Peering down the misty street, Jake spotted Lafe squatted on his haunches on the walk in front of the tonsorial parlor and bath house, scratching Cur behind the ears.

As he rushed along, preoccupied, Jake bumped heavily into a young woman as she left the door of a dressmaker's shop, jarring loose a bundle from her arms. Jumping in an attempt to catch the parcel before it hit the wet boardwalk, he bumped the young lady again and kicked the package with the toe of his boot, sending it skittering along the wet planks.

"Oh, sorry, ma'am. . . . Oops . . . sorry again."

Mumbling an apology, Jake bent to retrieve the bundle. Starting to straighten, he noticed the girl's face. He halted, half standing, in stunned and speechless surprise. Still in a crouch, Jake was staring into the strikingly beautiful face of a grown-up Ellie Warren.

There was a hint of concern in the most remarkable blue eyes Jake had ever seen as Ellie looked quizzically at the odd young man in buckskins.

"Are you all right?"

She can speak.

"Ellie? Ellie Warren!" Jake stood up, extending the bundle.

Ellie took the wet parcel gingerly with her fingers.

"Miss Ellen Warren, yes. I am afraid you have the advantage of me, sir."

Before Jake could compose himself to speak, Ellie crossed to a buggy at the curb, springing lightly to the padded bench. She clucked twice, flicked the reins, and drove off down the street. He watched the wagon disappear round a corner.

Suddenly the day was brighter, the grass greener, the air fresher, and there was music in the breeze. Ellie had gone, but Jake could still see her face before him.

Ellie Warren, all grown-up. I'll be hornswoggled. Wonder why she didn't recognize me?

Glancing at his reflection in the wet pane of the dressmaker's window, Jake saw a burly young rustic in soiled buckskins covered with trail dirt and badly in need of a shave. Removing his drooping hat, he ran his hand through his tousled blond hair.

"Well, no wonder," Jake said aloud, attracting the stares of a passing couple.

Jake and Lafe simultaneously pushed back their chairs from the table in the dining room at the Government House, and each took a cigar from a tin proffered by the red-jacketed waiter.

Lafe had thoroughly enjoyed his beef steak, though he argued that elk was mighty hard to beat. Jake had chosen a less expensive seafood platter of locally available Dungeness crab, smoked Chinook salmon, clams, and fried rainbow trout. Cold milk and hot cherry pie preceded the coffee that sat steaming in dainty Wedgwood cups in front of them.

Lafe was dressed in a new plaid cotton shirt and blue denim britches supported by wide galluses, all selected from the shelves of the general mercantile. Jake wore a denim jacket over a black-and-white checkered shirt and gray pants, resurrected from a carpetbag of his own that Geoffrey Cutler had stored with his books. A new gray hat with a wide brim and a short, flat crown sat on the chair next to him.

Jake smiled and puffed his cigar as he stared at his partner. Lafe'd had his face shaved, leaving a drooping, walrus-like mustache. Jake had never seen the mountain man without a beard, and it just did not look like the Lafe he knew. Jake had hardly taken his eyes off him during dinner. Lafe kept rubbing his cheek with the back of his hand, fascinated by the unfamiliar smoothness.

"I'd like for you to go with me to meet the Pettigrews, and to see Ellie."

"I'd have to be hog-tied to miss it."

"To be honest, I'm a little hesitant about seeing them again. I left before without so much as a good-bye."

Jake lowered his eyes and stirred black coffee with his spoon.

"Hesitant, my saddlesores. Call it what it is. You're plumb scared."

"Yes, you old nag. I'm plumb scared."

Lavinia Pettigrew opened the door in response to the gentle rap.

"Jake? Jacob Eriksson, is that you?"

Lavinia stood a moment, frozen in surprise, then took both Jake's hands in hers and pulled him into the room. Lafe stood awkwardly in the open door, gripping his hat in front of him.

"Oh, excuse me. Mrs. Pettigrew, my friend and partner, Lafe Cawkins."

"Mr. Cawkins, come in, come in. I have wanted to meet you ever since . . ." Lavinia turned toward the kitchen. "Caleb, come in here. You'll never guess who has shown up on our doorstep."

Caleb Pettigrew came from the kitchen door to greet Jake warmly. Introduced to Lafe, he pumped his arm enthusiastically with a firm handshake. After observing the customary formalities, they all moved to the parlor.

Excusing herself, Lavinia disappeared through the hallway to brew a pot of tea while the three men sat smiling in awkward silence.

Evaluating Jake with his eyes as if the younger man might break, Caleb asked, "Jake, have you been . . . er, uh . . . well?"

"Sober is the word, Caleb," Jake replied, smiling. "Yes, I'm fine now. Living in our little canyon in the mountains, it's easier to resist temptation than to find it."

They laughed then and launched into animated conversation. Lavinia returned with a china pot and four cups on a brightly polished wooden tray, placing it on the marble-top side table.

"Needs to steep for a minute or two."

She sat on the settee next to Jake and patted him on the leg. "It is so good to see you, Jake. We've often wondered how you were. We've missed you."

Lavinia turned to Lafe. "Mr. Cawkins, I've waited a long time to meet you, and to thank you for what you did for Ellie."

Lafe colored slightly and nodded.

Jake then told them about his chance meeting with Ellie that afternoon, laughing at his own clumsiness, and expressing genuine delight in learning that Ellie could talk again.

"She didn't recognize me, but I understand that well

enough, as trail-worn and disreputable as I looked when I bumped into her."

Lavinia got up and served the tea, adding cream and sugar as each requested.

"She probably won't know either of you, Jake, in any circumstance . . . and I pray that she doesn't. Ellie woke up one morning about two years ago, able to speak, remembering nothing. She has no memory whatsoever of anything that happened out there, not after the wagon was stopped in the snow. We have told her simply that her parents died there, and that she was brought to us by a friend. But no details. She has accepted that.

"I suppose the reality of that horrible experience was too frightening for her young mind to tolerate. She has shut it out completely."

Stunned, Jake and Lafe whipped their heads around, looking at each other.

Glancing about, Lafe asked. "Don't she still live here with you, ma'am?"

"Oh, surely. She's just sitting with an elderly lady friend tonight, whose son, Harley, works for Caleb at the freight company. He is on a haul to the coast. Ellie will be home in the morning."

"Will you stay the night?" Caleb asked. "We've plenty of room, be happy to have you both."

Jake declined quickly. "No thank you, sir. We've made previous arrangements."

Lafe looked at Jake knowingly, and nodded approval.

"You must come to dinner tomorrow then, and meet Ellie," Lavinia said. "If she recognizes either of you on her own, that's well and good. If she does not, please . . . say nothing. I'm not certain how strong she may be, even now. She is on her way to becoming a happy, well-adjusted girl, and I want nothing to jeopardize that.

"After dinner, perhaps you can join us all for a dance being held in the Grange Hall."

They sat and visited awhile longer, talking of politics, the Indian problem, the burgeoning growth of the population. Lafe was a talker, and the Pettigrews took an immediate liking to him. Finally the two mountain men took their leave, thanking their host.

Once outside, Jake said, "Let's ride out a ways and find a place to camp. I've enjoyed about all the town living I care to for one day."

"Couldn't suit me better, partner."

They had camped the night some five miles out, in a grove of poplars at the edge of a creek bordering on a wide meadow. Morning was a steely streak on the eastern horizon when Lafe started a fire, put coffee on to boil, then ambled out across the meadow, headed for his standing appointment with the Great Spirit. Long legs flushed quail, rabbits, and pheasants from the grasses in his wake.

Jake gave the little mouse-gray mustang a rubdown with a handful of meadow grass, then turned to Lafe's big buckskin and repeated the process. Retrieving his rifle from between the blankets of his bedroll, he slapped on his old hat and started at a leisurely walk in a direction opposite the one Lafe had taken. Cur, busy dunking for minnows in a backwater pool of the creek, noticed Jake's leave-taking and ran after him, barking for him to wait.

As Jake strolled the green meadow with the big dog casting back and forth through the tall grasses ahead, he was mindful of the rich personality of the valley around him. He paused there to listen and to meditate.

Having stopped at the edge of an impenetrable thicket of blackberries, the vines heavy with fruit, Jake filled his hat with the juicy, sweet delicacies and headed back to camp. He paused briefly to inspect the blossoms of a penstemon plant. When boiled, the tea was an effective treatment for sores and burns. Cur had gone back to camp ahead of Jake and was allowing Lafe, sitting with his ever-present cup of coffee in hand, to scratch behind his ears. The dog snorted occasionally as the smoke from the man's clay pipe curled in his direction.

Lafe and Jake breakfasted on blackberries and left-over dinner rolls cadged from the restaurant the previous evening. After tidying camp and carefully dousing their small fire, they sat in the sun at the edge of the chuckling creek and talked of their visit with the Pettigrews, of the growing Indian concern among the settlers, miners, and townsfolk, and of the startling changes taking place in the country. Living a different lifestyle, and with different interests than the farmers and miners and residents of the towns and villages that now dotted the countryside, the partners could more easily identify with the plight of the tribes that were slowly but inexorably being crowded from their homes and off their lands. There were no black and white issues, they agreed. No heroes or villains. No right or wrong to the overall transformation that was taking place, just a powerful conflict of priorities. Each of them, however, in the privacy of his own thoughts, was prone to side with the red man, and the prospect of growing civilization left them with long faces.

There was, of course, fault on both sides of the controversy. Miners in the mountains near the California border hunted the Indian like game, for sport. Understandably finding little amusement in the practice, the Indians retaliated.

There had been reports of Indian raids on isolated travelers, secluded settlers, and freight shipments. There were rarely survivors to name the assailants, and the methods employed by the attackers reminded Jake of those used by Malachai Winter and his crew of cutthroats when they had descended upon the Warren wagon. He mentioned the similarity to Lafe.

"That could be. I've had thoughts along them same lines, but there'd be no way on this green earth of proving it." Lafe swatted at a pesky honey bee, attracted to his smooth face by the lingering aroma of bay rum.

"If that pair that got away at the canyon, Winter and One-Eye, are still a'blowin' and goin' up to their same old tricks, they're mighty cagey. The only way a man would know for sure would be to come up on them in the act, like we done. And being once caught, they'll be all-fired mindful of that, you can bet your best buckskins."

Breaking camp, they headed back to Salem. Lafe wanted to ask around town about his old friend, Joe Meek, reported to headquarter in the capitol. Jake had decided to go to the offices of the newspaper, *The Salem Statesman,* to look through some back issues and catch up on the news, then hole up in Cutler's office in the Government House to get reacquainted with his books. During his years of debauchery, he had shunted aside all else in his self-destructive obsessions with whiskey, cards, and women. He felt he had a lot of catching up to do.

Jake spent the time on the ride back into town trying

to convince Lafe to go to the dance at the Grange Hall that night.

"Drat it, boy, I just wouldn't fit in at such a shindy. The most genteel gathering I ever been to was the Rendezvous at Green River, with that crowd. And they'd of thrown that whole bunch out of Sodom and Gomorrah."

Finally Lafe relented, agreeing to put in an appearance at least, but he reserved the option of slipping away at any time. They agreed to meet back at the Government House in time to wash up and change clothes for dinner at the Pettigrew home.

"One more thing," Jake said in mock solemnity, "if we're going to continue to partner together."

"And what might that be?"

"Let your beard grow back."

Lafe saluted Jake with an obscene gesture and they parted laughing.

Chapter Twelve

Lafe showed back at the hotel early. He had been unable to find his friend Meek who, someone had told him, was in Oregon City, paying his respects to one of the leading citizens of the Territory, Dr. John McLoughlin, former chief proctor of the Hudson's Bay Company.

McLoughlin had been instrumental in the settlement of the Willamette Valley, loaning money and supplies to farmers in need against the policies of his British-led firm. He resigned his post with the Hudson's Bay Company in 1845 and moved to land he had previously claimed in Oregon City. Revered by many, he was often called "the Father of Oregon."

Returning from an hour of browsing through back issues of the newspaper, Jake answered Lafe's beckoning wave and joined him in the dining room for pie and coffee. When they had finished, they strolled to a gunsmith's shop. Lafe wanted to have a closer look at a rifle he had noticed earlier in the display window. While there, Jake traded his pistol, selecting a new model 51

Colt, the Navy's .36 caliber percussion revolver. The Colt was a lighter gun than his Adams, just over two pounds, with a shorter, seven-inch barrel. It handled smoothly and easily in his fist. He also laid in a supply of the new cartridges made of combustible paper, or linen, with both ball and powder in one unit, speeding reloading. Lafe bought the rifle he had admired, a new model Sharps .50 caliber. Using a Lawrence primer, it also fired the new-style cartridges and had a fast action. They sauntered out of the gun shop and down the boardwalks of Salem, bristling like a two-man army.

Taking a handful of books from the office of the hotel, Jake and Lafe walked to the banks of the river, Cur leading the way. After test-firing and practicing with their new weapons, they deposited themselves under a big shade tree and blissfully read the afternoon away.

That evening, Lavinia Pettigrew met Jake and Lafe at the steps of the porch and ushered them inside. As they seated themselves in the parlor, a melodious voice cried out from the top of the stairs.

"Aunt Lovie, have you seen my cameo brooch? The one you gave me for my birthday last year?"

As he recalled the chance meeting of the day before, Jake's pulse quickened and he could feel his ears turn red.

"Your Uncle Caleb took it to the watchmaker's to have the clasp repaired. Don't you remember?" Lavinia called back. "Come down, dear, our guests are here."

Ellie Warren bounced down the stairs with youthful enthusiasm, looking for all the world, to Jake, like a princess stepped from the pages of a Shakespearean play. Her hair was golden, though not so light as his own, and hung in ringlets about her face. Her radiant smile caused one cheek to dimple pertly. Slightly out of

breath, her full and shapely breasts strained at the
bodice of a simple print dress edged in delicate lace.
Though her figure was petite, her body was that of a
woman grown. Yet, it was her eyes that set Jake's heart
pounding. Strikingly blue like the deep waters of a
clear mountain lake, glistening with tiny flecks of
golden sunshine. Eyes alive and penetrating, with an
inner light of lively intelligence. How different they
were from the lifeless, sad eyes of the little girl on the
mountain, those eyes that had been dulled by pain and
left devoid of any sign of feeling or emotion.

Her skin, smoother than a dove's wing, wore the
healthy tan of a girl who loved the outdoors. Her saucy,
upturned nose was sprinkled with barely perceptible
freckles. Her lips were full and soft, with the slightest
hint of a pout. If she had an imperfection, Jake could
not find it. He considered Ellie Warren to be the most
alluring woman he had ever seen.

Woman? Shame on you, Jake, he silently repri-
manded himself. *She's just a girl, no more than seventeen. You're a good six years older.* His mind heard. His
heart would not listen. Jacob Eriksson was in love!

Jake found himself wishing he was taller, more handsome, more dashing. He wished he was richer, widely
traveled, better schooled in the social graces.

Their eyes met and held for a long, awkward moment.

"Ellen, this is Jake . . . Jacob Eriksson."

"We bumped into one another on the street yesterday, Aunt Lovie." Then, to Jake, "My, Mr. Eriksson,
you are much taller when you aren't crouching," she
said smiling, a mischievous twinkle in her eye. She put
out her hand to him.

"And this is Mr. Cawkins."

Ellie turned grudgingly from Jake's admiring gaze

and shook hands with Lafe, his walrus mustache framing a wide grin, punctuated by the missing tooth.

"Proud to make your acquaintance, Miss Ellen."

Caleb came in from his day's work, depositing a handful of account ledgers on the buffet as he entered. Shaking hands all around, he said, "Mr. Eriksson is the gentleman who brought you down from the mountains after your parents died, Ellie."

Ellie blushed deeply and blurted out, "Oh my! Oh dear!" I am so sorry. No wonder you thought I should recognize you yesterday. You must think me very rude, and completely without gratitude. I am sorry. How can I ever make it up to you?"

"No need for an apology, Ellen. You were very young and quite ill at the time. Please don't bother about it." Then he added, "Save me a dance this evening, and we'll call it square."

"You shall have it," she exclaimed, clapping her hands.

They all talked enthusiastically through dinner. Ellie wanted to know all about the adventurous and romantic life of a mountain man. Lafe was more than happy to oblige her, embellishing greatly upon the glamorous aspects, and carefully omitting the more sordid and violent details. Neither Jake nor Ellie touched much of the food on their plates.

Suddenly, Ellie looked at Jake and asked, "And what have you been doing, Jake, since you so gallantly rescued me?"

A hush fell over the table as the chatter ceased. A spoon rang loudly against a cup in the awkward silence, as startling as a petard in church. All eyes were turned toward Jackass Jake.

After a pause, Jake replied, "I made some bad choices there for a while, Ellen, and they led me down some wrong trails. I've been lost. I'll tell you about it sometime, when we know each other better."

The strained atmosphere slowly abated and they talked awhile longer in a more reserved manner. When the meal was finished, Lavinia and Ellie cleared the dishes from the table and disappeared into the kitchen. The men retired to the parlor with cups of coffee. Caleb handed out cigars, then settled himself into a velvet-covered, high-back chair.

"Jacob, I can't tell you how satisfying it is to see you well. I admire you greatly for the changes you've made in yourself. Not many men could have done it."

"I'm afraid none of the credit's mine, Caleb. Lafe, here, dragged me physically out of the gutter . . . made me listen to some tough facts about myself. I got willing to change, and he guided me back to health and right thinking. And I'm full of gratitude."

"Nevertheless, I can see you are a better and stronger man for the battle. We are all of us tempered by the fires of trial and hardship. I salute you. I salute you both."

Lavinia and her niece came into the room, each with an armload of coats.

"It's time we left for the dance."

They all slipped into their coats, except Ellie.

"Aren't you coming, Ellie?" Jake asked.

"After a bit. I have an escort calling for me."

An escort? Jake's heart sank and he stiffened with unwarranted jealousy. Of course she would have a suitor, as lovely as she is. Nonetheless, he was in a dark mood as he rode next to Lafe in the back seat of the carriage.

Lafe smiled knowingly.

People poured into the Grange Hall from miles around, greeting old friends and craning their necks as they entered to see who had arrived before them. The ladies carried their covered dishes to place them among others on the long tables, then circulated around the hall to see who was wearing what and who was with whom. The men greeted each other, passing sly winks as they showed the bottles hidden in their coats and boot tops. The musicians and callers milled around the band area under colorful bunting streamers, tuning their instruments and making preparations. It promised to be a gala evening.

Once inside the hall, Lafe's misgivings evaporated and he entered into the activities with gusto. He would later brag to Jake that he had been the "belle of the ball." Clusters of townsfolk gathered round as he regaled them with hair-raising tales of his heroic exploits in the mountains, of hand-to-hand combat with scores of hostile warriors all after his scalp, of rescuing maidens from the jaws of certain death. He told of grueling feats of survival, in which he had been pitted against the violent forces of nature. He dramatically described unarmed battles with ferocious beasts. All the yarns he spun did have a basis in fact. He and men of his kind, cut from the same cloth of courage, had blazed trails that eventually led to the opening of the West. With his embellished stories that night, he painted himself as one of the heroes in the epics of Walter Scott, exaggerated to a degree that his listeners would know full well that he was having a bit of fun with them. But Jake had seen the stuff of which Lafe was made, and thought he sold himself short, if anything. Jake knew the mountaineer to be a man who had been where the bear walks and the buzzard roosts. He knew him to be tough where it really counts—in the mind—in his beliefs, convictions and principles. And in his loyalties. Lafe was tough all right. Tough enough to be tender. Tough enough to care.

The mountain man had the fluid grace and coordination of a natural athlete, honed by years of stealth on rugged trails. Once he got the rhythm of it, he was whirling around the dance floor like a honey bee around a blossom. One attractive widow, a dressmaker with carrot-red hair, was his favorite partner, and they became an entertaining fixture on the dance floor.

At a break between dances, Lafe walked to where Jake was standing by the buffet table, a long affair made of planks laid atop barrels and covered with cloths, heaped with those delicacies brought by the ladies in attendance. Cakes, pies, doughnuts, cookies, sweet rolls, pickled meats and vegetables, smoked salmon, cheeses, and nut breads. The variety seemed endless.

"You and me'd best drink from the ladies' punch bowl," Lafe said, winking.

Sure enough, there were two large glass bowls of punch constantly being refilled from a washtub under the table. Sidling over toward the "men's" bowl, Jake could smell why Lafe had warned him. As gents passed by, they emptied their flasks, bottles, and fruit jars into the bowl, giving the pink punch a definite rusty cast and the kick of a Missouri mule. Jake smiled his gratitude and filled his cup from the unfortified bowl. Then he walked back to join Caleb and Lovie, just returning to their seats after a turn around the floor.

Little square wooden tables, each spread with a cloth, were scattered around the perimeter of the hall. A wide assortment of chairs, gleaned from numerous kitchens, were placed four to a table. Wooden benches, farther back against the walls, were peopled by folks balancing plates on their knees or staring expectantly toward the crowd.

"Whew! Sure don't remember tunes lasting so long," puffed Caleb. "That is an activity best reserved for younger folks."

"Nonsense. You did beautifully," Lovie cooed, "and you are as light on your feet as you ever were."

"You're not seeing it from my point of view," Caleb said, rubbing his calf and wincing. "Jake boy, you're young and virile. Grab yourself a young lady and get out there on that dance floor, why don't you?"

"Oh . . . I'm not much of a hand. Maybe later."

Jake glanced toward the entry. Where was she? The evening was wearing on, and Ellie still had not shown. Perhaps something had happened. Her escort might have been delayed, or worse, would fail to show up at all. Might be she was still sitting at home, hesitant to come alone. He was about to suggest just that possibility when Ellie floated through the door, radiant and beautiful.

Ellie Warren's curls were piled high atop her head, baring a slender neck, gracefully bowed and strikingly white. Her dress was an eye-popper. White organdy with pink ribbon woven through eyelet at the neck and sleeves. A deep rose-colored, crocheted shawl was draped across her shoulders. A host of heads, male and female, turned in sequence to appraise her.

Ellie's escort was a clean-shaven young fellow, about Jake's age, trimly built and wearing spectacles. He was well groomed, in a dark brown suit and cradling a beaver hat in the crook of his left arm. He carried himself well, smiling graciously as he took Ellie's wrap. Jake's heart sank with disappointment and feelings of inadequacy. He had hoped the suitor would be a gangly youth with a poor complexion. Well, they were quite some distance away. He could still hope for pimples.

Another man, slightly older, accompanied the young couple—tall, well set, large through the chest and shoulders. He was immaculately attired in the manner of a southern gentleman. Jake could not make out his features, as his face was turned toward the opposite wall. There was, though, something ominously familiar about the man.

Ellie spotted the Pettigrews' table and stood on her toes to wave across the crowded room. She pointed them out to her escort, who nodded and tugged at their companion's sleeve. Following Ellie's pointing finger, the big man turned. His eyes locked with Jake's. Cold cat's eyes that Jake could never erase from his memory.

Jake's face blanched in shock and he leaped to his feet. His knees struck the underneath edge of the table, upsetting his punch cup and dumping the contents into Caleb's lap. Caleb jumped up, knocking his chair clattering backward, blotting at the errant liquid with his handkerchief.

"Caleb! Don't you know who that is with Ellie?"

"Certainly, her escort, Jonathan Samson. He is a young lawyer here in town."

"No, no . . . not him. The big man."

"Yes. Yes, of course. Harrison Beale, Jonathan's employer. A business associate and a friend of mine. What's wrong with you, Jake?"

"Caleb . . . that man is Malachai Winter. The man who . . . took Ellie!"

Caleb Pettigrew stared incredulously, shaken and appalled at Jake's ridiculous outburst and insane accusation. He lifted the handkerchief soaked with Jake's spilled punch to his nose and sniffed suspiciously.

"That is complete and utter nonsense, Jake. You're seeing shadows. I've know Harrison Beale for years. He is one of Salem's leading citizens. A successful lumberman, involved in community affairs, and a perfect gentleman. Why, he has even been a guest in our home, on several occasions."

"Damn it, man, he held a gun to my head while he terrified your niece. Do you think I could be mistaken about that?"

"Please, Jacob, not now," Lavinia whispered in a pleading tone.

The new arrivals crossed to the table. Ellie, smiling brightly and innocently, began introductions.

"Jake, this is Jonathan Samson, and Mr. Bea—"

"Mr. Winter and I have met." Jake stepped forward and stared defiantly at the big man.

"I am afraid you are mistaken, my friend. My name is Beale. Harrison Beale. And I'm certain I have never set eyes on you before."

Beale's steel-gray eyes blazed with undisguised hostility. Jake returned his glare with equal antagonism.

"Come, Ellen, I believe this is our dance."

Jonathan and Ellie moved away as he steered her through the milling celebrants. Smiling humorlessly, Beale excused himself, brushed past Jake and moved toward the refreshments.

Jake lunged to stop him, but Caleb quickly grabbed his arm. As Jake stood seething, Caleb placed a hand on his shoulder and said sternly, "You are our guest here. I am going to insist that you embarrass us no further. Mr. Beale is a family friend and business associate, and not the man you believe him to be. You are badly mistaken. It has been years since that terrible incident, and I'm sure it has been much on your mind, but Jake, you must admit, you were . . . well, not yourself during a number of those years.

"Believe me, son, I regret having to bring that unpleasant fact to your attention. But please, do us and yourself a favor. Take a short stroll outside and compose yourself. Then come back inside and let us all enjoy the balance of the evening."

Jake turned angrily to leave. Lavinia stopped him with a hand on his arm.

"Jake, if you pursue this accusation, I'm deathly afraid that the entire tragedy will come to light."

Jake pulled his arm from her grasp and said hotly, "And that's exactly what ought to happen, ma'am. That man is a mad-dog killer!" He jerked around and stormed out through a side door.

Lafe watched as Jake stomped out. He hurried through the crowd after him. By the time Lafe reached the exit, Jake was two hundred yards down the road, heading purposefully toward the center of town. Lafe ran to overtake him.

They sat together in the damp grass at the side of the road as Jake told the mountain man everything that had happened and all that was said, almost to the word. In Lafe's calming presence, Jake's temper cooled to a more manageable level.

"Now ain't that one to write home about? Are you right sure it was Winter?"

"Good Lord, Lafe, you don't believe me either? Of course I'm sure. The bloody renegade had a gun stuck in my ear. That kind of thing makes a man's memory keen as . . ."

"Whoa, partner, all right. Don't get your dander up again. You seen him face-to-face before, not me. If you're sure, I'm flat positive. Plumb ticklish. What you aim to do about it?"

"Stick *my* gun in *his* ear. Force him to own up to his crimes. I'll blow his swelled head off if I have to!"

"No. That won't work, and you know it. That's your anger talkin'. What makes you think if the Pettigrews, who are your friends, can't swallow your story, anyone else is apt to? You'd be offerin' up your neck for sure. Winter has laid his cover well, and judging from what you tell me just happened, is above suspicion here.

"I'll say this for the mangy coyote . . . he's got a toe-sack full of gall. To risk rubbing elbows with Ellie and the Pettigrews after what he done calls for a mighty rare conceit. He no doubt figgers this to be a grand and sinister joke, for he plainly thinks of himself smarter than us peons . . . and above the rules and laws set down for common folks. He's painted himself as an upright pillar of the town, and so figgers he's safe from exposure. Beyond reach. But no man is, and it falls on us to prove it."

Lafe paused to light his pipe, and to give his young friend more time to settle down.

"Winter's vicious, and lower than slug slime. We know that. But as yet, partner, we're the only ones that know . . . and that gives him the edge. You and me, we're loners, and strangers to boot. We got no one to back us in this. We dasn't go off half-cocked, or he'll come out winners, still a wolf on the loose. We got to plan careful and tread light until he tips his hand.

"You got him worried now, for he knows *you* know. He'll try to discredit you first off, and kill you as soon as he figgers it's safe to do it. You keep a wary eye on your backtrail, boy, for he'll be coming . . . and he won't come alone. That ain't his way. Winter won't take no unnecessary risk, but he's got to get you. And that there may be our saving grace. We at least know what he's got to do, and can plan for it."

"That's all fine and good, Lafe, but you're forgetting about Ellie. She's in danger and doesn't even know it."

"No, she don't know it, and that's just why she's safe for now. As long as she don't recollect what took place out there, she ain't a threat to him. She'll be safe enough. Winter dasn't harm her here . . . he'd be messin' in his own nest. You got to bide your time.

"He knows you know who he is and what he's done, and that you'll be watching him. And knowing will make him nervous. Nervous men make mistakes, and Winter'll make his. I want us to be there when he stubs his toe."

"It galls me to say it, but I suppose you're right. So what do we do now?"

"Well, first off, we ought to get back to that shindy." Lafe knocked the dottle from the pipe into his palm. He held it there until it cooled, then tossed it to the breeze. "The more Winter sees you around, the goosier he's going to get. Go back in there and apologize. Tell them you must of been mistaken."

"Apologize? In a pig's eye! Why the blazes should—"

"Simmer down, now. It'll chafe some, but you got to do it. It's apt to throw the two-faced, twice-named booger off balance. Then ask that girl to dance. That oughtn't be so hurtsome, if I can read sign at all. And again, it's going to make Winter squirm. He'll wonder and fret over what you're saying to her.

"Attack, boy, attack. But use your wits. Keep a cool head."

Shoulder to shoulder, Lafe and Jake walked back to the Grange Hall.

Chapter Thirteen

After the dance, Jake and Lafe decided to rent a room at the Government House in order to stay abreast of Winter's activities and get a lay of the land.

Jake slept fitfully that night. He twice got up to pace the floor, the second time almost stepping on Lafe who, being unable to get comfortable on the too-soft mattress had pulled his blankets down to the harder wood surface. Jake grinned in the inky blankness of the room.

They dressed before dawn and went downstairs to the restaurant for breakfast. Both men ordered deer sausage and eggs, hot biscuits, coffee, and gooseberry cobbler. They ate in silence. As they rose to leave, Geoffrey Cutler hailed them from his office door.

Jake followed Lafe behind the counter and into the office. Cutler shut the door behind them. He poured three mugs of coffee, then sank his overstuffed frame heavily into an overstuffed chair.

Cutler stroked his beard, then asked, "Jake Eriksson, just what the dickens you been up to?"

Jake shrugged.

155

"Somebody wants you out of town, either on the run or feet first," Cutler said, then explained. "An old saddlemate of mine that I was on a survey party with once came busting in last night, mad as a hornet. It was around one o'clock. I was still up, working on some food orders.

"Zeb—my friend—lost his whole outfit fording the Snake awhile back. Came out of the river with nothing but a wet backside and a long walk ahead. He made it this far, looking licked like something to be swallowed, and I been trying to fatten him up some. Letting him stay in one of the old rooms.

"Anyways, Zeb's been all over town, working at whatever he can get, trying to build up a stake. Then he's bound back to Missouri. Folks know he's hard up against it, and you can tell just by looking at Zeb that he's a powerful tough hombre. Well, he was standing at the bar of the Silver Otter, sucking on a beer, when this big yahoo sidles up to him . . . offers him two hundred dollars gold if he'd do a little job for him.

"Zeb asks him, joking, 'Who do I have to kill?,' and the feller says, 'Man named Jacob Eriksson.' "

Jake and Lafe jerked to attention and looked at each other in surprise.

"Zeb don't know you from a Flathead squaw, Jake, but hard up as he may be, he took hard exception to the idea that anybody might think he'd hire out his gun. So he ups and busts this gent's nose for him.

"That jasper picked the wrong man this time . . . but there's no shortage of those around who aren't so particular. If it was me, I'd light out."

Lafe looked at his young friend and slapped him on the knee. He grinned widely.

"He's jumpier than we thought, partner, and wasting no time. He's running scared."

They rode out of town in buckskins toward the foothills in the distance.

Lafe figured it might be best to disappear for a few days, allowing Winter time to give pause as to where they had gone and where they were apt to show up next. Then, when the renegade started to relax a mite, they would ride in to upset the honeypot again. Maybe have Sunday dinner with the Pettigrews. Winter would mess his britches at that, sure.

As the two riders cleared the town limits, Cur came racing up behind the horses, barking excitedly. The dog looked as if it had been dragged through a knothole. One ear was torn, and he was covered with scratches. His scruffy coat was matted and muddy.

"Welcome to the peaceful hamlet of Salem, boys." The mountain man laid back his head and guffawed.

Riding cross-country, Jake and Lafe cleared the valley at dusk and headed up the slope, eyes alert for a safe spot to camp. The crickets were tuning their fiddles when they finally pulled the saddles from their horses and turned them out on a patch of grass, ground-tying them so they would not stray. Unrolling their bedrolls, they pulled off their boots and sat down heavily on the edges of their blankets. Both were tired from the long day's ride, but glad to be away and free of the excesses of town living.

Chewing on dried salmon, the partners talked in low tones—not of the situation in town, but of paths to follow, rivers to ride and mountains to cross. They talked of all those gifts of nature, so freely given. Gifts to see and to touch. Gifts to breathe in deeply and to listen to quietly. Gifts of the soul and of the senses. They stretched out on top of their blankets. Jake Eriksson and Lafe Cawkins slept soundly, a part of the world around them.

One-Eye Charlie Riddle had answered an urgent summons from Harrison Beale. As was their custom on such occasions, they met at a carefully hidden shack in a wooded hollow near the river, nine miles out of town.

The call had come right ahead of hard times for One-Eye. The last wagon raid had yielded little profit, and by the time he had given the rest of Beale's boys their cuts, the bitter old man of the mountains was left with precious little to keep the bottom of his purse warm until the next job.

He had made do, right enough, for he needed precious little. One-Eye was a loner, eating mostly off the land, sleeping wherever he chose to drop his robes, steering shy of towns and settlements. He hadn't any use for people, hated all Indians, and owed allegiance to no man. Powder and shot for his guns, bacon, coffee, salt, tobacco if it was to hand, an occasional jug, and once in a while a can of peaches for the sweet tooth. Fill this spartan shopping list and One-Eye was content.

Charlie Riddle's needs were few, but he was scraping bottom now. The pickin's had gotten slimmer as more people crowded into the territory. Of course, that need not be the case. The reverse should be true, and would be, if Beale were not such a damned stickler.

"Don't be seen. Don't be heard. Leave no one alive to bear witness. Cover your tracks and stay out of sight." It was the same song before every dance. The man could try the patience of a saint, and there was nothing saintly about Riddle. As he rode to this rendezvous with Beale, One-Eye decided that this would be his last dealings with the man. Beale was getting too darned high-handed, and Charlie Riddle would knuckle under to no man.

Whenever Beale sent word, Riddle knew there was killing to be done, whether a raid on a freight wagon, or an isolated settler, or to get rid of someone who had become a nuisance. The need was the same.

Killing was a simple thing, and Charlie had no use for a man that did not do his own. Beale was able. One-Eye had seen him in action, and he was a mighty capable man with a gun. But he was an overly careful man, too, forever after the sure thing, always taking care to stay hidden. A skulking coyote.

Beale had been livid over that fracas a few years back that left Lafe Cawkins and his young partner still kicking. Now they had turned up again, both of them. One-Eye would have bet his horse that the young'un had died in that rockslide in the mountains near the camp. He had seen him fall, and the pack mule on top of him. But now, here he was, looking fit and fine as the hair on a baby's backside.

It was him, the young feller One-Eye was being paid to shoot, as Cawkins had not gotten a look at Beale's face. But the killer knew that he would have to put Cawkins away first. One-Eye knew him, and the man was a real bearcat. Once the mountain man was out of the way, killing Eriksson would be as easy as flinging a papoose up against a stump.

One-Eye noticed that Beale was behaving unnaturally when he entered the shack for their appointment this time. More concerned. He was nervous and testy. Not like him at all. The man was generally confident to the point of arrogance. So the little killer seized the opportunity to hold out for twice his usual fee. He figured he was giving the man two killings, anyway. Haw! That singed the big man's feathers.

Now One-Eye was perched in the rocks above the spot where Lafe and the boy were camped. He would do the job and head out of the country. Maybe toward Yellowstone or the Wind River country.

Riddle had picked up their trail outside Salem easy enough. He followed only long enough to determine their likely destination. Then, as Lafe and Jake moved at an easy pace, One-Eye circled wide and waited. He watched as they stopped for the night, then picked his vantage point. His ambush was set.

Killing was easier than trapping had ever been as a way for One-Eye Charlie to make a living. Now he waited, chewing on a wad of tobacco, for day to break.

Lavinia Pettigrew sat in bed, taking her hair down for the night. Her husband lay beside her, his back turned, one arm folded under his head on the pillow.

"Caleb, I'm worried. What if Jake is right? Is it possible, at all possible, that Harrison Beale is the man?"

He craned his neck around to look at her.

"That's ridiculous. You know Beale as well as I do. He's a hard man in some ways, in business and in politics. Intolerant, too, perhaps . . . and a bit superior. But certainly, he is not a killer, and he has always been nice to Ellie."

"I know dear, but still . . . the way he looks at her sometimes. And you know how nervous and upset she seems when he's around. We've commented on it repeatedly. She always excuses herself and finds some reason to leave. She has never liked him, and that's not like Ellie. She likes everybody."

"Lovie, that doesn't even make sense. You're thinking like a woman."

"Caleb Pettigrew, is that supposed to be some sort of insult? I am a woman . . . remember?

"All I'm saying is that if there is the merest possibility that he is not the man we've thought him to be, we dare not take any chances."

"There is no possibility. None. Jake's just mixed his memories over the years. Now please, let's get some sleep. I have a long day tomorrow."

He's right of course, Lavinia thought. *Still, can one tell a person's true character by the way he looks and talks or dresses? What does a killer look like? How does a child molester behave during the course of a normal day?*

Lavinia tossed restlessly throughout the night, dreaming of a frightened little girl with sad and lifeless eyes, her mouth opened wide in a silent scream.

When Jake opened his eyes, he was staring into Cur's hairy muzzle. Pushing the dog's massive head aside with one hand, he complained good-naturedly, saying, "Cur. Stay out of my face. We don't play that little game anymore."

Jake rose to a sitting position and stretched lazily. Judging by the glare in the clearing, he had overslept. Turbid, pewter-colored clouds hung heavy on the treetops, but no rain was falling. Surveying the camp, he saw that Lafe was gone. Jake knew where without wondering. He pulled on one boot and was reaching for the other when a shot rang out, the crisp report resounding through the trees.

Then Jake spied Lafe's new Sharps .50 leaning against the tree next to his own rifle. Alarmed, he pulled on the other boot and rushed to grab up both guns.

"Cur, find Lafe. Go get Lafe."

The big dog leaped away across the clearing and into the trees, heading upslope, with Jake in hot pursuit.

Lafe lay motionless, facedown in the grass atop a knoll. Jake halted at the edge of the brush, scanning the area. He could see no sign of enemies, though there were a hundred places to hide.

Cur sat at the side of Lafe's still form. The dog whined and looked back at the thick stand of brush where Jake was hidden—giving away his position to anyone watching. A bullet exploded the branches two feet to the left of where Jake stood. He whipped his head around toward the sound of the shot, trying to locate the rifleman. Deciding a jumble of rocks up the mountain to his left the most likely spot for the attacker to be, Jake moved quickly to the right, calling Cur back to cover.

Circling the knoll from farther back in the trees and sending the dog away into the woods, Jake moved carefully to a point where he could again see his downed companion, who lay as he had, twenty feet out from the safety of the forest.

He was concerned for his friend, but Jake knew if he were shot down too, it would do Lafe no good. He had to keep his composure and proceed with care and cunning. He stared hard at Lafe's unmoving body, trying to detect signs of breathing or movement, but could not discern much from that distance. Jake could afford to wait no longer, he had to chance it. If the mountain man was bleeding, hit bad, each minute would weigh heavily on his chances. A patch of ground fog would help mask Jake's movements the first few feet. He focused in on a large fallen tree, perhaps ten feet to the south of where his big partner was sprawled on the grass. With luck, he could rush out, grab Lafe's buckskin shirt at the collar, and drag his body behind the log to shelter before the rifleman could draw a bead and pick him off.

Luck? It would take a heap more than that. Try a certified miracle. Jake hoped that old Great Spirit was on His toes this morning.

Running in a crouch, weaving erratically, Jake reached Lafe and stretched to grab him with his left hand, both rifles clutched in his right.

"I ain't hit. Get to cover," Lafe barked under his breath.

Relieved, Jake dropped the Sharps in the grass and ran for the protection of the fallen tree, diving headfirst the last four feet. As he landed, a shot tore into the log above his back, filling the air with a cloud of bark, splinters, and dry needles. Glancing back over his shoulder, Jake saw that the spot of flattened grass where Lafe had been playing 'possum was deserted, the rifle gone.

For several minutes there was no movement, no sound. The forest began to stir again, the birds chirping and flitting through the green fir branches. Lafe called out in a hoarse whisper from the edge of the trees.

"Jake! See if you can draw his fire."

Jake crawled to the end of the log. Cautiously, he raised his rifle and put two rapid shots into the rock fortress up the slope, ducking back to embrace the ground as his fire was returned.

Abruptly a commotion erupted behind the barricade of boulders where the sniper was lurking. Growling, roaring, cursing, and shouting assailed the mountain air, then the boom of the big Sharps .50 bellowed from the edge of the woods.

The heavy bullet from the long rifle entered through Charlie Riddle's sightless right eye and carried the better part of the back of his skull into the mottled gray boulders behind him, painting them a brilliant vermilion red. The lifeless body of the little killer remained vertical for a moment, then fell, crumpling onto the rocky floor. Lafe went charging up the slope with Jake dogging his flying moccasins.

As they reached the redoubt, Cur greeted them, tongue lolling, tail swinging in rhythm to his happy heart's tune.

"You rugged rascal. You flushed him for us," Lafe said in proud praise.

The hulking hero of a dog had a deep gash on its head above the eye, where the sight on the barrel of the bushwhacker's rifle had caught him in full swing. He was spattered with blood that had belonged to the dead man. Cur, by the looks of him, was otherwise unharmed, having accounted himself well. Lafe looked sadly down on the lifeless body that now appeared so small and insignificant, nudging it with his toe.

"One-Eye."

"Yep. Winter's hired killer," Jake added.

Lafe indicated the dead man's rifle. "You want that?"

Jake shook his head. "I want nothing."

"Me neither. We'll bury it with him. He's apt to need it wherever he's headed. Ol' Charlie always was a hard man to warm to."

They went through the contents of the pouch that hung from a strap around Riddle's neck. A half-used twist of tobacco, a well-worn tinder box and a small canvas sack containing one thousand dollars in gold coin.

"Looks like Mr. Winter didn't get what he paid for,"

Jake observed. "I think it would be right neighborly of us to refund his money."

Lafe nodded in amused agreement.

Jake trotted down the slope toward camp to get a shovel, Cur skidding along beside him, while Lafe returned to the knoll to retrieve his hat.

The younger man was struggling with the dog, trying to hold its head still so that he could sew up the nasty gash across the animal's brow, when his partner walked grumbling into camp. His hand inside his hat, Lafe pushed a long finger through the new hole in the crown.

"This ain't no country for a bygawd hole in the roof. Reckon Mr. Winter could stake me to a new hat out of that purse?"

They buried One-Eye on the knoll, dragging one end of the fallen tree over the grave so that it could not be so easily dug into by marauding animals. Then Jake and Lafe searched out the spot where the little renegade had left his horse. They relieved the animal of its saddle and bridle, stashing them under a heavy growth of Oregon grape, along with One-Eye's rifle. They had thought better of burying it. Somebody in town, perhaps Geoffrey Cutler's friend, Zeb, would have use for an outfit and could come out and pick it up. They knew that the horse, a fine young sorrel mare with good lines, would not wander much farther than the nearest good grass.

Jake and Lafe stayed the night on the mountain. In the early morning, by a different route, they would head back to Salem—and to a confrontation with Malachai Winter.

Chapter Fourteen

Ellie Warren came bouncing down the stairs of the Pettigrew home and crossed to the buffet, taking a piece of hard candy from a milk glass compote. She was dressed for riding in a long-sleeve gingham blouse with a high collar trimmed in eyelet, and men's denim pants. Aunt Lovie had objected loud and long the first time she had worn the pants, but Ellie had argued how very much more practical and comfortable they were and had persevered until, finally, her aunt had given in, mumbling about the "younger generation." Now Ellie always wore them when riding.

The girl was worried about Aunt Lovie. She had not acted in her usual bubbly, carefree manner since the night of the dance at the Grange Hall. Lavinia was subdued and pensive. On several occasions, Ellie had caught her staring in her direction with an odd, concerned expression.

Going through the kitchen door, Ellie found Lavinia absorbed in her weekly baking chores, arms white to the elbows with flour with a smudge of it on the tip of

166

her nose. Lavinia wiped her hands on her apron and
spatted Ellie's hand as the girl stuck a finger in the
cookie dough.

"Going riding?"

"East of town today, I think," Ellie answered, licking
her finger. "Mind if I make a lunch to take with me?"

"Help yourself, dear." Lavinia paused. "Ellie . . .
have you seen Jonathan lately? Or Mr. Beale?"

"No. Not since the dance. I think they must be out at
Mr. Beale's lumber camp. Why?"

"Nothing really. I just thought it might be nice if you
spent more time with young men your own age. Don't
you agree?"

"Oh, Aunt Lovie. They're all such boors. Really.
Jonathan is nice, even if he is a little stuffy. I could
never be serious about him, of course."

Ellie wrapped her sandwich in paper and put it in the
pocket of the jacket draped over her arm.

" 'Bye. See you tonight."

Ellie skipped through the back door and crossed to
the stables where she had already saddled her pinto
mare. Lavinia Pettigrew watched through the screen
until her niece disappeared down the narrow street,
then returned to her baking.

Ellie Warren loved to ride alone along the lush, heavily wooded valley where the contrasting greens of its
hardwoods and evergreens joined in a happy symphony
of color with brash accents of whites, reds, yellows,
and blues of every shade and hue, contributed by the
blooms of wildflowers, berries, and shrubs. It elated her
to race across the undulating meadows, with the golden
hair that flowed halfway to her waist blowing free behind her. And she enjoyed being far from the confines
of town, exalting in the open country around her as it

was designed by nature in the beginning, free from people-generated sights and sounds.

Fearing for her safety, Uncle Caleb lectured her often against straying beyond sight of the buildings of the town. He warned of the dangers posed by renegade Indians and animals, or of a fall from her pony, all to no avail. Ellie needed to feel the freedom allowed her by these canters through the countryside.

Ellie paused in a marshy hollow to wonder at the delicate flowers on the blooming bear grass that grew there. She knew the Indians used the grass in weaving rain-repellent headwear of some sort, though she had never seen an example of the handiwork.

Riding to the top of a rise in the meadow, Ellie dismounted and, holding the reins loosely in one hand, allowed the little pinto to graze. As she stood gazing eastward toward the hazy blue mountains that prematurely halted the horizon, she spied two riders, too distant to identify. They emerged from a stand of poplars and onto the long meadow, moving at an unhurried pace. As a precaution, Ellie mounted her pony and rode at an easy trot to the screen of a grove of cedar trees, idly watching the advance of the approaching riders. As recognition dawned, she rode from cover and moved to intercept Jake and Lafe.

When they came together, Ellie smiled brightly and said, "Hello, you two. I haven't seen you since the dance," then added, "I thought you were staying in town."

Jake thought again as he looked at her that Ellie Warren was, by far, the loveliest creature he had ever seen.

"No big mystery. We just felt the need of a bit of fresh air." Jake frowned. "Should you be out so far, all alone?"

"I'm afraid I've wandered too far. I think I'm lost," Ellie lied, feigning coyness. "Would it be a great imposition if I were to ride with you gentlemen for a distance? Just until I'm not lost anymore?"

Lafe grinned broadly at her transparent ploy. Couldn't lose that little gal if you blindfolded her in a blizzard, he thought.

Jake sat a little straighter in the saddle.

"No bother at all, Ellie . . . we'd be happy to have your company."

"Ellen," she corrected. "Thank you."

"Well, I'm in a bit of a hurry, myself. I'll go ahead on. You two young folks foller along at your own pace. Come on, Cur."

Lafe advanced a few yards and turned.

"If you both get lost, I'll send the dog to fetch you."

Lafe rode away, grinning like a sheep eating sheepshowers.

They rode along, side by side. Jake's mustang nuzzled Ellie's little mare. She nipped him away.

"Jake . . ."

"Jacob," he corrected.

They laughed.

"All right, it'll be Jake and Ellie between us," she said. "May we stop for a while? I'm a bit tired from riding."

They stopped in the shade of a big oak that stood as a lone sentinel guarding a small brook. The crystal waters of the stream chuckled merrily down a slight slope. A trio of squirrels scolded them for their uninvited intrusion. Jake brushed away fallen acorns, dapper in their nut-brown berets, and they sat on the ground, letting the horses crop at the sweet grasses in the meadow.

Ellie offered to share her lunch, and they munched and nibbled as they chatted.

"I just love this country. It's so grand, so beautiful. I'll never live anywhere else." Ellie swept the landscape with a marveling glance as she spoke.

"Yeah, me too . . . though I prefer the high country. The mountains and the forests."

"Yes, they are magnificent. I don't get to go there as often as I'd like. Would you take me sometime, Jake? To the mountains?"

Jake reddened at the invitation.

"Well, I don't know. I suppose so, if your aunt and uncle agree. Sometime."

Ellie smiled quietly, then became suddenly serious.

"Jake, why haven't you been to see me since the dance?" she asked. "You *are* the one who rescued me from certain death in the wilds . . . my personal white knight. Did I offend you in some way? Don't you care for me?"

"Yes, no . . . I mean yes, of course I care for you. And you certainly haven't offended me." He paused, flustered. "But you really don't know me, Ellie."

"I want to though, Jake, very much."

"There are some shadows in my past . . . mighty foolish and unpleasant things I've done that I need to set right . . . before I can consider myself fit company for a fine young lady like you, Ellie. You could get hurt."

A fleeting memory, blurred and uncertain, flashed unheeded through Ellie's mind.

"Your past? I don't even remember *my* past. I want to know you, all about you. I don't care about the past, and I don't believe for a second that you would ever hurt me."

"Maybe. Let's just let it stand for now. See what hap-

pens." Jake stood up and brushed the dirt from the seat
of his pants. "We'd better go. It's getting late."

They rode back to town in silence.

Harrison Beale sat at a big scarred desk in a rustic
office attached to the unpainted cook shack of the lumber camp. The camp was situated low on the eastern
slope of Mary's Peak, in the Coast Range of mountains
that separates the Willamette Valley from the Pacific
shoreline.

The "H. Beale Lumber and Exploration Company"
actually shipped very little lumber. The mill sat idle
most of the time. An occasional load of unprocessed
logs was hauled into Salem, on a wagon emblazoned
with signs bearing the company name, to parade
through the town to create an illusion of industry. The
"lumberjacks" had been selected more for their
prowess with firearms, their flexible morals, and their
collective disregard for the rules of society than for
their skills with ax or cross-cut saw.

The men were getting restless, complaining about a
recent lack of action and of being stuck in camp, de-
prived of the pleasures of gambling, whiskey, and saloon women to be had in the larger settlements. Beale
knew that he would have to come up with a workable
plan for a profitable expedition soon or the men would
begin drifting off toward greener pastures. Easy money
was the only criterion for loyalty among these rough
men and Beale must supply it, as was expected of him.

In his mind, Beale pictured Jacob Eriksson lying
dead and bullet-ridden and he smiled. The insolent
backwoods bumpkin had been an intolerable irritant, a
danger to everything he had worked to build. He might
have ruined it all with his insistent accusations. But

Eriksson and that big partner of his were dead by now. A "loose end" disposed of. One-Eye was a master at his trade and Beale had utilized him to profitable results many times over the years.

Riddle had overstepped his bounds this time, though, demanding his fee in advance at double his usual rate. That had infuriated Beale, and he thought now that perhaps the disagreeable little killer had outlived his usefulness as well. Another loose end to tie up.

Beale cursed himself. He should have pulled the trigger on that young upstart Eriksson immediately that first day in the canyon. He had been careless again in the incident of the rockslide, and still again later, in the Dalles—only wounding instead of killing Eriksson as he had intended. It was totally out of his character to be so slipshod time after time. Had he been thorough, even once, he would not be out a thousand in gold.

Harrison Beale forced his mind back to his present problem: a raid. A series of profitable raids must be planned and executed. The opportunity for plunder had never been better. Gold had been discovered in Jacksonville, far to the south in the valley of the Rogue, and that little community had exploded from one saloon and a scattering of miner's shacks to a boom town of "ten thousand men and four white women" in only a year's time. Raiding ore wagons was impractical. The raw ore was bulky and difficult to dispose of profitably and in secret. But they were milling the ore locally there now. The shipments would be rich and frequent.

Beale had cultivated a perfect source of information. Caleb Pettigrew owned a freight company and kept abreast of when and where goods were shipped throughout the Territory. On the pretext of friendship, and feigning interest in the commerce and growth of the community and the country, Beale often had long conversations with his unwitting host, in Pettigrew's office and even over dinner in his home. He had gained valuable information from Pettigrew many times that had led to some of his more profitable raids and robberies along the freight routes of the Territory.

Jonathan Samson, the young lawyer that handled his affairs, was courting Ellen Warren and Beale had primed him to be a listening post as well. The fact that Miss Warren lived with her uncle troubled him some. Beale had blanched in alarm when he first saw and recognized the girl in Pettigrew's parlor. Her memory loss had been an amazing stroke of good fortune. She had grown into a juicy morsel—a trifle older now than he preferred, but desirable nonetheless. Before he left the country he would take extreme pleasure in reminding Miss Warren of who he really was. He'd had her before, in the mountains, and he would have her again.

With luck, Beale figured, he would soon accumulate enough wealth from future, well-planned activity, combined with what he had already amassed, to leave this damp, dreary, uncivilized land and return east to the States. To New Orleans or St. Louis, where a man of his appetites and abilities could establish a self-gratifying lifestyle. There, too, he could use his own name, Malachai Winter, with impunity. He chuckled to himself, remembering.

Winter had borrowed the name Harrison Beale from his dear, departed stepfather. The pathetic little fool had married his mother, a New Orleans prostitute, to "reform" her and give her twelve-year-old son, Malachai, a father and a good home. Mr. Beale had partially succeeded with his mother. No longer needing the income, she had ceased selling her considerable feminine charms. Regrettably, she continued to give of herself, generously and frequently.

The boy would accept no control or guidance from his well-intentioned stepfather, though he accepted his generous financial support without qualms. One evening, Mr. Beale discovered young Malachai attempting to force the lock of his strongbox. He sat the boy down and lectured to him long and sincerely on the subject of morality, trying to show him the error of his ways. That night, Malachai bludgeoned his stepfather to death with a fireplace poker as he slept in his bed, his wife at his side. With the help of one of the woman's male friends, the boy and mother disposed of the unfortunate and trusting Mr. Beale's remains. They lived well on the deceased's small estate until it was dissipated, at which time his mother enthusiastically resumed her career. Harrison Beale is dead. Long live Harrison Beale.

Beale was reaching across his desk for a cigar when the door burst open and Jacob Eriksson barged into the room, flanked by Lafe Cawkins. Lafe, holding his big Sharps loosely cradled in his arms, stood at the door while Jake crossed to the desk to fling a small canvas sack of heavy gold coins into the chest of an astonished Malachai Winter.

"I believe this belongs to you, Winter."

Jake spoke in a conversational tone, more chilling and deadly somehow than if he had screamed his damning words.

"One-Eye couldn't do the job."

Winter sat speechless as the bag of coins tumbled from his lap to the floor.

"What's wrong, killer? You look like you've seen a ghost."

Winter regained his composure and glared at Jake.

"I haven't the foggiest notion what you are referring to, young man. I have never heard of this . . . One-Eye, is it?"

"Mannered. Cool. Oh, you are a piece of work, you lying snake. Save your posturing for the hangman. I'm sick of it."

"You're finished, Winter. Washed up. If you've got a grain of sense in that fat head, you'll ride north to Portland and book passage on the first boat out. I'll be watching your every move from here on out . . . me and my bunch. You won't be able to steal a stick of penny candy without us seeing you. From every window, every shadow, from behind every tree, we'll be watching . . . you and the scavengers who ride with you. You won't use the privy without us knowing.

"You're offal, Winter. You stink up the air that good folks breathe. You've preyed upon the weak and the helpless and the outnumbered for the last time. In other words, killer, you're gone or you are dead. Because I'll shoot you through your black heart, if it takes that . . . but I'd rather see you dangling at the end of a rope."

Jake turned and headed for the door. Like an enraged bull, Winter exploded from his chair and planted his fists on the desktop. Livid with anger, he screamed after Jake's departing figure.

"You . . . you impudent pup! Just who do you think you're dealing with, you nothing, backwoods upstart?"

Jake turned back to face the outlaw's harangue.

"If your big ugly friend weren't backing you with that cannon, I'd kill you, Eriksson . . . tear you to pieces with my bare hands." Spittle drooled from Winter's lips, dancing comically in midair as he trembled in tenuously leashed fury.

"It happens, slick, that my big, ugly friend is only here to see that your hired pack of dung-eating dogs stay in their kennel. That's all. I don't need any help to stomp the stuffings out of a rabid skunk. So come on out from behind that desk, and let's see just how much of you is mouth and how much is muscle."

Jake's voice was unruffled but the blood boiled hot in his veins. He had not been in a knockdown fight since he was a schoolboy. He'd had a passel of them then, defending his pa's name against much larger, tougher boys—strapping farm kids. He had learned one valuable tactic early on. Get in the first blow. Most boys will circle and bluster and shove until they work themselves into a frame of mind to start the ball rolling. Jake had been able to best more than his share of physically superior opponents by striking swiftly, while his adversary was occupied with these obligatory preliminaries.

Jake had natural quickness and agility, and was hardened by the daily demands of wilderness living. This blustering ape would at least know he had been in a fight.

But Jake was not fooling himself about Winter, either. He was a big bruiser. Just looking at him would be enough to scare a man with half a brain. One could see the power in his massive chest, arms, and shoulders. Malachai Winter would be a vicious and merciless opponent. But by now, Jake was well past the point of hanging back. He wanted this battle—needed it. Every attempt he had made at bringing Winter's criminal activities out into the open had been thwarted, and Jake himself made to look the fool. He took off his gunbelt and handed it to Lafe.

"I'd be obliged to handle this here little chore, partner, and tear down this weasel's henhouse for you," Lafe said.

Jake smiled and slapped the big man's shoulder. "You're just upset because he doesn't think you're pretty. Thanks anyway, Lafe. I want him."

Chapter Fifteen

Winter came smiling, like a beast from its lair, his eyes ablaze with maniacal rage. With his coat slipping off his shoulders to the floor, he charged around the corner of the desk. Jake hit him—a slashing overhand right to the throat, then a powerful left jab crushing his nose. Croaking and gasping desperately for air, Winter backed against the wall, his head tucked to his chest to shield his face. Blood gushed from the outlaw chief's shattered nose. He turned his back, scrambling to free his arms from the entrapping tangle of his coat sleeves. Jake kicked him savagely in the side of the knee to send him plummeting toward the floor, a wounded cry on his bloodied lips. Jake hurried Winter's fall with a two-handed sledgehammer blow to the back of the neck. Unable to stop his descent with his coat-bound arms, the bigger man slammed hard to the floor, the full weight of his hulking body driving his face into the unyielding planking.

Freeing one arm, Winter shakily pushed himself to

his knees. Once more Jake attacked, bringing a knee crashing into his opponent's jaw and sending him flying into the heavy desk. Stunned, shaking his head, the renegade crawled haltingly behind the desk on hands and knees, panicked and confused by the ferocious effectiveness of his attacker.

Like a great many very large men, Winter had seldom been challenged, his size alone serving to deter opposition. Then, too, his diversionary posture as a civic leader had occupied much of his attention. He had gotten soft, slowed by inactivity. Winter had sorely underestimated this young hellcat, who seemed not only unafraid, but eager to join him in battle. That frightened him. Winter was accustomed to acting from a position of strength, capitalizing on the fear of his victims—backed by henchmen who were hired to protect his interests and do his bidding. And like most bullies accustomed to uncontested victory, he did not have the stomach to face a man on equal footing.

Jake could have, should have, ended the matter then by following up his advantage, but an idealistic inner sense of fair play held him back, giving his opponent time to recover. In the heat of battle, Jake lost sight of the fact that he was fighting a man who would kill him at the first opportunity.

Winter knelt, panting and pretending submission.

"No more . . . please, no more."

"Remember what I said, Winter. I want you gone."

Jake turned to walk out of the room. Seeing Jake's back, Winter sprang from the floor with surprising swiftness, driving his departing opponent into the wall with a splintering, crushing thud. Jake's knees buckled and Winter locked him in an immobilizing wrestling hold, under his arms and behind his neck—and began to drive and batter Jake's head into the wall, again, and again, and again. Jake's skull exploded with pain as consciousness faded in and out. Winter freed one arm while pressing Jake's face to the wall with the other. He began pummeling Jake in the kidney and ribs. Ripping flashes of pain tore at Jake as he struggled vainly to free himself, helpless in the steel-hard grasp of his larger adversary.

In desperation, Jake braced himself against the office wall with one free hand and one foot, vigorously kicking the other booted foot back and down into his captor's shin. Screaming in sudden agony, Winter released his grip.

Jake locked the fingers of both hands together and, with a full swinging arc, landed a shattering hammer-force blow to his opponent's temple, once again sending a bloody, beaten Winter to the floor behind the desk. Jake leaned heavily against the wall, fighting nausea, regaining his senses and his wind. Once more, wearily, he turned to take his leave.

Roaring like a wounded bear, Winter came up from behind the desk, swinging a pistol into play. The office filled with the roar of a shot and the stench of brimstone. The pistol flew from Winter's grasp as Lafe's bullet plowed into the cylinder, twisting and breaking the outlaw's finger, caught in the trigger guard. Howling incoherently in frustrated pain and anger, the renegade leader hurtled through the door past Lafe and disappeared into the trees.

Backing each other, guns at the ready, Jake and Lafe eased toward their horses. The mustang sidestepped nervously at the smell of blood as Jake lifted a boot to the stirrup. Lafe grabbed the gray's reins, holding it steady while Jake pulled himself stiffly and with painful difficulty into the saddle. Lafe mounted, and they sped down the trail and out of sight.

After they were away, they slowed, riding solemnly and quietly. Lafe looked at Jake and clucked his tongue.

"You done a job of work today, partner. You know, though, you should of never let him up the first time."

"I know. That was stupid. I got the headache to prove it. But speaking of 'nevers,' that was a pretty chancy stunt you pulled, wasn't it . . . shooting for the gun in his hand? If you'd missed, he could have killed me."

"And I'd of mourned you something fierce, Jake ol' son. Besides which, that wasn't meant to be no fancy shot, just a quick one. Your 'big ugly friend' was meaning to gut-shoot him."

They rode on, laughing.

As Jake and Lafe rode back into Salem, a cloud drifted ominously across the sliver of a moon, throwing darkness in their path.

They rode directly to the livery to feed and stable the horses, then walked down the street to the Government House. Jake washed up, then they ambled into the dining room and ordered coffee, asking the waiter to send his portly employer to their table at his convenience.

Geoffrey Cutler came through the kitchen door with a fresh blackberry cobbler and three plates in his hands. After spooning the dessert, he sat down at the table.

"Jake . . . Cawkins. Evening to you. Thought you might give me your opinion on this berry pie.

"Say," he said, looking at Lafe, "your friend, Joe Meek, is back in town. He was in for supper tonight."

Lafe grinned. "That's prime. Thanks, Cutler. I'll track him down first thing in the morning."

They told Cutler of their run-in with Charlie Riddle, and about the horse and outfit, which they offered to his friend Zeb.

"One-Eye dead? You boys made a lot of Indians mighty happy, I'm thinking . . . and yeah, you bet your boots Zeb'll want that rig and pony. He'll surely give you his thanks, until you're better paid. I know he's been itching to get on down the trail."

"You think he might be willing to stick around for a few days? We might have need of a good man."

Jake then told Cutler of his encounter with Beale, as he was known, eliciting a broad grin from behind the red, kinky beard.

"Hot damn! You two jaspers believe in making hay while the sun shines, don't you? If I was fifty pounds lighter and ten years younger, I'd throw in with you myself.

"Let me warn you, though, Jake . . . be careful," Cutler added, "because Beale has a lot of allies here. Powerful men. They don't know you like I do and wouldn't believe a word of it. They'd probably run you out of town instead of him. So for your own sake, don't raise a big ruckus talking against him until you've got some hard proof."

Jake and Lafe finished their coffee, said good night and climbed the stairs to their room.

Two days after the incident at the lumber camp, Jake was riding his horse at an easy walk north along the river. Having decided to give his own horse a well-earned rest, he was atop a rented bay gelding. Cur was running back and forth, casting around to see what manner of varmints he could flush from the brush.

Lafe had ridden out with Joe Meek early that morn-

ing to do some fishing and, undoubtedly, a lot of yarn-
ing and recollecting with his old friend from the mountain years.

After reading awhile in his room, Jake had gotten
restless. He had gone to the freight office to talk to
Caleb, to try once more to convince his friend that he
had not been mistaken in his identification of Harrison
Beale as Winter, the renegade. But Caleb had not been
there. He had taken a wagon and one of his teamsters to
Oregon City to recruit more drivers. Pettigrew's business was on the grow, and he had added two wagons
since the first of the year.

The Free Land Act, which brought thousands of new
hopefuls streaming into the territory, the discovery of
gold at Jacksonville in the valley of the Rogue, and the
general vitality and industry of the vigorous, adventurous men and women who populated this bustling country, all contributed to the unexpectedly rapid expansion
of Caleb Pettigrew's business of transporting goods
and commodities up, down and across the length and
breadth of the Oregon Territory.

At any rate, Jake had been let down at finding Caleb
gone, for he had primed himself for an appeal to his skep-
tical friend. So he decided that a long ride in the countryside would be just what the sawbones ordered. Might be
that he could relax and forget the whole frustrating ball of
wax involving Winter, at least for an afternoon.

The day was overcast and a mist was falling, but it
was mild and pleasant and he enjoyed the solitude.
These gray, drizzly days had always been his ticket, giving him a strange peace, and a quiet sense of well-being.

As Jake dropped into a depression, where a creek
emptied into the river, a man suddenly burst from the
brush on top of the rise in front of him, gun drawn.

Hearing a noise behind him, Jake turned in the saddle. Another gunman covered his back.

Boxed. Jake had been preoccupied and careless. Now he faced the heavy price that all creatures pay for a lack of vigilance in wild country.

"Ride easy, Mister. You don't need to die just yet. The boss man wants to do that his ownself."

Catching a movement with the corner of his eye, Jake shouted, "Cur!"

The big dog rushed through the grass like a charging buffalo bull. Cur leaped at the man on the rise as Jake whirled his mount toward the other and leaped from the saddle. Jake hit the ground rolling and came up with his Colt in his hand, firing twice in rapid succession. The twin .36 slugs from Jake's blazing Navy Colt flew true, lifting the surprised gunman backward off his feet, dead as he landed in the grass.

Two shots rang out from the rise where Cur was battling the first bushwhacker. Jake heard the dog's yelp of pain. He turned in time to see Winter's hired gun flee into the brush.

As Jake hurriedly waded the creek, reloading on the move, he could hear hoofbeats racing away. By the time he reached the top of the rise, the fleeing horseman was disappearing into the late afternoon haze. Rushing quickly to his dog, Jake bent and touched the big beast gently. Cur opened his eyes and raised his head, looking soulfully at his master.

"Easy, old friend."

Cur had an ugly wound high on his shoulder. Jake probed around and guessed there were no bones broken. Using his hat to carry water from the creek, he bathed the animal's wound.

"That bullet's going to have to come out, boy."

Jake carried Cur carefully to the protection of the trees on the river bank and, using his pocket knife, dug out the chunk of lead from low on the squirming, protesting animal's withers. He bound the wound with a strip torn from the tail of his shirt.

The rented bay had bolted at the first sound of gunfire, likely halfway back to the barn by now. Jake gathered the dog in his arms and started the long walk back to Salem.

Lafe rushed out to meet him as Jake stumbled wearily out of the darkness, carrying the wounded dog.

"I figgered you for a goner, boy. Your horse come in over two hours ago, but we couldn't backtrack him in the dark. What happened?"

Jake's feet were raw and blistered. He was exhausted from the long walk, and from carrying the seventy-pound dog all those miles, but Lafe insisted on hearing all the details before he would allow Jake to go to bed. Over coffee at the Government House, Jake told him what had happened.

"Lavinia Pettigrew has been asking to see you," Lafe said, "and she seemed upset."

Jake could hardly hold his head up, he was that tired. "It'll have to wait until morning."

In the room, Jake gingerly bathed his suffering feet, then fell across the bed, too tuckered to undress.

An hour past dawn of the following day, having had a long hot bath, Jake limped down the stairs to the lobby.

Lavinia was waiting for him. Jake escorted her into the hotel dining room and they took a table against the back wall. After her negative response to his offer of breakfast, Jake ordered tea for her, coffee for himself. Lavinia seemed unduly nervous and fretful, worrying with the sleeve of her blouse, playing at her teacup with her spoon. Her generally infectious smile and vibrant personality were conspicuously missing. There were dark circles under her eyes and she looked drawn and tired. Starting awkwardly, she blurted out her reason for meeting him here.

"Jake. I'm very concerned . . . about Ellie."

"Hey, look Lovie, if you're talking about my running onto her outside of town, I can assure you that noth—"

"Oh, no. It has nothing to do with you. Not directly, anyway. My dear Jake, I would trust you with Ellie's safety and well-being above any other. I know you care for her. I can see that when you look at her. I can sense it when you're around her.

"It's just that I've been doing a lot of thinking about what you said that night at the dance . . . about Harrison Beale being the man—the man who hurt Ellie before.

"I can't sleep for thinking about it, Jake. I keep seeing that poor, terror-stricken child you brought us from the mountains. Withdrawn, lifeless, unable to speak of her tragedy. I remember the long months, well over a year, before she was able to utter a sound, or smile, or laugh. Even to feel. The more I think about it, the more I worry . . . and the more convinced and positive I become that you may be right."

"No maybe to it, Lavinia, it's true. What does Caleb say?"

"Caleb has closed his mind to it. He won't even discuss it with me.

"Mr. Beale was there yesterday, at the house. Caleb is out of town, and I didn't want him inside, but he insisted that he had come only to pay his respects and could stay but a moment, so I let him in.

"He looked simply awful. He'd had a bad fall from his horse. His nose is badly broken, his lips are split and swollen and his face is bruised and puffy. And his right hand is in bandages."

A twinkle of mischief, more representative of Lavinia's usual effervescence, crept into her eyes.

"I notice you have some cuts and bruises yourself, Jake. Have you been riding Mr. Beale's horse?"

Jake just smiled.

"So what happened when you let him in?"

"Ellie was in the kitchen, and we all three sat at the kitchen table and had tea. He asked a few questions. . . . How long would Caleb be gone? Where had he gone? What was he hauling? . . . small talk, mostly. Then he left.

"Jake, he was a perfect gentleman all the time he was there, but the way he looked at Ellie gave me cold chills. It may just be an overactive imagination on my part, but I don't believe so. I think Ellie felt it too.

"He didn't look at her like you do, with respect and admiration. This may sound foolish, but he looked at her like a starving animal might look at a piece of fresh meat, with an appetite out of control."

"What do you want of me?"

"Could you spend some time with Ellie, Jake? Keep her occupied, away from Harrison Beale and the people around him? Just until Caleb gets back?"

"Sure. Be my pleasure. But Lovie, let me caution you. Don't tell Ellie about your suspicions. She might react differently toward Beale. If he should even suspect that she might know the truth, her life could be in real danger."

Gales of laughter rattled the chandelier in the dining room of the Government House Hotel. It was the dinner hour, and curious patrons turned their heads to stare at five men engaged in boisterous conversation at a big round table in a rear corner of the room.

Lafe Cawkins, Geoffrey Cutler, Zeb Proctor and Jake Eriksson were listening to Joe Meek's embroidered recollections of a trip he had taken in '43, the year of the first great influx of settlers into the Oregon Country.

". . . that ol' grizzly was so big, when we cut him open we found three pilgrims inside, and boys, they was still in their wagon . . . with a full team of horses."

Once again the table rocked with laughter, and the fabled mountain man continued.

"Well, we headed south out of Oregon, heading for Monterey, and I told the boys . . . Zeb was along . . . I said, 'Boys, when we get down amongst the Meskins, I'm a'gonna become a *doctor.*'

"They all laughed at me, one of them bein' so tactless as to remind me that I couldn't even read or write. But I wasn't put off, no sir. I dug more arrowheads and rifle balls outa various hides than any ten citified gents with that there fancy diploma.

"So I done it. I set up shop and done quite well for a while, with patients lined up from Monterey to Santa Fe. And I'm right proud of the fact that I cured purt'nigh as many as up and died on me. Besides, I got no doubt them that died was better off for the experience."

More laughter as Meek finished off with, ". . . and boys, folks been calling me *Doctor* Meek ever since."

Jake was sure Meek must be the most colorful of all that special breed called "mountain men." He was a handsome man of impressive height, stocky build, and ruddy complexion. Meek's long hair was thinning rapidly on top of his head, and his full, frizzy beard was showing traces of gray, but his powerful presence and magnetic personality overshadowed any physical characteristic of the man. Joe Meek had become a mountain man at eighteen, and had worked at being a trapper, hunter, guide, and scout. He was related, (a cousin perhaps, Jake wasn't sure), to President Polk's wife. Presently, he was a U.S. marshal of the Oregon Territory. Lafe, who was quite a talker himself, had barely gotten a word in edgewise all evening. All those at the table were thoroughly enjoying themselves.

Zeb was wanting to go out in the morning to bring in the horse and gear that he had inherited from the late One-Eye Charlie Riddle, so Jake offered him the use of his horse.

"He isn't used to anyone but me riding him. Might try to get a little rank with you."

"If'n its got hair and all four legs, I can ride it, Jacob."

Lafe told Marshal Meek about Harrison Beale, or Malachai Winter, telling only of the murder raid and the innocent emigrant couple that had been killed, carefully leaving out any mention of Ellie or of her involvement. If word were to leak out about what had been done to her, not only would Ellie's life be in danger, but, unfair as it seemed, so would her reputation. They were talking about Winter now.

"By all rights, I can't just up and put a man in the lockup on your say-so, Lafe . . . though I don't doubt a word of it. We got no hardrock proof.

"If'n I was to jail every feller in Oregon that has something from his past he don't want known, there wouldn't be enough hands left in the whole damn territory to do the milking in the morning. But I'll tell you this, I'll put out the word, quietlike, and I'll be keepin' a eye peeled my ownself." Then he whispered to Lafe, "If'n we can't catch the varmint at somethin', we'll just shoot him."

Lafe and Meek took turns swapping lies, Cutler added a few of his own, and the wide-ranging conversation continued well into the night.

Chapter Sixteen

Driving Caleb's buggy, Jake and Ellie emerged from a covered bridge, heading onto an open meadow west of the river.

Lavinia had packed a picnic hamper with fried rabbit, deviled eggs, thick slabs of nut bread and two ripe pears. They were going to Ellie's "secret place," a shaded glen in a deep cleft between two hills where a small waterfall had formed a deep, clear pool.

They asked Lafe to go along with them, a half-hearted request at best, but he had refused, claiming a prior commitment. Jake had secretly thanked the Great Spirit for the favor.

Cur, rapidly recovering from his wound, sat stiffly in back of the buggy, sneaking furtive sniffs at the seductive hamper in the seat beside him.

The day was overcast and a light rain was falling, but the young couple chatted away as if it was a sunny day at the beach. Jake had promised to read for Ellie from a book of poetry by Robert Browning, and she had asked him to teach her to shoot a handgun.

"You'll have to get your aunt's permission," he told her, and Lavinia had readily agreed.

Upon reaching the glen, the young couple alit from the buggy. Jake admonished Cur not to start lunch without them, then they walked down to look at the falls. The mayflies had hatched, and trout broke the surface of the pool with regularity, sounding much like popcorn starting to make. They both regretted not bringing tackle along, and the pan-size brookies taunted them for their oversight. After relaxing for a long while by the waters, they strolled back past the buggy to find a likely spot for their shooting practice. Cur jumped down from the buggy seat, yelping as he hit the ground. The big dog limped after them, eager to take part, whatever the activity.

Setting an empty cracker tin on a rock, Jake showed his pretty protégé how to cock and fire the little purse gun, a two-shot, "over and under," short-nose pistol with ivory grips, that she had borrowed from her Aunt Lovie.

Ellie aimed at the target and fired, squealing at the frightful noise. Her shot sent the tin flying, having hit left of center and near the top. A good shot. Like a lot of women shooting for the first time, Ellie had simply pointed as she would have pointed her finger, and fired. And, as with most things, that initial natural action is the most successful. They practiced for another twenty minutes or so, Ellie becoming more knowledgeable and less proficient. Tiring of the game, she asked Jake to show her how well he could shoot. Showing off a little, he put on an exhibition of marksmanship that left Ellie stunned and delighted. She had seen men shoot before; had even seen a gunfight once, that ended with a man wounded. But this skillful display was on another plane. She was impressed.

They carried the hamper of food down by the falls and spread a cloth on the ground—just as the skies opened. Running and laughing through the downpour, they rushed to the protection of a large rock overhang and fell panting into the dirt-floored shelter. Cur lay watching in dry comfort from beneath the thick boughs of a large cedar, fifty yards away.

Ellie's smile faded slowly as a look of earnest interest replaced it. She placed her hand on top of Jake's and looked into his eyes.

"Tell me about this 'past' you're so ashamed of. I'd like to know. I need to know all about you . . . for a very special reason."

Jake turned red in the face and became sullen. Blasted woman, he thought, why did she have to go and spoil it all? Then Jake recalled the principles that Lafe had tried to teach him. Moral codes and self-imposed rules of conduct he must follow in each and every area of his life if he was to stay free of the self-centered thinking that, left unchecked and uncorrected, could drive him back to drinking—and to a lonely death in a trash-strewn alley somewhere. One of those basic principles was honesty, with himself and with folks he cared about. Jake decided he had to tell her. He had to tell it all, even if Ellie broke and ran. He could only share the truth, then allow her the freedom to judge for herself.

So Jacob Eriksson told Ellen Warren the story—of the shame of Jackass Jake.

She sat without speaking, thinking of all she had heard. Ellie sensed the basic decency of the young man sitting beside her. She had listened as Jake told of things he had done that now shamed and saddened him, but she heard more. She heard the guilt, remorse, the loneliness and pain that had stalked and plagued him through those misspent years. And she heard the growth and resolve and strength in the man he was becoming.

With tears coursing down her cheeks, Ellie put her hand on the back of Jake's neck and pressed her lips to his. Jake reached his arms around her, pulling her close to him, kissing her warmly, deeply, hungrily.

Locked in embrace, they shifted their bodies so that they touched full length. He pulled her tightly against his chest and they pressed their thighs hard together. His caressing hands wandered fervently over the gentle hills and valleys of her thrusting body. Jake kissed her gently, but passionately, at the smooth, white base of her neck, on the lobes of her ears, on her closed eyelids.

Ellie's breathing was rapid and heavy as she huskily murmured, "Jake, oh Jake . . . I love you, I love you, I love you . . ."

Panting with passion, Jake became suddenly aware of his excited state and of the insistent throbbing in his veins. Pulling abruptly away he sat upright, swiping at his eyes and face with his palm. Then he turned to face Ellie, who lay heavy-lidded and flushed.

"Ellie . . . I'm sorry. I forgot myself. Forgive me."

She smiled, sitting up slowly.

"There's nothing to forgive, silly. I started it." Then, squeezing his hand, she whispered, "But I'll not apologize."

They sat for a long time in remembered propriety, Ellie leaning back against his chest, his arms cradling her, the fingers of their hands intertwined.

"I love you, Ellie. I've known it for quite a spell. But we've got to wait. Before I can do anything about us, I have to do something about me . . . make something of myself. And I've wasted some good years. I don't have anything to offer you now."

She tilted her head to look into his eyes.

"My darling, you carry inside you all I could ever want or need. I love you. The rest will come. We can do it together."

Suddenly remembering, Ellie cried out, "Oh yes, I have something to tell you, Jake. Something exciting. About *my* past."

Immediately concerned, Jake watched her and waited.

"I think my memory of those lost months of my childhood is coming back. A bit at a time, but surely returning.

"I remember being trapped in the snow. I recall the hunger . . . and poor Papa having to butcher the mules, one at a time, so we wouldn't starve.

"And I think I remember your canyon. Not what happened while I was there, or you, or Lafe, but what it looked like . . . high rock walls, the little cabin. I remember the smell of wildflowers. And a coat. A patchwork coat of beautiful furs. Is any of that right?"

Filled with dread, Jake grasped her shoulders and pulled her to face him.

"Ellie, please listen to me. Do not tell anyone what you've just told me. No one. Your Aunt Lovie, if you simply must share with someone, but please, don't tell anyone else."

"I don't understand. Why not?"

"I can't tell you right now. You'll just have to trust that, in this instance, I know best. It's very important. Will you promise me?"

Puzzled, disappointed at Jake's reaction to her wonderful revelation, she recognized the strain and worry in his face.

"All right, whatever you say. I promise. But . . ."

"But what?"

"I've told Dr. Fox already. He was delighted. I thought perhaps he should know."

"Blast it!

"All right, listen . . . it can't be helped now. I'll talk to the doctor when we get back into town."

"I still don't understand. You're being very mysterious."

"Part of my charm."

Jake gave her a warm smile and squeezed her hand.

The rain had stopped, only a light mist remained falling. The forest was shaking itself, coming alive after the downpour. The birds were the first to resume their normal activity, announcing melodiously to the rest of the wood that the storm had passed. The young couple crawled hand-in-hand from beneath the overhang, then stood facing each other. Jake slid his hands around Ellie's waist and locked them behind her, bending to kiss her gently on the lips.

"You hungry?"

"No."

"Neither am I."

"We can't take all that food back. Aunt Lovie would be hurt."

Cur dined well that evening. Sides bulging, he slept contentedly in back of the buggy all the way back to town.

Jake unhitched the horse from the buggy and wiped it down. Leading the animal to its stall, he dumped a portion of oats in the trough, fastened the rope between the posts at the rear of the stall, then hurried to the back door of the Pettigrew house. Making his apologies and promising to return in the morning, Jake hurried through the darkening streets to the doctor's office. The lamp in the office was out and he could see no light coming from the window of the upstairs apartment. He tried rapping on the door.

"Dadgum it."

Frustrated, Jake glanced up and down both sides of the street, where lamps glowed like fuzzy fireflies in the gathering fog. He walked rapidly down the street, head swiveling, his eyes searching. Jake came to a sudden halt in front of a bakery, four doors down from Fox's office. Through the sweating window he saw the doctor seated at a small round table, a cup of coffee in his hand, savoring a fresh doughnut, hot off the rack. A bell jingled as Jake opened the door.

Jake poured himself a cup of coffee from the pot sitting on top of a potbellied stove and accepted a doughnut from a large, genial woman of color standing behind the display case. With the doctor's permission, he seated himself.

"Sir, I'm Jake Eriksson."

"Certainly, I remember. You are the young man who brought Ellen Warren to her uncle from that terrible business in the mountains. I ministered to some injuries you received later in a nasty fall—broken ribs, cuts, bruises." He brushed crumbs from his shirt front. "What may I do to be of service, Mr. Eriksson?"

"Thank you, sir. I have something important to ask of you. Ellie . . . Ellen, has told me she is starting to recall some of the details of that incident. I am asking you not to tell a living soul about her memory returning. She could be in grave danger if the wrong people find out."

"Young man, I am not in the habit of discussing my patients with strangers. You included. Of course, it is understood that anything Miss Warren has discussed with me is strictly confidential. I will tell no one."

Jake sagged with relief, saying, "Thank you, Doctor. No offense. Have a pleasant evening."

"Oh, Jacob," the doctor added, "I did mention something of the matter to Harrison Beale. He is a family friend, and he came in after Ellen had gone. He had seen her leave, and was concerned she might be ill. You might wish to warn him, as well."

Jake's face drained of color as he wheeled on his heels and rushed from the shop.

Should Ellie be told everything now? Would she be in more danger, or less, if she knew? Would she be so affected as to retreat into her world of silence again? As the questions bombarded his mind, Jake became progressively unsure, more confused. He recognized suddenly, and with much relief, that he should not attempt to make any decisions without the counsel of cooler and wiser heads. First he would talk to Lafe. The mountain man had common sense. He would know what to do. Jake walked purposefully toward the hotel.

Cur appeared out of the thickening fog and trailed along at his side until they neared the livery, where the big dog took its leave to retire for the evening. Lafe was standing outside the hotel in the fog, smoking his clay pipe. When Jake explained the situation to him, they sat on the edge of the boardwalk to talk it over.

Lafe and Jake mulled over the options and alternatives and the possible results, consequences, and repercussions of any action they might take. But, in the end, quite logically, they concluded that whether or not to tell Ellie the whole truth was not their decision to make.

That responsibility belonged to Caleb and Lavinia Pettigrew, her guardians. Jake and Lafe must tell the Pettigrews what they knew, including everything that had happened of late—the ambush by One-Eye, the brawl with Winter, Ellie's returning memory, and the doctor's loose-lipped comments to Beale. Then it was strictly the Pettigrews' decision.

They might have saved themselves a lengthy and painful discussion. That night, Ellie Warren sat bolt upright in her bed, stifling a scream of horror. She remembered everything.

Shrouded in the foggy mists of morning, Ellie Warren walked alone through the lanes of a cherry orchard just past the outskirts of town.

Her face was drawn and pale. Her eyes were rimmed red from weeping, and dark circles bore mute testimony to her weariness and torment. An uncaring fog crept silently through the trees, furnishing a nightmarish setting for the young woman's anguish. Ellie walked down the long, straight rows of evenly spaced trees. Their ordered precision seemed to offer a regimented stability and direction to her mind, now so filled with tumult and confusion.

Ellie was a tough-minded young lady with a solidity born of self-confidence and personal esteem, but the sudden flood of horror-ridden memories tossed and hurled her emotions into a dark turmoil, where voracious monsters of the past lurked in ambush. She clung desperately to her sanity.

In graphic detail, Ellie's mind's eye saw her father being blown from his feet as he extended his hand in gracious greeting to the leader of the ma-

rauding pack of degenerates that had descended upon their pitiful camp. Her mother next, dragged screaming to her feet by a thrashing tangle of arms and grasping hands, wailing, "Ellie! Run! Run!" as they ripped the clothing from her slight frame, mauling and groping her, fighting and pushing one another in frenzied lust.

Only the leader stood back, aloof from the writhing mass of depravity and violence. He had loomed over Ellie, a huge shadowy presence, his feral eyes burning into her with greedy carnal appetite.

A sharp, tortured cry from her mother had snatched Ellie from the trance in which she was held captive by those demonic eyes, and she had fled in panic toward the woods. In a few giant strides the man had caught her, bludgeoning her to the ground with a meaty fist. Then he had cruelly dragged her by a skinny arm to the murky privacy of the timber, where he had viciously violated the screaming, trembling wraith of a girl she had then been.

Her attacker brutalized her, again and again and again, and Ellie felt that he would never stop. The intense physical pain became a mere undertone to the terror that gripped her. He insulted and despoiled the very soul of her, robbing her of her right to human dignity.

Then, defensively, Ellie had hidden from the cruelty behind the walls of her mind, where the man could not follow. She watched safely from a tiny window as the debauchery progressed over the long, long hours and days that followed. She

*felt pity for the little twelve-year-old girl out there,
caught beyond the safety of the walls.*

Ellie remembered all these things, as her sense of reality was challenged by her own emotions. She was al-
ternately filled with feelings of fury and paralyzing
fear; of bitter resentment and of ominous dread.
Though her logic and intellect denied them, she was
also wracked by feelings of personal guilt and shame.
She knew that she was utterly and completely blame-
less. That was fact—irrefutable. But one's feelings do
not always coincide with what the mind knows to be
true.

And the questions. What will others think? Will they
whisper and point? Will Jake still love her, knowing she
has been so misused? Ellie fell exhausted to the ground,
weighted down by the conflicts boiling inside her.

"God help me."

Sobbing hopelessly, Ellie Warren fell asleep.

Chapter Seventeen

The fog thinned, then dissipated as the sun climbed higher. A distant crow called raucously to its mates, an invitation to breakfast in a far-off blackberry thicket. Muted sounds of the increasing activity in the streets of Salem filtered through the branches of the cherry trees above the prone and unmoving figure on the orchard floor.

Ellie woke in a welcome state of calm, newly armed with brave resolve, her mental torment eased.

The young woman now knew that she had been in a self-enforced exile from reality, blotting out, in defense of sanity, an experience too overpowering in its horror for her to face. As that abused girl, she had retreated to the safety of a silent world within her own mind, where no menace could follow. Then, as she began to regain the lost abilities to feel, to love, and to trust, Ellie ventured cautiously out of that tightly woven cocoon of safety, testing reality a bit at a time, much as a bather tests unfamiliar waters.

Last night, with that dream of revelation, Ellie's

mind abandoned the last bastion of security from pain
in favor of the real world—with its brutality and evil,
but also with its magnificent rewards of gentleness,
beauty and love—available to those who are brave
enough and strong enough to accept them, and the risks
inherent in them.

Could she face that most intimidating of all antago-
nists: truth? Ellie was sure that some untapped inner re-
source would be there to supply the strength and
courage she would need. She was ready to face whatever might come and to handle it then and there, to the
best of her ability. It was all she could do. It would be
enough.

Ellie returned to the house and walked into the
kitchen to find her Aunt Lovie.

"Harrison Beale is the man who killed my parents.
The man who kidnapped and molested me. He is
Malachai Winter!"

It had been two days since Malachai Winter had
learned from the good doctor, through the pretense of
concern as a devoted family friend, that Ellen Warren
was regaining her memory. Would she remember everything? Would he be identified as responsible for that unfortunate incident in the mountains? There was no way
he could be certain, but Winter dared not take the chance
that his role would remain secret. These unthinking fools
would surely hang him on the word of a mere girl. Western men were ridiculously sensitive about their women,
pampering and protecting them. Winter had seen more
that one poor fellow killed simply for rutting with a balky
wench. Stupid sentimentality. If not for the rapturous
pleasure they carried in their bodies, there should be a
bounty on every one of the insufferable wenches.

Confound it. Now Winter would be forced to abandon his meticulously fabricated identity, his carefully nurtured reputation—everything. Years of planning and building for the future, lost. The orphan girl must bear the blame. And that upstart yokel, Eriksson. If he had not come around stirring things up, the girl might never have remembered the incident. They must die, both of them, for their interference. But not quickly or easily. A very special retribution must be devised for those two.

Winter had liquidated all his assets that very day. Jonathan Samson, his young lawyer, delivered the cash to him at the lumber camp.

"Here it is, Mr. Beale. Quite a sizable amount to leave lying around. Want to tell me what's going on?"

"Simply moving my base of operations for a time, Johnny. Nothing for you to bother about. I'll be in touch."

"I'm afraid that won't do, Beale. I have a healthy share coming from your last ventures. I've done a thorough job of covering up your shadier enterprises, and I want what's coming to me."

"Well now, sonny. That's only fair."

The sound of the shot that killed the young barrister was lost, echoing through the deserted camp.

Winter had gathered his men and was now leading the small army into the mountain fortress he had established and maintained for just such an eventuality. The outlaw chief was confident that the "stronghold," as he had christened it, was brilliantly located for his purpose, in a well-hidden cavern, high on Bearbones Mountain. Sentinels could be posted to cover all possible approaches.

Winter learned of the place from a Klamath brave

who fled his village in disgrace, escaping into the forests with the angry tribe hot on his heels. The Indian had molested the wife of a tribal leader, then killed the man in the ensuing dispute. Walking Otter had enlisted in Winter's band of raiders. He had shown his leader the trail to the stronghold, a winding labyrinth of cutbacks, fords, and inconspicuous passages through seemingly solid faces of rock. Winter was so delighted with this secret hideaway that he wanted no other person on earth to know of its existence. That is the how and the why of Walking Otter's disappearance.

This hiding place had been Winter's insurance. It was now his only recourse. So he led his band here, establishing a base of operations strategically located near the trade routes between the gold fields to the south and the supply points in the settlements to the north. He had spies in both areas to keep him apprised of shipping schedules and cargo manifests.

The world had stripped him of his respectability and of his identity as Harrison Beale. So be it. They would soon come to know—all of them, the whole sanctimonious country—just who they were dealing with. They would know and fear the name of Malachai Winter.

Malachai Winter had vanished from the valley without a trace.

Following Ellie's disclosures, an enraged Caleb Pettigrew, backed by Jake, Lafe, and Zeb Proctor, had ridden thundering into the lumber camp at Mary's Peak in search of the renegade. The camp was deserted and stripped of everything of value. They discovered the body of the young lawyer, Jonathan Samson, in a shallow grave behind the cook shack, but could find no clue as to Winter's whereabouts.

There were numerous reports of Winter having been seen among bandits raiding supply routes to the south. If true, he had abandoned his penchant for anonymity and was taking an active part in the attacks.

It had been two months and more since the outlaw chief had disappeared. Jake and Lafe were in the hotel dining room, facing a pressing problem of their own. They had been in Salem much longer than originally planned, and by now they had almost run out of money.

"Wealth don't make a man happy, I reckon, but I don't turn no somersaults over poverty, neither," Lafe said. "It ain't at all filling. Time has come to go among 'em. Besides which, I've had enough city living to last me two lifetimes.

"Trouble is, Jake, I don't cotton to living in the high country by my ownself again, neither."

Lafe paused to light his pipe.

"Partnerin' with you has spoiled me . . . and you sure can't go traipsing off to the high lonesome with me, leaving little Ellie alone, makin' muffins."

Jake bristled. "You're my partner, you ugly cuss, until one of us puts his possibles in a pine box. Besides, I've got nothing to offer Ellie. Not yet.

"What I do have is an idea. If it works, it could be the solution to our immediate fix, and a start on our future. See how this sets with you. I think it's a solid plan."

"Run 'er out."

"You recollect that big herd of wild ponies we saw a year back, up on the high plateau around Warm Springs?"

"Sure. Not far from the cabin. Go on."

"There was some mighty fine horseflesh in that bunch. They should still be in the general area, and more of them. I figure we can take some men and round them up . . . cull the runts and the older horses, sell off most of the rest. There's a crying need for good horses all over the valley. We ought to have a ready market."

Jake settled in his chair, awaiting Lafe's reaction to his plan. Lafe motioned to the waiter to warm their coffee.

"They'd have to be broke to be of use to most of these pilgrims. My old bones is gettin' too brittle for me to go forking any wild-eyed mustang that'd just as leave be somewheres else."

The younger man grinned and nodded his understanding.

"Thought of that, too, partner. Zeb Proctor worked horses in Texas and did some mustanging in the lower Basin before he came West. I've spoken to him. He'll handle that end of it on shares. And he knows where there's a couple of good hands we can hire for wages."

"I don't know about herdin' nothing but beaver, Jake, but would five hands be men enough to handle a herd of any size on the trail?"

"Zeb says it can be done, considering the nature of the trails we'd be taking, and figuring we'd geld the stallions and gentle some of the leaders before the drive. If we do lose a few head, we can go back after them when we get the main herd secured."

"Sounds to me like you've already done a heap of thinkin' on it. I'm game, I reckon."

"That's not all. Last time we rode south, down around the Umpqua . . . recall our being so taken with that high valley near Cinnamon Butte?"

"I do, and I think I see where you're headin'."

Jake nodded. "I've never seen a spot better suited to raising horses. It's a perfect place to build a home. There's good grass, plenty of water and it's protected from the weather. We can hold back the best forty, fifty head of this gather, keep or buy a good stud, then drive them down there and start us a herd.

"I'm thinking of something permanent, Lafe. A real home, not just an eight-by-ten cabin. The valley is well away from where there's apt to be any folks crowding in, and that'll suit us both. This country is growing at a rapid rate, with no end in sight. There'll be an increasing need for good horseflesh from here on out, as I see it. It's something we can build on, partner. It's a future for both of us . . . and for Ellie, someday, if she'd cotton to it."

Lafe leaned back in his chair and said, "I expect I'll soon be getting' a mite long in the tooth to go wadin' icy cricks runnin' trap lines, so . . ." He slapped his hands on his knees. "You sold me, I reckon, you silver-tongued devil."

The big mountain man had been watching his young friend as he laid out his plan. With great satisfaction, Lafe observed that their relationship had changed, was still changing. When they had come down off the mountain to Salem, only a matter of months ago—even up until the time of the shootout with One-Eye—Lafe had been the definite leader of the two. That was different now. Now they were truly partners. Equals. Jake was taking on responsibilities in their partnership and in his own life. The lad was growing up—becoming less interested in himself, his own little plans and designs. Lafe had watched Jake, the man, getting more and more involved in finding out what he could contribute.

"When do you want to start, Lafe?"

The big woodsman checked his pockets.

"I'm packed. Let's go."

Caleb was enthusiastic about their plans. Learning that Jake had been right about Beale being Malachai

Winter had removed any doubt in Caleb Pettigrew's mind that the young man was completely over his past problems. He no longer doubted Jake's veracity or his strength of character, and he had seen evidence of his capabilities. He had become one of Jacob Eriksson's greatest champions.

Ellie Warren was like a beloved daughter to the Pettigrews, and both Caleb and Lavinia were delighted at the growing bond they saw developing between her and young Jake. They felt parental concern for Ellie's future happiness, another reason that Caleb avidly supported the horse-catching venture.

As a freighter, Caleb was acutely aware of the need for good horse stock throughout the valley and beyond. Saddle and pack animals, teams for wagons and carriages—especially to the south, where raiding Indians had all but eliminated the availability of good animals. He offered to put out word of the roundup along his company's freight routes.

"I can assure you there will be a long list of ready buyers waiting here when you return."

The horse hunters made their arrangements and said their good-byes. Ellie had burst into tears, almost causing Jake to reconsider his plans. He realized, though, he could not pass up the opportunity the project promised. It was for her benefit as much as his own.

The small caravan left Salem, starting southeast for the Santiam Pass and the plateau beyond. Two pack mules carried food, supplies and ammunition. Each of the five men had a spare mount. It would have been preferable to have three or four fresh mounts per man. The job they were facing was a back-breaker, and hard on working stock. But getting hold of more horses would have meant a delay, and time was short. It was important they catch the wild ponies in the open, in large bunches, before the animals split into smaller groups to seek out the sheltered gullies and canyons in preparation for winter. The hunters were already cutting it close. To complete their gather as planned would require two months, maybe more.

While still high on the mountain, they spotted the first big herd, about fifty head strong, far off on the flat. Before the day was out, they had located six bunches more, all about the same size or with slightly fewer horses running in them.

"Zeb, you're the only mustanger and broncbuster in the crew. What do we do first?"

Zeb sent a spurt of brown tobacco juice in pursuit of a scurrying beetle on the trail.

"First off, we got the catch corral to build. That'll take several days. Then we locate all the water holes in the area we're gonna work.

"Mustangs is wily critters and will shy from the least sign or smell of danger. We leave our sign at all but a couple of tanks so they'll steer clear from them and water where we pick for 'em to. At them holes, we need to cover our sign well. Can't even be a stick out of place. We mask our smells and lay hid. We let 'em come in and drink their fill before we start after 'em. Their own full bellies will slow 'em down, and we'll run 'em into the catch corral.

"Joseph's the best we got with a rope, so we leave him at the corral to rope the stallion of the bunch as we run 'em through the gate. After the capture, we geld the stud."

Zeb grinned as he saw Lafe wince. "That'll keep his mind off stirrin' up the mares . . ."

"I'd reckon," Lafe put in.

". . . and they'll gentle down with him out of the picture. Nothin' to it, Jake, except a heap of work and a sight more luck."

Lafe knew of a canyon nearby which, upon inspection, proved to be an ideal location to hold the horses for the drive back. Narrow at the entrance, the canyon fanned out to take in an area of forty acres or more. The lone exit could easily be barricaded with a fence of a few small pole logs. There was ample water and plenty of graze. In fact, a small bunch of wild mares and foals were already in the canyon. While clearing brush away from the entrance, the horse hunters discovered a large, cavelike hollow in the side of the north wall of the canyon. It would provide a fine shelter and night camp. They stashed their supplies and food on a natural shelf in the hollow and laid in a store of wood for the cookfires.

The better part of the first week was spent readying the catch corral in the canyon, with Zeb directing the work. They would need to break a few head for remounts, so they built a small bucking pen with a gelding chute and a snubbing post.

An eight-foot-high gate would close off the narrow mouth of the canyon. Fanning out to the right and left of the gate, three hundred yards in each direction, the men constructed walls of brush that would funnel the pursued herd into the trap.

On the sixth day, the crew started the gather. The back-busting pursuit of wild ponies was hard, dangerous, grueling work, sapping every remnant of energy and determination from the men and their mounts. They would crawl gratefully to their bedrolls each night, dreading the sun's rising. But after the first few torturous days, they hardened to the grind, and their

moods lightened. They made jokes again at the campfires and began to approach their daily labors with a
spirited zest, thinking anew of the rewards ahead.

The mustangers weeded out the older stock, the runts
and those with poor lines, and gelded or released the
stallions. As a result, the growing population of horses
in the trap was a fine-looking collection. Every few
days, the men stayed in the canyon all day to rest their
mounts. On those occasions, they would walk among
the herd, talking in low tones, touching the mares and
young horses when they were allowed. This practice
had a positive, cumulative effect, gentling those animals that had already been gathered, and calming the
newcomers as they were brought in.

The crew gathered around the bucking pen to watch
Zeb top the first mustang. It was a big grulla mare that
Zeb said looked like a real "kidney buster." The wild
mare was blindfolded with a gunnysack. Pete held its
head, twisting its ear. Zeb took the bucking rope and
swung quickly into the saddle before it could crab sideways on him. As Zeb hit leather, Pete let go of the ear,
jerked the blindfold and skittered for the fence. Nothing happened. The grulla stood trembling as the men
watched expectantly.

Then the horse exploded!

The mare came unwound, spinning in circles, then
catapulted skyward, twisting sideways in the air. Its
nose was almost touching its rump. It drove into the
ground with a bone-jarring thud that left Zeb's face
drained of color. He fought to keep its head up. It
soared again, dodging sideways and landing with a
grunt, snaking its powerful neck side to side. The enraged mustang stood straight up and fell backward, trying to free itself of the alien presence on its back. Zeb

jumped free, then climbed back aboard before the mare could regain its feet.

The wild mare uncorked again in a head-whipping, hard-driving buck that jarred even the spectators' teeth. It spun in tight circles, throwing Zeb into an almost horizontal position as he clung to the saddle horn with a white-knuckled fist. Then the mustang slowed, crowhopping around the corral. Finally, it settled into a trot.

Zeb hastily dismounted and walked mincingly through the backslapping, admiring wranglers. He plopped down on a rock to blow.

"Now I recollect why I give up this nonsense."

It had been one heck of a ride.

Zeb and Pete Jasper, a wiry young Negro man of seventeen, bucked out a few more of the animals for remounts to spell the horses that were brought with them from Salem. Zeb was a tough and able broncbuster and horse handler. Young Pete admired Zeb's skill with the animals, becoming an eager student. He showed remarkable tenacity and before a week was out, through blind adherence to the instructions that Zeb gave him, he was seldom being bested by the game little mustangs.

The other hired man, Joseph Mankiller, was three-quarter Indian, a skillful rider, an excellent roper and a good hand.

The days were crammed full of dust and sweat and saddle sores, and the time passed swiftly. The horse hunters had done much better and gotten on faster than anyone had figured. With less than seven weeks gone, they were ready to start the herd on the trail back to the valley. They had collected over four hundred head of prime horseflesh. By the time they had driven the herd from the canyon to the pass at the summit of the mountains, the horses were well broken to the trail, handling easily, the few stragglers usually catching back up to the herd on their own.

After talking it over with Jake, Lafe decided at that point to quit the drive and head northeast. He intended to pay his respects to old Wolf Robe, probably for the last time. Lafe figured to be back before the first hard snows clogged the passes.

Jake waved his friend off down the trail, then pushed the herd toward the valley below, flush with success, driving his future before him.

Chapter Eighteen

Winter squinted one eye and peered through the
mariner's glass he held to his face. From his place of
concealment atop the ridge above the pass, he watched
as Lafe Cawkins reined his big buckskin mount around
and started back down the mountain, the direction the
herd had just traveled. The renegade chieftain concen-
trated on Lafe's unexplained departure for a moment,
broke into a big smile, then beckoned urgently to one
of his cutthroat band behind the rocks.

Pointing out the departing figure of the mountain
man, Winter issued instructions to a big, seedy man that
had scurried to his side. The summoned outlaw repeated his assignment back to his leader, like a student
confirming his lessons. Then he hustled down the
slope, gathering two other men of his mold. The three
renegades stood in hurried conference, mounted their
horses and disappeared into the thick timber down the
mountain.

He watched until his henchmen had gone, then Winter settled back against a rock, taking a cigar from his

inside pocket. He bit the end from the cheroot, swallowed it, and put a flame to the tip. Drawing deeply, he exhaled in a failed attempt at a smoke ring.

The bandit leader had become obsessed, almost maniacally so, with concocting a campaign of vengence against Jacob Eriksson, the man he blamed for his fall from respectability and prominence. Unable to assign to himself any shortcoming, he *needed* the young mountain man as someone to blame for his failures. He did not take into account that his own criminal actions had been his downfall. Nor did he seem to realize that his preoccupation with revenge was negating the effectiveness of traits that had, until recently, enabled him to succeed in those nefarious pursuits for so long— caution, cool-headedness, and a priority for profit. Two men on his payroll of felons were assigned to full-time surveillance of Winters' elected nemesis, Jackass Jake. His hard and handsome face broke into a smug smile.

"Without Cawkins around to wet-nurse you, Jacob Eriksson, your life is mine." He chuckled aloud. "Yes sir, Jackass Jake is dead meat!"

Lafe rode along the base of the mountains, heading north. He made good time traveling alone. In the shadows of a crisp, still evening, he stopped to make camp at the foot of Olallie Butte.

The next morning, Lafe planned to cut cross-country. In five days, with luck and if the weather held, he would be in Wolf Robe's lodge on the banks of the Snake, where it empties into the Columbia, north of Waiilatpu.

The old Indian had saved Lafe from a miserable death and, more importantly, had given him reasons for living and a set of principles to live by. It had made all the difference in Lafe Cawkins' life. It saddened him to think of the old man finally facing the end of his journey.

Pouring the last of a pot of coffee onto the sizzling coals of a small fire, Lafe went to his blankets and slept, dreaming of sunny days on a shaded porch overlooking lush meadows filled with prancing horses.

Minutes after Lafe rode away on his private pilgrimage, shots rang out from the ridge above the herd, peppering the ground behind the horses and sending them off in a headlong rush toward the valley.

"Stampede!"

Riding point, Zeb Proctor was knocked from the saddle by the milling, confused animals. He scrambled behind a boulder as the thundering mass of horseflesh rushed by in a panic, then watched in horror as a grulla mare, the one Zeb had bucked out that first day, hit a hole and turned a cartwheel. The mare landed on its back, its neck popping like a cannon shot above the roar of the stampede. Pete Jasper, Joseph Mankiller, and Jake chased after the blindly charging ponies. As they passed the rock where Zeb was crouched, Jake paused and tossed him a rifle.

"I'll be back with a mount for you," Jake yelled out.

As the herd reached the foot of the pass, the wild ponies fanned out over the valley, slowing, but still running. Spotting Zeb's riderless horse, Jake caught him up by the reins, then motioned Pete and Joseph to his side.

"Pete, you go south. Joseph, north. Watch where they go, but let them gentle down. I'm hoping most of them will drift back together. Don't spook them any more than they are. I'll go back and pick up Zeb, then we'll catch up to you. Now, ride."

Zeb was stomping mad and cussing a blue streak when Jake cantered up and transferred the reins of the little dun mustang to the frustrated wrangler. Handing Jake his rifle, Zeb swung into the saddle.

"Them backshootin', rotten, fatherless weasels. Jake, dang it, as soon as the racket passed, I could hear 'em laughin'. Laughin', mind you. Hell, we could of all been killed or busted up."

"Could you make out who they were?"

"Shoot, no. Never even seen 'em. But Jake, I swear to you, I heard 'em . . . laughin'! Let's take out after them. I'll give them good-natured skunks somethin' to bygawd laugh at."

"Calm down, Zeb. There's nothing I'd like better, but we got horses to catch. First things first. Let's go to work."

Jake knew full well who was likely behind the stampede.

Preacher Stark raised the Ferguson rifle to his shoulder and sighted down the barrel at the blanket-shrouded form lying in the camp.

The outlaw had waited impatiently, chilled to the bone, for the first gray of dawn to arrive so that he could make his kill and get back down to the stronghold. Why in blazes did Winter always assign him to a job where he would be stuck out in the dadgum woods, away from his warm bed and hot food?

Preacher squeezed off his shot. He saw the figure buck with the impact. One more in the head for good measure. He fired again.

After reloading, Preacher got to his feet and moved toward the camp, motioning for his hidden companions to come in. He walked stealthily with his rifle in firing

position to the still body on the ground. Ripping off the
blankets, he rolled Lafe Cawkins over onto his back.

The head was swamped with blood. Stark flipped the
coat open with the barrel of his rifle. The buckskin shirt
was so bloodsoaked he could not tell exactly where his
first shot had scored, but it had dang sure done the job.
The mountain man showed no signs of life.

"Let's hit for home, boys. Our bonus is made."

They rode away into the cold morning fog.

For the next four days, the wild horse hunters rode
from dawn to dusk, working harder than ever, rounding
up the scattered ponies. As Jake had hoped, the biggest
share of the scattered horses reassembled into bunches
of their own herd instincts. On the morning of the fifth
day they started them again for Salem, shy about eighty
head as near as they could figure. The grulla mare and
nine others had died in the stampede in the narrow
pass. By the time the herd was halted for the night only
twenty head were missing. When the men had the herd
safely corralled in Salem, Jake planned to send Joseph
back to bring in what stragglers he could find.

The herd was six miles out when Jake spotted Cur
racing across the meadow, headed straight for him.
Jumping from the saddle, Jake braced himself as the
big dog leaped, all lapping tongue and wagging tail.

"Cur, you old rascal. I've missed you, big fella."

At dinner that night in the Pettigrew home, Jake was
pressed to relate every detail of his horse-gathering
venture. He told of the sniping shots in the pass and the
resulting stampede, the miraculous recovery of so
many of the horses and of his strong suspicion that
Malachai Winter had been responsible for the attack.

"Of course he was behind it, that son-of—"

"Caleb. Please."

"It isn't profanity when applied to that degenerate scoundrel, Lovie. Just descriptive."

True to his word, Caleb Pettigrew had collected a list of anxious buyers as long as his arm, from the Columbia to the Rogue. Jake and his crew would have their work cut out for them for many weeks, breaking and delivering the horses.

Having found that he could face life's challenges successfully, Jake was feeling good about himself and his abilities. He squeezed Ellie's hand under the table.

Ellie had not said much during dinner, contenting herself with listening to and watching the man she loved. Now she wanted very much to talk to Jake and to be alone with him. She helped Aunt Lovie with the dinner dishes, then joined the men in the parlor.

"Wouldn't you like to take me for a ride, Jake?"

Caleb objected. "Not tonight, honey. Jake and I have business to discuss. Besides, it's raining."

"It's always raining. We can put the top up on the buggy, Uncle Caleb."

"But . . ."

Lavinia shushed her husband as Jake helped Ellie with her wrap.

The fog burned away, leaving the day cold and bright. The motionless figure of Lafe Cawkins lay as his attackers had left it. Queued-up vultures circled high above the man on the forest floor, some unseen force staying them from swooping to enjoy the banquet below. The body lay without movement all through the first day and the next, and the following night.

From far back in the dark void to which he had retreated, the mountain man looked out upon the bloody shell of himself and willed it to move, to waken, to live. A tiny beam of light forced itself through the blackness to stoke the minute spark of life that stubbornly remained.

Lafe opened his eyes.

The first sensation the mountain man felt was bone-chilling, mind-numbing cold. Struggling to rise, he leaned his head forward and slowly raised his upper body to rest back on his elbows. His skull burst with flaming rockets and pulsating lights. Nausea swept over him in a wave, and his head pounded explosively, rocking his entire body. He squeezed his eyes shut tight and steadied himself through sheer might of will. Opening them cautiously, he looked down at the dried mass of blood that covered his body.

Cold fear gripped him. *Am I dead?* A racking spasm of intense pain coursed through his violated body.

Nope . . . sure ain't dead, unless I led a lot worse life that I thought. He tried to sit fully erect, but another sharp wave of pain slammed him down and he fell twisting and turning into nothingness.

Lafe could see the gnarled old hands of Wolf Robe pull him from the blackness into the twilight. The old Indian knelt beside him and clasped his hand.

"Wait, my son, until Three Bears comes to help you."

Then Three Bears came running, gathered Lafe into his arms and carried him toward the source of the light. The Indian held him aloft at arm's length, pushing him ever closer and closer to the intensifying brightness.

Lafe regained consciousness. His big horse was nuzzling at his hand and he could feel snowflakes melting on his cheeks. Opening his eyes, he looked around. It came to him where he was. That he had been shot he knew, but who in tarnation, and when?

The buckskin nuzzled him again and whickered. The horse must have eaten everything within reach, then pulled loose its picket. That indicated to Lafe that he had been unconscious for at least one day, perhaps two.

Further scrutiny of the campsite told him his saddle was gone. And his rifle. He decided that it could not have been Indians who had attacked him. They would have taken the horse too. Why hadn't his assailants taken the horse? Probably afraid somebody would recognize it. His saddlebags, covered with his blood, lay where he had used them as a pillow. That was good. He had a bit of jerky in there and a few hard biscuits. Lafe's sidearm and long knife had been removed from his body. He thought, though, he could recollect having a large folding knife in his saddlebags.

Water. Those who had tried to kill him had taken his canteen. He would need water soon. Lafe remembered a stream, just a trickle, where he had the buckskin staked out.

It was snowing softly but steadily. He must find shelter. If he froze he wouldn't need the blasted water.

Lafe tried to get up, but the agony was too great and he was too weak. He dared not force himself. Might black out again and that would likely be the end of him. He began to crawl, dragging his saddlebags and blanket, able to manage only a few feet at a time before he tuckered out.

The mountain man felt his head. There was a large, long opening in his scalp along the side. He could feel the bone. Aside from the head wound, Lafe had been shot in the back. That bullet caused an exit wound the size of a fist in his right side near the base of his rib cage. The bloody cavity was filled with bone splinters, no doubt from a rib. They must have caught him from the rear while he slept on his left side.

"Sneaky, rotten bushwhackers. I look like I been guest of honor at a hog butcherin'."

Lafe started to crawl again, consciousness washing in and out like a tide. Reaching the stream he drank deeply, rested, then drank again. Scraping mud from the sides of the stream, Lafe plastered his wounds as best he could. He did not know if it would help, but Dr. Meek swore by it.

A large fallen tree formed a bridge over the flow of water and Lafe could see a slight hollow underneath the trunk across the stream. He rested, then reached across the brook, holding his blanket out of the water to drop it on the other side. Next, the bags. Dizzy and out of breath, he rested again. He dragged himself through the water, blew for a while, then crawled to the depression beneath the log. Not big enough. Had to hollow it out some. Cupping his hand, he began digging in the soft earth and humus that the fallen forest giant rested upon.

Finally, he scratched out a chamber roomy enough to hold his lanky frame. Lafe dragged himself into the hole, pulled a large fir branch over the opening and slept, exhausted by the effort.

Lafe Cawkins woke in the middle of the night in a womb of total darkness, not knowing where he was or what had happened. His throat was parched, craving water. Realization slowly returned, followed in short order by the omnipresent pain.

"Lafe, ol' son, looks like you might've drawn the

black bead this time." He spoke aloud, not knowing his own voice.

"Great Spirit, if you ain't too busy, I could use a hand. Looks like I got hold of a rock, here, that I ain't going to budge without you help me out."

Lafe knew well that in nature there are no rewards or punishments. There are consequences. He must plan each action carefully, and conserve his small energies to survive.

He had to have water again. He grudgingly pushed the covering branches aside and, laboring painfully, crawled from the depression. Lafe's wound had stiffened while huddled in the hole, and each movement was a victory over the agony his body felt.

"Backshootin' varmints could have left me the canteen."

After slaking his thirst, Lafe added fresh mud to his wounds, crawled back to the hole and struggled inside. Drained of all strength, he slept again.

The light was high in the sky the next time the mountain man awoke. The sun was shrouded heavily with clouds that were swollen with the sinister promise of snow. Lafe was burning up. Fever. Should be no infection, though, as he had no lead in him of which he knew.

The world outside his shelter was blanketed in white. Not yet deep, less than an inch. Digging into the pouch of his saddlebags, Lafe pulled out the folding knife and opened the six-inch blade. He could dig some dry wood for a fire from the underside of the log above his head.

Gnawing a piece of jerky brought a wave of queasiness. He put it back. Later. Lafe tried eating some snow, but could not quench his insistent thirst, so he resignedly crawled the lengthening distance to the stream and drank. Crystals of ice were beginning to form at the edges. He hoped it did not freeze over. Drinking until he could hold no more, Lafe started the grueling trek of a few feet back to his shelter, crawling with increased difficulty. He was gaining a whole new respect for lizards and other crawly varmints. Back in his snug haven, he slept again.

Lafe woke with a start. Something, or someone, was pulling at the branches that covered the entrance. Wolves? A bear? The killers returned? He opened the blade of the knife and held it in his trembling right hand. Light flooded into the hole as the branches were pulled away. Lafe squinted at the sudden brightness and automatically thrust his left hand over his eyes, causing himself to cry out at the sudden, painful movement. His eyes accustomed themselves to the light, and he found himself looking into the face of his friend, Three Bears.

The Cayuse told Lafe to stay protected in the hole while he built a suitable shelter. When the Indian had completed a lean-to and built a fire, he returned to the log to find that Lafe had passed out. He reached in and gently pulled the mountain man from the depression, wincing with grief at the spectacle of his friend's wounds. Three Bears carried Lafe to the lean-to and carefully laid the long, limp body on a bed prepared from fir boughs spread with a blanket. Then he heated water in a container fashioned from birch bark, and tenderly bathed the wounds. The Cayuse brave applied a salve of herbs and bear fat that Wolf Robe had sent with him.

Lafe had still not regained consciousness. His instinctive drive to survive had relaxed at the sight of his friend and, no longer alone, his mind allowed him to rest.

Three Bears covered the gravely wounded man with a buffalo robe. He stood a moment, watching his un-

conscious friend's labored breathing, then, taking his
bow, walked off into the trees. He returned ten minutes
later with a fat rabbit he had bagged with an arrow. He
dressed the kill and prepared a broth. At the inviting
aroma of food, Lafe opened his eyes. He looked at
Three Bears.

"What are you doing here? How'd you find me?"

"Wolf Robe sent me. It came to him in a vision. He
saw three men stand over you. He saw your wounds. He
heard you call to the Great Spirit. 'Go to your friend,'
he told me. 'Go to Bear-Upon-the-Mountain. Bring
him to me.' Wolf Robe told me where to find you."

Five days they stayed in camp, the Indian tending the
wounds of Bear-Upon-the-Mountain, strengthening
him for the journey to the land of the Cayuse. He fed
his wounded friend with broths and stews from fresh-
killed game, herb teas, and honeyed bran from the
stores of Wolf Robe's medicine bag. Three Bears made
a travois and hitched it to the buckskin horse, then
strapped Lafe down. They started slowly across the
plateau.

Far away, in his lodge, Wolf Robe smiled.

Chapter Nineteen

Snows clogged the mountain passes and crowned the peaks with glistening glory, but commerce in the protected, temperate valleys went unimpeded.

The late autumn air was rent with the indignant screams of high-bucking horses, leaping and twisting with explosive fury, denying their destinies under saddle or in harness. The emergence of a land growing, a land peopled with men who moved on horseback and in horse-drawn wagons and buggies and drays, created a demand that brought eager buyers streaming to the holding pens.

The busy days melded into weeks with scant notice and the weeks stretched into months. The herd of captured horses was dwindling. The successful venture was nearing an end. Jake, by all rights, should have been in a festive frame of mind, but as time passed he grew more and more concerned.

He had heard no word of Lafe Cawkins. Where was he? He should have returned weeks ago. Had he delayed too long in the land of the Cayuse and gotten snowed in? Jake pondered what could have happened. He might have been thrown from his horse somewhere out on the plateau, gotten caught without water, or run out of ammunition with Indians closing in. There was much that could happen to a man alone.

Where does one begin to look for a lone man in a land as vast and varied as the Oregon Territory—a land large enough to swallow armies without a trace? Along the high ridges? In the deep canyons? On the expansive, barren Great Basin? In any of the hundreds of the gorges of raging rivers, or along the streams where the beavers build?

Lafe was a knowing man, tough and capable. Given time, he could fight or wriggle or claw his way out of most any fix—but Jake worried all the same.

He knew full well what the crusty mountain man's reaction would be to worrying over things that might never happen.

"Jake," he would say, "no sense frettin' over things we got no control of. Better to use our energies on what's before us to do."

Jake grinned. Even when he was not around, Lafe Cawkins gave him the guidance he needed. With that thought in mind, Jake laid plans to ride south to survey the valley where he and Lafe planned to settle and build for the future. There was snow, but a man could make it on horseback with little trouble. He would take two horses, his gray mustang and a big blue roan they had captured on the plateau. And a pack mule. He made a list of supplies and left it with the storekeep to fill, then walked to the Government House to ask Cutler to hold his room.

Cutler and Zeb were in the dining room, hunched over steaming cups of coffee. Jake joined them, accepting a cup from the waiter, and told them of his travel plans.

"I'd ride along with you, Jake, but I got a run to make myself," Zeb said. "Now that all the ponies is broke, Pettigrew's hired me to ride shotgun on a freight shipment to the gold fields. He's lost his last two wagons of goods to them no-count raiders."

"Why don't you wait until Zeb gets back, then?" Cutler asked. "Or you could wait for Lafe to turn up. I hate to see you ride out alone. The Modocs are raiding down in Klamath County, and Winter's bunch is all over that country down there."

"Don't get all lathered, boys. I'll ride careful. I've got two good horses and two good guns . . . and a big dog that's a posse all by himself. I'll be as safe as an ugly girl's box supper.

"Lafe's always told me that a man is more apt to stay on his toes when he rides alone, not depending on others to do his watching for him, and not needing to worry about his trailmates."

"All right, you mulehead. When you leaving?"

"First light tomorrow."

"Why can't I go with you? I can ride with the best of men, I'm young and I'm healthy . . . and a lot tougher than you seem to think, Jacob Eriksson."

"Ellie, your place is here."

"My what? Did I hear you say, 'my place'? If I'm to believe anything you've told me, sir, my place is with you, and the place you're going is to be as much mine as yours. Or have you changed your mind?"

"No. Of course not. The valley will be our place. Yours, mine, and Lafe's. But the trip is far too risky for a woman, conditions being what they are. Besides, you know good and well that Caleb and Lovie would never allow it. It just isn't proper."

"We could at least ask them."

"No. You're not going. That's final."

Ellie whirled and stomped from the room.

When Lafe Cawkins came to, he was lying in a slender shaft of diffused light angling through a smoke hole in the roof of a Cayuse lodge. A pungent odor, an herbal scent, hung heavy in the close air of the primitive shelter. He recognized that he was at home, in Wolf Robe's lodge, but for some reason he could not remember the hour, the day, or the moon. Not even the season. Where were the others? Had they gone off on a hunt without him?

A sudden jolt of searing pain in his lower side caused Lafe to roar out in agony. His hand went to the wrappings that bound his torso, where the pain had originated, and his mind was snatched abruptly back to the present. He was not still that young white man, taken in and living among the Indians. Apparently, though, judging from the startling and painful wake-up call, he was still alive.

He remembered, then, that he had been savagely attacked and left for dead, and that Three Bears had appeared at the scene of the ambush to snatch him from the jaws of death, sent to aid him on the strength of old Wolf Robe's vision. Lafe lifted his hand to the wound in his scalp. It, too, had been tightly bound. He felt as if he had been wrapped for shipment.

The buffalo-hide flap at the lodge entrance was flung wide as a Cayuse maiden came rushing inside to investigate Lafe's scream of pain. There was a frown of concern wrinkling her brow.

"Lie quietly, Bear-Upon-the-Mountain. You are very sick."

Her straight black hair glistened, even in the dim light of the lodge's interior. Her dark eyes were as large and soft as those of a young doe. A sweet, musky scent preceded her arrival at Lafe's bedside.

"Who . . ."

Lafe's incomplete and raspy query ended in a cough that jarred his wounds, spawning a sharp intake of breath. He groaned through clenched teeth as his eyes filled with tears.

"Shhh," the girl cautioned, a finger to her pursed lips. "Do not try to speak. I am Sun-Shining-on-the-Waters. The Care-Giver is my grandfather. You are in his lodge. You are in my care."

Lafe nodded carefully. The girl moved quickly to pour a small portion of a thick liquid from a bottle into a small bowl. With a small, strong palm to the back of Lafe's neck, she held the lip of the bowl to his mouth, nodding expectantly.

"Drink this. You will sleep again. It will take away the pain."

Sun-Shining-on-the-Waters sat back on her heels, her legs folded beneath her, her hands clasped in her lap as she watched her patient's eyelids grow heavy. Not until he had lapsed into the deep, even breathing of restful sleep did she draw quietly away.

"You will live, white man. Your body is strong. Your spirit cannot be conquered. Grandfather has told me."

The night was clear and crisp.

Jake was camped under some lovely willows on the banks of the Calapooya River, near Tidbits Mountain. He shot a rabbit for supper, roasting it on a green willow spit over a low fire. He savored the last morsel and threw the bone to Cur, who waited impatiently at his feet. Wiping his fingers on his buckskin shirt, Jake dug out his pipe and filled it. He freshened his coffee, then leaned back against a sturdy willow's trunk to gaze at the stars and enjoy his smoke. Jake never felt quite this content or at ease when he was in town.

The face of Ellie Warren crept into his mind's eye, smiling out of the starlit sky. She was a fine young woman, Ellie. Jake had been taken, at first, with her stunning good looks—a beautiful face and a body that made his blood race just to think of it. But there were other, deeper reasons he loved her that convinced him that he wanted to spend the rest of his days with her at his side. She was a woman to walk beside a man as an equal partner. A lover, yes, and just as important, a friend. If they both were committed to it, they would enjoy a rewarding and lasting relationship based on truth, understanding, and respect. It was a pleasant thought to dream on.

Emptying the bowl of his pipe into the coals, Jake banked the fire and pulled his blankets back in under the trees. He was lingering in that zone between wakefulness and slumber when a low rumble of warning from the dog brought him instantly alert. Jake could not spot anything, but he drew back into the darker shadows under the low-hanging branches, handgun drawn and ready. Several minutes passed before the shadowy form of a lone rider leading a pack animal loomed at the dark edge of camp. Jake tensed and stifled a growl from Cur.

The rider advanced tentatively.

"Come in with your hands empty and a smile on your

face, stranger." He spoke softly and calmly as he pulled the hammer of the Colt in his fist to full cock.

The silence in the dark clearing grew heavy as the intruder sat motionless in the saddle, unresponsive to Jake's challenge.

"Speak up and come in, Mister. It's too late in the day for grave digging."

"Jake? Where are you?"

"Ellie? . . . Dang it. What are you doing here?"

"I'm going with you. Can you come out to where I can see you?"

Jake stepped grumbling from the trees, stuck his gun in his belt and crossed to stir the coals of the fire. He added fuel. A small flame caught to bravely light the dark clearing.

"Just what in the everlovin' blue-eyed world do you think you're doing, Ellen Warren?"

"No need to snap at me. I told you. I'm going with you. I left Uncle Caleb a note. They won't worry knowing it's you I'm with."

Jake was angry. "I brought only enough supplies for one. You're going back."

"I had Mr. Finley at the store duplicate your order. I brought my own."

"Doesn't matter. I'm sending you back in the morning."

"I won't go. I'll follow you."

"Then I'll take you back to town!"

"And as soon as you're out of sight, I'll follow you again. I am going with you, or behind you if you insist upon it. I want to see our valley."

"Dadgum it, Ellie, you . . . you are . . . stubborn." Jake fought back stronger language.

Jake cut some branches from a willow, thinking while he worked what fine switches they would make. He directed her to spread her blankets on top of them and get some sleep.

"We'll discuss it again in the morning."

After tending Ellie's horses, Jake pulled his blankets back into the clearing and laid down, seething with frustration. After a time the silence in the camp brought forth competing serenades from crickets and frogs, with an occasional hoot of appreciation from a neighboring owl.

"Jake?"

"What now, Ellie?"

"I'm hungry."

They bucked drifts of snow to the ridge above their valley and looked down on a wonderland of crystal-coated splendor. Regal evergreens stood in white-robed elegance to receive glittering crowns, delivered on golden shafts of sunlight that darted like thunderbolts from occasional rifts in the swift-moving cloud bank above them.

Tall peaks surrounding the site on three sides offered effective protection from the cold winds and heavier snows that would ravage the surrounding heights in the dead of winter.

The valley was deep, and the young couple picked their way carefully down a treacherous, well-used game trail to the floor below. The snow was no more than ankle-deep on the flat meadows where a large stream ran deep and clear in its rocky bed. The flat was dotted with groves of fir trees mixed with birch, aspen, alder, cedar, and pine.

As they moved farther into the heart of the canyon,

Jake and Ellie were treated to the sight of a tall, slender waterfall loosing a silver ribbon from the top of the bluff at the other end of the crescent-shaped valley. A wide, flat table of rock some forty feet above the meadow that comprised perhaps four acres flanked the falls.

Pointing, Jake told Ellie, "That's where we'll build our home."

"Oh, Jake, I've never seen any place quite so beautiful. It's perfect. Like a dream come true."

The location was remote. Supplies would need to be hauled in by packhorse or mule, but the very remoteness held appeal for them both, and would for Lafe as well. Nature would supply many of their needs. Game was plentiful in the surrounding mountains. Fish abounded in the lakes and streams. There was timber aplenty for lumber and an abundance of stone for building material.

They camped three days in the secluded valley— chatting, making plans, locating the house, barns, corrals. Jake built a lean-to in a thick stand of fir trees, sheltered, dry and warm.

That last night, the young lovers had an extra entrée on their menu, a squirrel that Ellie shot with her little purse pistol. Jake had been afield and came hotfooting it back when he heard the echoing report. She stood there, holding her prize aloft by the tail, smiling proudly.

"Probably frozen solid," Jake said, teasing her, and they laughed, unable to stop until tears filled their eyes.

Jake and Ellie sat for a long time in front of the fire that night, huddled together for the pleasure and for the warmth. They talked of their future together. There must be tall sons and beautiful daughters. They would make a home filled with books and a zest for learning, with love and tolerance and respect for all who lived there. The joys and triumphs would be shared, multiplied by the sharing. The sorrows and fears and adversity they would share, too, and let that sharing ease the hurting.

"I hate to leave tomorrow."

Ellie poked at the fire with a stick, sending a column of orange embers spiraling into the dark sky.

"We'd better, my little runaway, or your Uncle Caleb will have 'Wanted' flyers out on me."

They laughed, as young people laugh when in love.

Her glowing, dark-honey complexion contrasted attractively with the intricately beaded flow of the white buckskin gown she wore on this, her wedding night. Sun-Shining-on-the-Waters walked to kneel beside Wolf Robe, who sat cross-legged on the ground facing the circle where the dancing of the nuptial ceremony and celebration that followed had taken place. Shakily, the old Indian reached to cradle her face in the leathery palms of his gnarled hands. The deep crevices of his face arranged themselves into a toothless smile.

"You are beautiful, my granddaughter. You have made me proud." Wolf Robe's voice wavered as he spoke.

"I honor you, Grandfather."

Towering above his Cayuse bride, Lafe Cawkins beamed a proud smile down upon them. The mist that had welled in the mountain man's eyes captured the flickering reflections of the dying fire behind them. Sunshine, as Lafe had come to call the girl, had been at his side throughout the long and difficult period of his recovery, nursing him, tending him. Somewhere along the way, they had realized that they were in love. It had made the old man very happy. Wolf Robe craned his neck to address the rough-cut white man that he had come to love as he had loved his own family.

"Walk with me, my son."

Lafe bent to take Wolf Robe's extended arms, pulling the frail old man to his feet. They walked together, away from the influence of the fires of the village, along the chuckling run of the river.

They continued in silence for a time, then Wolf Robe halted, standing quietly, watching the reflections of the moon dance upon the swift moving waters. Finally, he spoke.

"I shall walk out alone at dawn, into the hills, to sing my death song."

Lafe answered with a sharp intake of breath.

"No, Uncle, it is too soon. You are needed here. We need your wisdom and your counsel."

Wolf Robe smiled sadly and shook his head.

"I am tired, my son. The Great Spirit has made a place for me in His lodge. Whispering Willow, my wife, waits for me. My strong sons, who died in battle, have readied my pony and wait to ride with their father. I will be young again, and strong. It is time.

"Your strength will protect my granddaughter, your wife. Your kindness and your wisdom will guide her. I have stayed too long here because of my concern for her. By taking her into your lodge as your wife, you allow me to go. It is good."

Lafe rubbed a forearm across his eyes. He cleared his throat. "It has been my honor to walk the path of life that you blazed for me, Wolf Robe, my friend. Your way was straight. The journey has been good."

"And you, my son, have gladdened my heart by

showing the way to another. You have given of yourself, and that is the measure of a good man.

"Now . . . walk back with me. It is your wedding night. It is not a night to spend with an old man."

Chapter Twenty

J ake and Ellie climbed the trail out of the valley, pausing halfway to look back—and forward in time to their
future together.

They led their mounts up the narrow path afoot, Ellie
in the lead, the extra horse and pack animals between,
Jake in the rear with Cur at his heels. As Ellie reached
the top and momentarily disappeared from sight, Cur
growled menacingly.

"Don't worry, boy. We'll catch up."

Jake topped the ridge—and stood facing the covering guns of Malachai Winter!

There were two of them. Winter, and a tall shabby
man as towering and menacing as the renegade chieftain himself. Both men's pistols were trained on Jake.
Winter held Ellie Warren hostage, his beefy arm
around her neck.

The bandit leader was changed. He no longer resem-
bled the dapper and confident Harrison Beale. His jaws
were covered with an unkempt beard. His hair hung to
his shoulders, stringy and unwashed.

"We meet again, Jackass Jake. Let me assure you that this time the pleasure will be entirely mine." Winter's eyes burned with madness born of hatred. "Cover him, Preacher."

Winter holstered his pistol, then tore open Ellie's heavy coat, still holding her by the neck, and thrust his hand inside her blouse. Ellie cried out in pain and fear.

Rage flooded through Jake's body in an uncontrollable wave and he lurched forward.

"No, Jake," Ellie screamed.

Jake halted a split second before Preacher Stark's finger would have closed on the trigger to loose a shot through his brain.

"You scum," Jake bellowed. "You coward. Let her go. Face me man to man if you've got the stomach for it!"

"Still the feisty little upstart, aren't you, Jake?" Malachai Winter drew his gun again, keeping a tight hold on Ellie. "I'm going to thoroughly enjoy killing you . . . piece by piece. But first, I want you to know what's going to happen to this haughty little wench of yours. It's nothing we haven't shared before, is it, my dear?

"I shall take my pleasures with her, here in the snow. Pleasures, Jackass Jake, that you have never imagined."

"Shut your filthy mouth."

"And when I become bored of it, I'll turn the leavings to Preacher, here . . . let him paw and maul her a bit. Then, I'll put a bullet between her eyes and leave her dead and ravaged in the snow . . . just like I did her mama. How does that set with you, Jackass Jake?"

The last thread of control snapped in Jake, and in one blurring motion he swung around in a crouch behind his gun, firing into Preacher Stark, striking the outlaw in the leg and spinning him into the snow and over a bank.

As Jake turned back to face him, Winter fired his weapon. A searing sledgehammer seemed to smash into Jake's shoulder, propelling him backward to the snow-crusted ground. Now filled with bloodlust, Winter pushed his screaming captive aside and closed on Jake for the kill.

Cur charged with a snarling roar, leaping for Winter's throat. The dog's massive jaws clamped onto the side of the startled renegade's face. Sharp fangs sank deep to strike bone. Winter screamed, clubbing the beast away with the butt of his pistol. He clutched at his shredded cheek. Blood streamed through the fingers of his leather glove and down his arm.

The delay caused by the dog's attack was sufficient to allow Jake to struggle to his knees and swing his Colt into play. Deadly reports from opposing guns overlapped in furious thunder.

Winter teetered ominously above Jackass Jake, bleeding from his grinning mouth. Badly wounded, Jake struggled to raise his pistol. He heard a nauseating click as the hammer fell on an empty chamber. Winter looked into his enemy's eyes, still smiling—then fell dead in a heap across Jake's legs.

Preacher Stark then came from behind dragging his wounded leg. He pulled his gun level with the back of Jake's head. A shot sounded, sending an angry echo across the snow-clad mountain top.

The surprised renegade raised his hand to the hole in his forehead, where Ellie Warren's bullet had killed him.

Ellie dropped the smoking derringer into the snow and rushed to Jake, racking sobs shaking her body. She cradled his head in her arms.

"Jake . . . Jake . . . speak to me. Say something."

He looked into her tear-stained face.

"See if you can drag this big ox off me, will you?"
Then Jake passed out.

The first thing Jake Eriksson saw when he opened his
eyes was the ordered pattern of flowered wallpaper.
Crisscrossed lines that formed tiny diamonds boasting
delicate blue and white daisies in their centers. He
smelled the freshly laundered case on the pillow under
his head.

Jake saw Ellie, sitting asleep in a rocker at his bedside, her head hung forward on her chest, her blond hair
cascading over her shoulders. He opened his mouth to
speak. A weak, inaudible squeak emerged. He reached
over to touch her hand. Bolting awake, Ellie looked
down at him and smiled.

"So, you've finally come back, eh? Thought you
might be planning to hibernate through the winter."

"How . . ." He cleared his throat, rusty from a long
silence. "How'd I get here? Who brought us in? I can't
remember."

"I brought us in. I told you I was tough."

"Yeah. You are. You're quite a girl, Ellie Warren."

"Actually, you did most of it yourself, my love. You
rode the whole way, but you were delirious. Apparently, you thought you were back on the Oregon Trail
from Independence. You talked of your father and
mother."

"I do remember the firefight. You were great."

"You were the courageous one. I love you, Jake."

"I love you too." His eyes filled with grateful tears
just as his stomach announced its' need for food. "I'm
hungry."

"I'll get you something," Ellie said, rising. "There's
someone here to see you."

Lafe Cawkins came in the door of the room as Ellie squeezed past. The mountain man displayed a wide grin that featured the gap left by his missing tooth. Cur trailed close behind him.

"Lookin' a mite puny there, partner. Can't let you out of my sight. You don't take proper care of yourself. I'd best haul your skinny backside up into the mountains and put some meat on your bones."

Lafe grabbed Cur in midair as the big dog leaped for the bed.

"Hear tell you went and made a hero of yourself. How you feelin'?"

Lafe pulled off his slouch hat, exposing the pink scar tissue that had replaced the hair along the right side of his scalp.

"I'll be all right," Jake said. "What in heaven happened to you? Looks like you been scalped by a cross-eyed Indian with a rusty knife."

"Long story. Tell it to you later." Lafe turned serious then. "Old Wolf Robe is dead, Jake."

The rough-hewn mountain man's eyes filled with tears and he turned his face to stare at the wall.

"I'm sorry, partner. I know you thought the world and more of him." Jake squeezed Lafe's arm. "I never met the man, but I learned a heap from him just the same, through you . . . most of what I know regarding how to live a proper life. We're both better men because of Wolf Robe. I'm sorry."

"Shucks no, don't be sorry. He wasn't. He was hankering to see what was on the other side. There, he'll be buck young and strong again. A brave warrior who'll never grow too old to ride the trails or walk the mountains."

Lafe got to his feet, saying, "Don't go 'way, Jake. I got somebody I want you to meet."

He stepped into the hallway. As soon as Lafe was out of sight, Cur jumped onto the bed and laid his big head in Jake's lap.

Lafe came back, leading a beautiful young Indian girl by the hand. She dipped her head shyly and looked at Jake through large and lovely eyes, black and shiny as a raven's feather.

"Jake, this is Sunshine . . . my wife."

"Your wife? Well, I'll be double-dog damned. You ornery rascal, congratulations! No wonder you were gone so long." Jake took the girl's hand. "Mighty proud to meet you, Sunshine Cawkins . . . I'll be hornswoggled."

"She's Wolf Robe's granddaughter." A deep pride showed in Lafe's eyes as he explained. "She took care of me, nursed me back to health. We got to know one another. I liked what I seen and I reckon she did, too . . . though that's one I can't figger. We was married Indin fashion. It made ol' Wolf Robe mighty happy."

Ellie walked in carrying a tray. A bowl of lamb stew and a thick slab of cornbread, hot from the oven. A smaller bowl of sliced peaches and a glass of buttermilk.

"Jacob Eriksson, get that filthy animal off the bed. No wonder they call you 'Jackass Jake.' "

He had an inkling then that he would never shake that handle. And that was all right.

Jake had been badly shot up and had some broken ribs, but he was young and strong and he healed rapidly. Dr. Fox had just left the room, telling Jake that he would be fine, but to stay in bed another two to three weeks. When Ellie walked in, Jake was sitting on the edge of the bed.

"Jake, have you lost your mind? Get back into that bed."

"Quit hovering, woman." He looked around the room. "Find me some pants."

"I'll do no such thing. Get back under the covers. You have guests. Lafe and Marshal Meek."

"Joe Meek? Well, bring 'em in."

They lumbered into the small bedroom, the two legendary mountain men, looking miscast amidst the frills and prints and laundered linens. Jake shook hands with the marshal, they passed some small talk, then Meek reached inside his coat, pulled out a thick envelope and extended it to Jake.

"What's that?"

"One thousand United States dollars.

"The Freighter's Association had a reward out for Malachai Winter. And that other one, Preacher Stark. When you up and kilt them two, the others lit out . . . the hull pack of wolves. You're a bona fide hero, son."

Jake pushed the envelope back toward the marshal with the palm of his hand.

"I reckon not. I won't take money for killing a man, not even a scoundrel like him."

Meek started to protest. Ellie stepped forward and plucked the envelope from his fingers.

"He was no man. He was a beast . . . with a bounty on his pelt. I'll take it. It will educate the children he would have denied us."

It was a double wedding.

"Jacob Webster Eriksson, do you take Ellen Elizabeth Warren as your lawfully wedded wife?"

"I do."

"Lafe Cawkins, do you take Sun-Shining-on-the-Waters as your lawfully wedded wife?"

"Yes sir, I purely do."

To honor the newlyweds, Caleb and Lavinia Pettigrew hosted a potlatch, a large banquet, the custom borrowed from the Indians of the area, featuring tables heaped with foods from nature's local larder—elk, venison, and bear meat, Chinook salmon, both smoked and broiled, pan-fried speckled trout, sturgeon roe, cracked Dungeness crab, steamed mussels and clams, shucked raw oysters freighted fresh from Puget Sound, breads and cakes made from wild grains and sweetened with honey, fresh berries and berry pies, pears, cherries, apples, nuts—the menu appeared endless.

Aunt Lovie cried through the entire affair. Ellie could not stop laughing.

Caleb presented Jake and Lafe with leather-bound volumes of the works of Washington Irving and Daniel Defoe.

Joe Meek, Geoffrey Cutler, Zeb Proctor, Pete Jasper and Joseph Mankiller paid their respects. Dr. Fox was in attendance, sporting pie stains on his shirt front, and Sean Michael Sweeney closed the doors of his Golden Egg Saloon and came from Tuality Crossing.

The celebration continued into the night, long after the guests of honor had departed to their upstairs beds.

Lafe and Jake spent the next three weeks in the canyon, supervising the building of the house, the barn, and the main corral by a crew furnished as an additional reward by the grateful members of the Freighter's Association. Jake suspected that Caleb had been the spur to their generosity. With construction completed, the partners returned to Salem to retrieve their anxious brides.

*   *   *

Spring reigned again over the vast Oregon Territory. Warm winds off the blue waters of the Pacific rushed to wake the flowers and rouse the seedlings from their winter beds. Birds busied themselves in song as they gathered building materials for their nests. The creatures of forest and field greeted the fresh abundance of nature with practiced nonchalance. Only the very young, of every species, found it impossible to contain the sheer joy they felt at being alive.

Four riders, cast in silhouette by the rising sun, rode bravely into the future—a journey made one day at a time.

Epilogue

If, when hiking the backtrails in a remote area of the Cascade Mountains, you should happen upon a deep and hidden valley, high on the shoulders of those mountains—enter that valley.

And if, while walking near the waterfall that plummets like a crystal ribbon from the rim of the bluff high above, you should spot an unusual mound of stones; a cairn formed stone-by-stone by the loving hands of the children he fathered—you will have found the final earthly destination of Jacob Eriksson, Jackass Jake.

Sharing that same cairn is the mountain man, Lafe Cawkins, a companion of Jake's for all their years. Two common men who struggled together for a small victory over their own personal demons.

But do not look for markers, for as with so many others of their time, the signatures of these men were left only upon the land. Their monuments, the sons and daughters they bore; their legacies, the principles they lived by.

The shame of Jackass Jake was long ago erased and forgotten.

The valor of Jacob Eriksson, and of the thousands of men like him—the unsung and unheralded who forged an attitude of daring by facing the frontier, embracing the land for its proffered bounty, and returning to that land their sweat and toil and tears—lives on.

Jake and Ellie had two strong sons, Frederick and Marcus, and a lovely daughter, Lavinia.

Jake died in 1873, at the age of forty-five, killed in an ambush by Modoc Indians in the lava beds country south of the valley as he returned from a horse-selling trip in California. The Modocs, under Captain Jack, were engaged in a battle against the army at the time, in one of the final Indian campaigns in Oregon.

Ellie lived until 1907. She passed away in her sleep at her daughter's home in Sacramento, California. She was seventy-three.

Lafe crossed to "the other side" in 1875, age unknown, of wounds received in a wrestling match with a cougar that had been harassing the herds of horses in the valley. His wife, Sun-Shining-on-the-Waters, shot the big cat off him with a rifle, at a distance of two hundred and fifty yards. She buried the pelt with her husband.

Lafe and Sunshine had one son, Jacob.

Sunshine Cawkins returned to live with her people, the Cayuse, near what is now Yakima, Washington, following the death of her son, of influenza, in 1884. Her date of death is not known.

They lived their lives, all of them, in harmony with the magnificent land around them, accepting nature's laws and temperament, trying each day to put back into the land, and into life, at least as much as they accepted from it.

God, grant us the serenity
to accept the things we cannot change,
courage to change the things we can,
and the wisdom to know the difference.
> —Pastor Friedrich Christoph, 1782